CrimeSpree

CrimeSpree by Rich Hayden

2015 Rich Hayden

ISBN# 978-0-9963969-1-2

Chapter 1

The profound revelations

What year is it? No, no, don't answer that. It's not a question. It's more of an exclamation of utter disbelief and it's where this all began. What year is it? Really? Are you kidding me? What year is it!? I can understand losing the time. That's pretty easy to do, we all do it once in a while. Shit, sometimes you're having such a good time that time itself seems to melt away, simply because its presence no longer matters. But then there are other times, like right now, for instance, when time becomes unignorable. It is with you at every breath, every beat of your heart, and every tick of a clock's second hand now holds a gravity that before you would have never thought possible. But we'll get back to that later. For now just indulge my rant. I mean, it's the least that you can do.

So, where was I? Oh yeah, missing time. I can see forgetting what day it might be.Three-day weekends are a bitch like that. I'll even give you the benefit of the doubt if you can't quite recall what month it might be. After all, there is probably a list of legitimate reasons for a temporary brain dump like that. For instance: leap year, excessive drinking or maybe a coma. But losing a whole fucking year? Now that's something that I can't quite wrap my mind around. But there I was, sitting on a bar stool, when I experienced the first of the two profound revelations.

People tend to think that enlightenment arrives when they find themselves placed among wondrous surroundings. Beaches, mountaintops, an enchanted glen, maybe, some such shit like that. This may very well be true, but it wasn't in my experience. I was in Oklahoma, well, I think so anyway. I was lost, exhausted, and starving. And by starving, I am of course referring to the American definition of starvation. That is to say,

Rich Hayden

I hadn't had a snack in about eight hours. Anyway, I was very near that skinny and oddly rectangular portion of Oklahoma, but I could have just as easily been in Texas or Kansas. That really doesn't matter though, does it? At that moment, all I really cared about was getting the hell out of my car and putting something greasy in my gut. The diner that I straggled into promised to sate my desire for gristle and caffeine.

The road was dusty and the air was hot, like it had been set on fire. Rain water was something that apparently didn't exist in this part of the country. The wind that swirled through the treeless landscape blew grit and other fine particles of dirt into my eyes and between my teeth in the brief time that it took me to exit my vehicle and enter the restaurant. What a shack. It was an old trolley car, or maybe it was a worn-out trailer home. I don't really remember, but it looked like the whole thing was just an accident. What I mean to say is that it didn't strike me that any plan was ever laid to open a diner using a renovated old vehicle. What it actually felt like, and I'm pretty damn sure this is how it went, is that some old hillbilly chick wandered into an abandoned structure and started cooking shit.

As I sat there at the counter and drank coffee that could have passed for asphalt, I ordered food from a waitress whose tag revealed her name to be Darlene. She was probably closing in on fifty and was surely the owner, as she barked orders at the other two girls who worked there, both of whom were younger and had better skin. I had no doubt that Darlene made them pay dearly for that offense. Her wild hair was blond and frizzed, and her lined face was painted with every color of the rainbow. The legs of chunky Darlene, varicose-laden as they were, were dressed with nothing more than a pair of hot pants and a heavy set of high heels. Her gigantic boobs tested the limits of her shirt buttons, and the deep creases which ran across those sun-ripened jugs could have carried the rivers out to the seas. Once I ordered my breakfast, suffered my share of friendly sass, and

4

removed my eyes from those crispy cannons, I viewed the motley lot that filled the little establishment.

The world grows older, technology emerges and advancements are made, but creeps and weirdos never change. And to think, if I hadn't torn the GPS from my dashboard and splattered it across the highway after it sent me down the exit to nowhere, I might never have found this quaint little hole. But there I was, with the fringe, the legends, the people that developed society tends to forget about. Oh they still exist, the unrefined, those left unpolished by the many hands of modernity. Today we have cars, very expensive cars, that can drive themselves, computers the size of dimes, and three successful manned missions to Mars, but there in Darlene's diner was some fucker in the corner playing spoons.

There was a raggedy couple seated uncomfortably close to me whose only shared interests were making out and, I strongly suspected, crystal meth. There was a guy placed mercifully at the opposite end of the diner who engaged the salt shaker in spirited debate. It was a surreal exchange to witness, to state it very mildly.

"How are you?" he chirped to the combination of glass and sodium.

Predictably, the coarse saline had little to add to the conversation, but this mattered not. The small, inanimate object was still offered pleasantries before finding itself as the muse for a deranged argument. And argued with it was. Politics, the weather, labradoodles, you name it. This certifiable fellow had opinions to spare, and the poor shaker could do nothing but sit there, all salty and wrong.

There was an older gentleman seated down the row from me who looked as bright as he did warm. Not to mention very out of place, given all the normality that he exuded. The ringing call of the spoon virtuoso was ever-present, and then there was this guy who would have scared the god right out of me. Provided that I had any to start with. For as soon as I

5

noticed him, most everybody else in the place just fell into one common blur. So let me tell you about this dude. I'm guessing he was a truck driver, as there was only one rig parked outside and he was proudly sporting a Kenworth cap. It was heavy with stains and had a bill that was nearly devoid of its skin. His boots were black and dusted with the floating earth that whirled around outside. His impressive height was already exaggerated by the boots, while the straight-leg jeans that he wore made him appear to be seven-feet tall. He was stuck inside a pale blue t-shirt and, although he was thin, the veins in his arms rippled over the muscles like the roots of an old tree discontent in its placement. He had a droopy mustache, the kind that you could use to scrub rust from a chrome bumper, and he wore a large set of dark sunglasses.

I've never been so afraid of a pair of eyes that I couldn't see, but as I dunked my toast into my coffee, I saw him raise his head in my direction. Behind those blackened shields I couldn't see his eyes, but I knew he was looking at me. He could have been looking anywhere, but oh no, he was staring right at me, through me. His glare gave me a feeling I had never felt before. It was foreign, unsettling, and exciting. It spoke of something primal, something nearly forgotten in today's polished America. This was a sensation that probably would have passed and eventually it would have been forgotten altogether, but then something else happened. With his stare, that trucker upended a barrel of gasoline in my mind. This act alone would have proved harmless, but then a squirmy clown weaseled himself down next to me and struck a match. Oh what a fucking inferno that little spark would become.

What year is it?

Yep, that's what he asked me, and though I knew the answer well, I didn't have the mental wherewithal necessary to form simple speech. He looked barely human. He was more like a twitching collection of bones that had been strung together with atrophied muscles and loose flesh. His sunken eyes were dark and distant, and his rotten teeth smacked off his tongue as he sucked on a muffin wet with jelly. He smiled a lot, although I doubt there was a shiver of happiness in his body, and when his hands weren't busy with the muffin, he cracked his knuckles incessantly. He asked me again for that very vague and broad measure of time and again I said nothing. I just continued to study this fool and was made a bit uneasy when I deduced that he was not completely insane. At least he would have had an excuse. No, he honestly had lost track of time—a lot of it. It was in that moment that I truly understood for the first time just how it is that we, as human beings, measure and mark the passage of time. And for one reason or another we use pain, tragedy, and, most of all, fear as our marking stones.

Oh mighty fear, were we really that quick to forget your teeth?

But again, I find myself skipping ahead. So, after watching this simple creature slick jelly onto his fingers, onto his wallet, between the folds of his bills and then into the agitated hands of Darlene, I figured it was time to move on. I gave a final glance around the room and took in the finer details of the ramshackle restaurant. I marveled at how all white eventually yields to yellow, as evidenced by the hue of the walls and the forgotten glory of the checkered tabletops. As I directed my gaze through the glass of one of the windows, I struggled to decide upon whether or not I found the glare of the afternoon sun more unpleasant or the ragged, plaid curtains through which it seared.

My attention was momentarily grabbed by an old TV that was seemingly duct taped up above the door. It spewed forth a newscast that was muted. This was fortunate as I cared not for whatever brand of artificial panic was being sold. I watched as an aging blond with too much foundation on her face narrowed her eyes and furrowed her brow. She was relaying something terrifying indeed. I slid my vision down to the ticker and absorbed tidbits of information. The Chinese invasion of New Zealand, the ten-year anniversary of the cell phone crisis, the unveiling of the first Realdoll to feature Artificial Intelligence. Blah, blah, blah.

As I moved toward that noise box and all its colors, my eyes tripped over the uneven and cracked floor. I chuckled at the menagerie of homemade signs that were tacked up and taped all over the place. Some of the signs were constructed of nothing more than laminated copy paper and offered clever warnings to those who disobeyed proper diner etiquette, while others relayed nothing more than perverse little proverbs. I was awed again by the sight of those with whom I had just shared breakfast, and, with the sounds of a dozen clanging spoons at my back, I stepped back outside.

Okay, I'll give it to Darlene—she was really good at two things—making bacon and turning up the air conditioner. As the full force of the midday heat smashed into me, I immediately regretted the coffee and I felt the remains of the three pancakes crammed into my stomach as they started to bubble. As I walked to my car with a hand shielding my eyes from the spears of the angry star above, I clicked my remote numerous times, but my ride remained unresponsive. Feeling ill and fumbling with the key and the light that it reflected, I managed to put a couple of new scratches into the paint before springing the lock on the door. Ahh, faux-leather interior, the exact same shit that Satan uses for a loincloth, of this I'm convinced.

Little things tend to make me really happy, like when I find a couple of bucks in an old coat, or when a cute girl who is obviously younger than me is charitable enough to lend me a smile. I like matinee movies and I get totally stoked when I find pizza places that run a happy hour on slices. See, it doesn't take much, I'm not that hard to please. But would you like to know what really pisses me off? When I'm lost in Oklahoma-ish, low on money, out of friends, and the fucking car won't start.

Awesome. I turned the key, pumped the gas, punched the steering wheel and prayed to the thin air, and you know what? Nothing worked. Fuck you, thin air.

At this point I'm glazed by sweat and my hair is stuck to my face in an unkempt arrangement that made me look like an indie-rock songwriter who can't be bothered with things as trivial as a haircut. I was wearing a faded orange t-shirt that now looked quite pink, given all the sweat that dotted my pasty skin underneath, and the tan shorts I had on were probably a bit too small. I realize that I was cutting the figure of a strung-out homo at the time, but hey, cut me some slack, I had been in the car for god knows how long at that point. Just then, in my vulnerable state of mock faggotry, there came a tap on my window.

The sound jarred my attention and I turned to the dirty glass to witness the blade of a screwdriver as it methodically rapped on the pane. The handle of the instrument had been absorbed into a massive hand, and as I traced a knot of veins as they unwound themselves up the long arm, I felt my heart quiver with alarm. That creepy trucker and his armored eyes stared in at me. The motion of the screwdriver had stopped now and he remained as rigid and still as I, although I'm certain he shared not an ounce of the fear that had flooded my entire being. I was scared, nightmare scared, but there was no alarm clock primed to go off, and no distant ringing of a phone was going to free me from this vision. Yes, sir, this was indeed real, and though I knew it impossible, I felt like he was going to kill me. And what a terrible fear this was, for I sensed no reason for the murderous sensation that bled from the trucker. He didn't want to kill me because I was easy prey, he didn't want to kill me because I looked like a city queer. He just wanted to kill me to have something to kill. But that terrible act was supposed to be extinct, right? In that instant I was thankful for the drenching effects of the sun because I think I might have pissed a little. But then my dread was replaced by complete amazement.

"You need a lift?" he murmured.

I'll never forget those words, and it felt like an entire year had elapsed before I returned with an answer. I thought about the fact that I didn't even have car insurance, and as the car lay quiet, I was reminded of how much I hated that piece of shit. Not quite forgetting that I was swindled for a couple grand a while back just to call the heap my own. In that moment, I wanted to rage. My luck had been absent of any fortune lately and I was one nightfall away from being considered homeless. I didn't have a lot to lose, I figured, and it was painfully obvious to any common moron that I had nothing to steal and barely anything to offer. My tongue was dry and my lips were cracked so deeply that I felt as blood softened their narrow fissures, but still I spoke. I spoke one simple word that sounded wholly wrong to me then, although now I'm not so sure. Either way, right or wrong, I spoke.

"Yeah," I replied.

Okay, I've seen enough TV shows to know that this is about the point in the interview or the questionably acted biopic where the network flashes to some re-enactment of a tennis shoe contacting the step of a tractor. After which comes a batch of commercials, and then some more backstory on me. So to save the fine people at AnyBC some trouble, I'll fill in the blanks for you, how's that? Oh, that's right, you don't have a choice but to listen, and there isn't a goddamn thing that you could offer me to buy my obedience, so I guess we'll just plod along at my pace. I can do this all night long. It's about all I can do now. But by the time that this little charade has come to its abrupt and barbaric end, America will be left with the sour taste of my ass in her mouth. That's okay, I'm fine with that. I'm just here to set the record straight, after all, who can better articulate my misdeeds then me?

I never liked hide-and-go-seek until I figured out that if I only pretended to close my eyes as my friends darted off to tuck themselves away, I could find them much faster. I hated school, but once I refined the art of cheating on tests, it got a whole lot more enjoyable. One time, I even managed to hack into the school's computer network, at which point I took the liberty of adding a little sheen to my semester report file. I didn't like Becky Weaver, either. She was fifteen, three years younger than me, and a bit annoying. She wasn't all that attractive, but once I discovered that I could have sex with her and then never call her again, she became much more interesting to me. I mean, come on, her dad was a total no-show, so that was a bullet I didn't even have to dodge! That's right, America, I'm not a nice guy, but before you get all self-righteous, I ain't that bad either. Let's face facts already, everybody has fun and gets by at the expense of someone else. I just did it on purpose. Maybe I'm just that smart.

Once I became an adult—I'll refrain from referring to myself as mature—I worked tirelessly at not working. I had quick hands and a quicker tongue. Oh what a lucrative combination that was. I could swipe a tip jar or a donation box and receive a friendly thank you on the way out the door. I panhandled in hundred-dollar shoes and made more money around the holidays than most people working an ordinary nine-to-five could earn in a month. I stood in line at bank ATMs behind hundreds of people and indulged their need for small talk about their children and pets. You can't believe how many people leave their cards in those things when they're pleasantly distracted. From there I would load up on a bunch of crap I could pawn easy or unload at a flea market for fast green. I got pretty good at blackjack too, which was a great way to supplement my income with something that most people would consider after-work recreation. I just cut out that pesky work part. Seemed like simple enough math to me. And even when the cards betrayed me, I made up for that by running a short-lived scheme with a female dealer in a Pittsburgh casino who dragged around a hefty bag of low self-esteem.

11

Rich Hayden

As I got older my deceptions grew more complex and more profitable. I helped a like-minded fellow of avaricious tastes move a shipment of bogus painkillers around the streets for a time, and I got into the racket of manufacturing counterfeit cell phones. I fell in with some cons who thought up a brilliant valet parking scheme. We would park the cars where they belonged, return them unharmed, and we never once lifted a dollar or a single credit card. But don't kid yourself, we stole all the same. Bit by bit, we would remove small parts from the cars. A fitting here, a bracket there, anything that contained steel, aluminum, copper or brass. We even managed to score small amounts of gold from time to time. We never took enough to affect the performance of the vehicles, at least not right away. And by the time that these cars did break down, we were long forgotten in the minds of the drivers. This was around the time of the iron shortage, so scrap value was high in those days, but the work required was too much like, well work. Long story short, it wasn't for me.

I was caught up in a lot of unsavory practices back then, but there was one scheme that was clearly my favorite. It wasn't original by any means but it was all mine, and I worked it alone. This cut down on the risks and it maximized the profits. Maybe I was greedy, maybe I just didn't trust other thieves. Either way, I was doing something right, because this particular ruse had some staying power. I had an old pickup truck that I fitted with one of those removable magnetic decal signs, you've seen'em, I'm sure. Anyway, my sign detailed my services for asphalt sealing and repair services. I would knock on doors that I was certain would produce an elderly face, at which point I would stretch out my trap before them. I had a fancy letterhead contract and proof, a word I use loosely, of my insurance. Once those aged little bugs found themselves stuck to my threads, I would kindly ask for the small down payment that was required before the work could commence. Most handed over checks that amounted to a few hundred dollars, while some I swindled out of a thousand or two. A few of these craftier seniors balked at my claims, but this was a minor obstacle easily bested. To assuage their concerns, I would simply stroll out to my truck and smear a little tar over their faded driveways with a brush and a five-gallon bucket. *Holy shit, it will look like new!* Yep, that's what they thought as they dug into their pockets.

As you might have guessed, I never returned to do the work. To be brutally honest, I don't even know if asphalt and blacktop are two different words for the same thing or if they are, in fact, separate materials, and I couldn't care less. Surprisingly, this little con worked for quite some time and I wasn't even all that careful. Think about it—I never even put a phone number or web address on my magnetic sheet of lies and deceptions! But hey, you can't fool them all, and I didn't. Some of the crustier types threatened to call the cops on me, and a few were true to their word. Like that fucking mattered. I was gone in seconds once my trickery was brought to the light, and my sign was torn from my truck before I even left their neighborhood. And once there was too much hot talk of a tar-toting charlatan, I simply moved on to other schemes. So listen to this and pay attention: you can't discourage a thief from his trade, period.

Ahh, it's nice to reminisce about gullible old people and easy money, but alas, all things reach their end. Besides, that was a long time ago, my East Coast days, my amateur hour. I moved around the country after that. I wandered from state to state and ripped off anybody who happened to drift into my line of fire. I cashed in pretty big with a successful identity theft caper in Kentucky and stole thirteen cars during my lovely stay in Georgia. I lived in Indiana for a few years and managed to lead a moderately comfortable middle-class lifestyle by indulging my old personalities of panhandler extraordinaire and debit-card magician. The disappearing act was my specialty. I booked numbers in Kansas and was arrested. Hey, nobody's perfect. It wasn't all bad, though. After all, it was winter, and the state graciously put me up during those harsh months. That was so very thoughtful of them.

I met a lawyer in Iowa. This wasn't a legal thing, she was just drunk at a bar and I could smell the blood in the water. I'll have you know, my intentions were purely just to bang this chick, although so much more was wrought from my efforts. She was significantly older than me but had the body of a twenty-year-old, and I had her pegged to a T. She was the in-charge, independent, get-it-done type. Her name was Lucy Miller and she was all business, all the time, not to mention the top-rated attorney in the state. She worked fourteen-hour days, six days a week, and practically lived at the gym. But tonight, for reasons I still don't know, she was alone and hammered. What the hell was Lucy Miller doing in the Dirty Mug? That place was for scumbags. Even I was a little too good for the joint. But there we were, her and I, me and her.

"Hello, drunk girl," I said with a grin as I occupied the seat next to Lucy.

"Hi, bad guy," she replied with suspicion in her eyes and a giggle in her throat.

"So," Lucy began while sipping some manner of swill. "Why'd ya feel the need to come over and hit on me?"

"I haven't hit on you yet," I corrected with boyish charm splashed all over my face.

"Well, are you gonna?"

"Of course, that's why I came over here."

"Ah ha! I caught you," she said, waving a finger at me. "So back to my question that you have so rudely ignored, why'd ya saddle up next to me?" she asked, wobbling herself on the barstool for effect.

"I wanted to look down your shirt."

"You dog!"

"Wait, wait, wait," I said defensively with my hands out in front of me. "I came for the cleavage, but I think I'll stay for those eyes."

"You're despicable," she stated, still smiling.

"True, but I'm also quite charming and I make for good company," I said as I slid a bowl of cashews in her direction.

Lucy flipped one into the air, opened her mouth, and watched the nut travel to the floor after it bounced off her cheek. We both laughed and she dug her fingers into the bowl. She popped a few into her trap at short range and I motioned for another round.

"You getting that?" she quizzed as the beers approached.

"Of course, I'm a gentleman."

"A bawdy gentleman, maybe."

"A gentleman all the same."

"So what's your name?"

"I can't tell you my name yet, you'll assume too much. Instead, let me tell you that I'm a traveler, an entrepreneur. I am untethered, I am a global citizen, I am a gentleman, and I am hopelessly captivated by you."

"Wow," she said with sarcasm and a smirk and cashews in her teeth. "I could fall in love with you."

"Yes, you could," I replied softly, and she was just drunk enough to believe me.

If I think really hard about that night, I almost believe in fate.

Not so fast. You're not about to see me get all sentimental, at least not yet. And I'm certainly not going to show remorse for the things I've done, and an apology is that last thing that any of you could ever hope to squeeze from me. Alright, fuck! I'm getting a little worked up here. You gotta understand that it's a bit difficult to concentrate at a time like this.

Okay, where were we? Oh yeah, the leggy Lucy Miller. The lights were low and yellow and the air was thick with haze, as the Dirty Mug was apparently the last place in America that

15

still allowed smoking. They had one of those ancient jukeboxes that had the capacity to play about fifty CDs and, if my memory serves me well, the song *Such A Scream* was playing. There were three really drunk hillbillies who were attempting to play darts, a pair of grannies who gnawed on a patch of cheese-fries, one ferociously grumpy bartender, little ol' me, and the sloshed Ms. Miller.

The place was small, but with the absence of company, decorations, or any piece of furniture that anyone would even care to save, a bull could have rampaged down to the end of bar next to Lucy and disturbed practically nothing along the way. I bought her two more beers before she even fully realized that a gentleman, that's me, was the source of her continued alcohol. And you know what happened next? We hit it off. She was drunk, I was evil. Years, class, and morals all set us worlds apart and we got along like old friends. We were both liars. Maybe that was the bond, I don't know. Either way, I'm honest now, and she's dead. Moving on...

We flirted a little more, but we mostly just talked long into the night on all manner of subjects until that crabby bartender informed us that it was time to go. And by time to go, I mean to say that he wanted to leave, and, as a consequence, me and the Iowa super-lawyer had to split. Being the chivalrous fellow that I am, I drove Lucy's Mercedes deep into the suburbs and placed it snugly into a garage that rose up from the manicured landscape of her estate. Now let's pause another minute and consider the facts of the case. I had a Mercedes in my hands, an attractive and very passed-out woman in the passenger seat and a purse on the floor that probably held at least a few grand in cash and who-knows-what else in plastic. I wasn't a saint, but you can imagine where this could have gone.

As I think I mentioned before, Lucy was quite attractive and so I did not abandon my quest to get her out of her clothes. The conquest was quite easy, and, yes, I had a lot of sex with Lucy Miller that night. She was semiconscious most of the time, and, as a result, I didn't feel all that bad about it. Let's be real for a second anyway. She didn't walk into the Dirty Mug and order umpteen beers just to relax with a book. She knew what she was getting herself into, at least when the night began. Hey, if you bait the wolves, sometimes you get eaten.

This little moment right here is when the saga of me and Lucy Miller actually rises above the level of juvenile interest. Because when the morning arrived, I was still there, and more surprising was the reality that she really wanted me to stay. Maybe in her dreams that night Lucy had felt the gravity of loneliness as it pulls heavy on the hearts of the middle-aged. I guess it's possible that I reminded her of an old love. For all I knew, this might have been something that the no-nonsense lawyer did with regularity, or maybe she just wanted a boyfriend. Whatever her reasons, she kept me around.

That morning I made her a pot of extremely black coffee and a full breakfast plenty large enough for the two of us, although I did most of the munching. We stayed around her place most of the day and continued with our first date in reverse. There were the expected and awkward pauses in our conversations, and we both said things that sounded much sillier out loud than when the words were confined within our own skulls. But by nightfall, the mood lightened. She reminded me of a much younger soul as we snacked Doritos and watched a cheesy kung-fu movie on her ridiculously expensive couch. I saw her for who she used to be. A long time ago, before all the seriousness of adulthood and legal jargon had smothered her. It was terribly cute, and this is why I suspect that Lucy took such a liking to me. I enabled her to act this way. I didn't care about her caseload, neither one of us had any interest in discussing the law, and she knew right away that I wasn't going to judge or challenge her. She didn't see me as a threat. Apparently she wasn't clairvoyant.

Let's put off what inevitably came of our unlikely union for just a bit later and continue on with the sweet stuff for another spell. I like this part anyway. It makes me happy, or as least as happy as anyone in my situation could hope to be.

Later that same night, she took ten years off her face with a scientific method of makeup application and I made her laugh with myriad trivial anecdotes that someone of my limited education has no business knowing. Against good judgment she tossed me the keys to her car and we set off for town. We had dinner at a corner grill, which was nestled in the heart of an artsy district that was not nearly as high class as I had expected when we departed. We both had steak, she stayed away from the booze that night, and after we sampled a few desserts, Lucy picked up the tab. She said it was a thank-you for taking care of her the night before. Apparently, and how fortuitous it was for me, taking advantage of a drunk chick was good behavior where Lucy came from. After a few leisurely laps around that brightly lit urban square, our time together had come to an end. When we got back to her place, I parked the car but didn't accompany her inside. I simply walked her to the door and kissed her goodnight.

After having seen what true wealth can buy you, I viewed my apartment in a much shittier light. I didn't talk to Lucy for a few days, but during that time she texted me incessantly with daft little messages that possessed a schoolgirl's maturity. We saw each other when we could, which was usually a couple of times a week. When we shared a bed, I usually stayed at her place, although she wasn't above slumming and stayed at my pad a time or two as well. One night, as she lay next to me, staring up at the chipped plaster ceiling of my glorified studio, Lucy pressed me hard on what it was that I actually did for money. I didn't answer right away. I was quiet as I glanced around the room and took in all that my lies had earned me. The cardboard boxes in the corner, the faded carpet that needed swept, the crooked shelf of random books and scratched DVDs. I looked at the blank screen of my dying TV and then to the stack of magazines that bachelors tend to have next to it. Then I turned my eyes to Lucy as she lay cocooned in sheets that were as comfortable as tissue paper. She smiled at me, and so for a little spice, I decided to tell the truth, I told her I was a thief. I didn't go into detail and she wasn't interested in learning the finer points of my trade, but I offered enough light to give her a peek at my dirty game. I was an unsavory dude, and man did she dig it, for a while.

As the summer died away, Lucy did something that even I found unexpected. She asked me to move in with her. Okay, at this point I might have actually been in love with Lucy Miller, but I very clearly heard the devil as he screamed the word *JACKPOT* into my ear. I took to my role as ward quite well during my stay at the Miller palace, and for a while, things were merry. Our relationship was buoyed by the excitement of something new and that was enough to momentarily hide the differences that would one day unwind us from each other. It was nearly two years, I think, that I shacked with Lucy, and I can honestly say that I felt what it meant to be truly happy. She was happy, too, or at least she seemed to be. I can take a small solace in that now. After a while, though, it became unignorable that she was water and I was the slipperiest of oils. I wasn't gonna change, and, admittedly, she didn't have the energy to try and straighten me out. We started to fight about meaningless things, and, like a tidal wave over a village, the realization that the fun fling between the law and the law-breaker was over finally slammed into the both of us.

Our parting was amicable but sad, mutual but fraught with disappointment. I think we saw in each other all that could have been. In another time, under different circumstances and upon alternate paths we probably could have made it work. I'll admit that I took advantage of Lucy, and I did use her for the money, but I never stole from her. In fact, I cared so much for her that if I had stayed with her until the end, I seriously doubt that I would be here talking to you right now. Whether or not that's a good thing is a debate for another time, although at the moment things are quite bad for me. But what's done is done, you can't reshape the past. I left Lucy and a year later cancer sunk her into the grave. I'm just glad she didn't have to watch what has become of me.

I'm not made of steel. After the split between me and that beautiful brunette with the deep laugh lines around her mouth, I was a mess. I got the hell out of the Midwest and headed south. I spent an eye-blink in Alabama and made some quick cash, too, but my true destination was much further away. I drove all the way to Homestead, Florida with some clothes, a few hard drives full of my favorite movies and music, and a suitcase stuffed with cash that I had been stockpiling. By the time I reached the state's southern tip, I had run out of dry land. If I wanted to get any further away from Lucy and her memory I would have had to best the mighty Atlantic. And maybe I would have tried, but I was never much for the sea.

Enter the blur, the mush, the nothing time. Enter the dirt years. By thirty-five, I had no car, I had burnt through my money. I didn't even have a place to stay. The only possessions I had left were tightly wrapped up in a dingy old knapsack that accompanied me everywhere, just like a proper hobo. Most of the friends I once had were just fading memories now. Some I had lost to time, others to the sheer distance now placed between us. But let's be honest, I didn't run with the noblest of fellows. Most of those I once called friends were no longer so because I cheated them somewhere along the line or vice versa.

Even Mr. Have gets had sometimes, and back then, just like now, I have nothing.

To be successful at being a cheat, you need to be sharp. Not once in a while, not here and there, all the time. You get it? All the fucking time. And I betrayed rule number one as I rowed gleefully down a river of alcohol. I trolled the beaches in and around Homestead, slept among the fields, and sat upon the hot streets with a bottle in my hand. I didn't panhandle, I didn't beg, I just drank. I felt like a failure and I felt sorry for myself. I felt like all the bad I had done was coming back to haunt me. To be honest, I wasn't used to a slump and this was a big one. I couldn't handle it and so I sank deeper into the booze, and that's even before I called Lucy.

When I left Iowa and settled in Florida, I thought it would be a permanent vacation. I was destined to become a legendary beach bum with a silver tongue. I would go to nightclub parties in Miami, grace the sets of porn shoots, and play guitar with the other troubadours under the stars and before the black roll of the ocean at midnight. You might see me at a Dolphins game thanks to some prime tickets that I scored, or maybe that was me you spied out on the water. How did I get on that yacht? Retired in my thirties, living among the sand and foam and warm air of the Sunshine State. But you know that's not how it worked out.

What an idiot I was. I had no long-term way of making money or even saving it. I didn't possess a skill that could land me a legitimate job, and I had not the first clue of how to escape the mess that had finally caught up to me. Thanks to the bottle, I managed to get myself arrested a few times for petty theft, and I secured myself a prominent place on the radar of the local PD. The jig was up, the party was over. I wasn't as smart as I fancied myself and I wasn't as charming as I used to be. I was just a guy who was used to stealing shit and getting away with it. I was used to luck, just pure dumb luck, and that luck was gone. I used to have delusions of grandeur, but reality grew cold and clear and nothing about me was grand. In the sunniest place in America I felt my darkest, and at best, I was just a pathetic drunk with no friends. I couldn't even direct my alcohol-laden complaints to anyone else as most people steered well clear of me. Hell, no one really liked me beyond our first introduction anyway. Nobody except Lucy.

One ordinary day a storm blew through Homestead and the rains that came with it harshly reminded the sun that the sky doesn't belong to it alone. The high winds tore leaves from the trees and glued them to the roads like stickers across a teenager's notebook. Signs were bent, siding was torn from buildings, and water soaked every goddamn thing in sight. Debris littered every path and dotted everyone's lawn like confetti left behind after a massive celebration. But I never left the beach that was my sandy and sprawling home. I just laid there during the punishment and allowed the droplets to smash me into the sand as the air howled all around me. At the time, it felt like a cleansing. The wind pulling at my clothing, the roar of the ocean as it barked at me, and the absence of any other human soul. This was my storm, my moment of chaotic clarity.

Once the rage of nature had lifted, the rush of gusty winds and the sounds of tires as they cut through deep pools of cool fluid were offered to the gloomy sky. Sirens called from this way and that, and children milled about outdoors to splash around in the aftermath. I was returned to earth and to all its familiar sounds. I heard voices and saw indefinable people in the far distance. My lesson was fast and violent and then it was gone. I was back among the reality of my situation, and as I rose from the sand like jetsam plucked from wreckage, I clearly wondered if I had learned anything from this cryptic experience.

I walked along the beach all colored in burnt amber and gray from the glare of the sky above. It was weird, unsettling almost, for even after the sky had calmed its stir, the sun remained tucked away from view. This was odd. The sun is always just on the other side of a hurricane, but there was something about this little burst of a storm that had chased it away for good. Without purpose, I strolled through town, and the whole rest of the day was cloudy. No, not cloudy, dark. I scraped together enough money for a coffee and sat out on the patio of a corner café. I was all alone and preferred it this way as I gazed calmly and with sober eyes out toward the first sparkles of a premature twilight that began to shimmer off the ever-present dew. As I viewed the gleam of wetted grass and droplets of water as they fell from road signs, I felt around in my pocket and rubbed the coins that were found there between my fingers. To my touch, they felt like just enough to make an awkward phone call.

Do you have any idea just how hard it is to find a payphone these days? Okay, I get it that everyone over the age of three has two fucking cell phones, but every once in a while, a guy like me comes along who needs a goddamn payphone. As I mentioned before, all my luck had been washed out to sea, or maybe it had just evaporated into thin air. Either way, it was gone, and this was evidenced by the fact that the first payphone I came across was nicely decorated with a tree limb. Fantastic, there's probably only four of these suckers left in the whole damn state and this particular relic had a branch rudely shoved through the center. So on I went, down slick streets that reflected shiny lamppost light, but it wasn't all bad, as I was given the gift of time. I had some time to think about what I was going to say to Lucy if indeed I ever found the fabled fountain of youth. Oh, that's right, I was just looking for a fucking payphone, but I digress. She would almost assuredly be surprised, and I would sound like a fool as I relayed a story to her about how lying out under a storm finally gave me a little perspective. I would tell her all the things that I couldn't say back in Iowa and she would be genuinely happy to hear them. She would probably tell me to board a bus to Iowa, and there she would pick me up so that we could give the unlikely theory of *Us* another go-round.

The third call I made was to her office. I know I probably shouldn't have called there, but that was how I learned that

Lucy was dead. I talked to some uptight douche named Steve and he relayed the news to me with the same emotion that someone uses to read aloud the finer details of a parking ticket. Thanks, fucker. That was the most devastating thing I was ever made to suffer, and it came at me in a slow monotone. But the worst part? Lucy had been dead over a year. She was just a rotten heap of flesh and bloodless veins locked inside a box. She was cold, stiff, and buried under the earth in a deadened womb of silence and darkness. It was an image that I couldn't beat out of my brain. So maybe you'll forgive me if I can't recall just what happened in the days that followed the very moment that the phone slipped from my hand and was left to swing helplessly out of reach of its mate.

For the first time in my life, I acknowledged the writing on the wall and got a job. It wasn't a good one, but it was the first step toward finally setting down the fantasy that I was destined to be some legendary drifter. Sure, I got by for a while and had some fun, but I ended up nothing more than the junkie who swears that he's gonna be that one exception to control the uncontrollable. So I entered the only rehab that a thief is offered, honest employment. I spent the better part of a year busing tables and washing dishes at a boardwalk restaurant, and you know what? I actually enjoyed it. I liked most of the people that I worked with, and this young little waitress named Carla, who was indescribably cute, took quite a liking to me. You probably thought that part about Carla was going somewhere, huh? Nope, that was all. She was fifteen years younger than me, a knockout, and I never once exploited her naiveté. Chalk it up to an exercise of my rehab, but in reality, Florida just held too many bad memories for me and I was in no rush to craft any more of them. Carla would have been a blast, but Carla would also have been very temporary.

I allowed myself to enjoy the camaraderie that came with the job but I permitted myself to do little else that didn't involve saving every last cent I earned. It took some time, but I eventually got off the beach and into a proper apartment. I had to go two hours inland to find anything that I could afford, and as a result, I left the boardwalk and the temptations of Carla behind. I quickly found another job working in the kitchen of some bar placed right in the middle of nothing.

It sat atop a road that couldn't decide if it was the nicest dirt road in the country or just the most neglected stretch of asphalt that America had to offer. Spanish moss hung from the trees that encircled the bar, and, as it swung low, that ghost-like growth swam across the brittle roof of the small building with each light kiss of the wind. The sounds of the swamps filled the outside air, while inside the stale oxygen was littered with the twang of country music. It was the scary kind, too, not the pop-country crap you hear on the radio, but real country songs about death and crime that tend to get red-necks excited. All the woodwork inside the stale bar was warped from years of humidity, and the windows were all either smoked out or covered over with signs that advertised cheap beer. It was always dark in there, a thin veil that scarcely obscured all the slime. There was never a shortage of unsavory characters inside The Gator Trap, and thanks to this company, I finally found myself on the wrong end of a raw deal.

I desperately wanted out of Florida. I wanted to settle in a state that I had never visited before and I wanted to start fresh. With a sizeable heap of cash tucked under my mattress at home, I had enough to afford a cheap car and still have a little left over for the unknown journey ahead. This was right about the unfortunate time that I met Mike the mechanic. His nickname was *Silent Running*, a nod to that obscure band from the 1980s, Mike and the Mechanics. *Silent Running* suited Mike perfectly well, because he very quietly ripped people off and, as a result, he was always on the run from the law. I should have known better. The warning was right there in the name, but Mike pulled me in anyway. Maybe it was because I saw a lot of myself in Mike. Maybe it was because I kinda like the song *Silent*

Running, I don't know. It doesn't really matter though, because a ripoff is a ripoff.

One evening after my shift was done at The Gator Trap, me and Mike wound our way through the outskirts of the Everglades. The growth, the sheer wildness of the place was overwhelming. As we drifted along upon narrow roads, I could smell the swamp and I heard the symphony of nature in all its undisturbed harmony. The deeper we drove, I watched as the trees lost their singularity as all eventually melded into one with all the stitching of moss and vine that hung tangled within their branches. I felt like we were a thousand miles from anything touched by man, and it was this primal feeling that would visit me again and move me to change the world. But that's something we'll discuss in a bit, because for now, I've got a shitty car to buy.

Me and that trickster Silent Running pulled into a trailer park that had been abandoned long ago. It was creepy. There were about a dozen or so mobile homes around but Mike was the only resident left. Inside Mike's rusty truck, we slowly bounced into the heart of the park. I looked out over the trailers like they were headstones left to crumble within a forgotten cemetery. One of the buildings had been tipped over, a few others were losing their battle with the embrace of the creeping swamp, and two trailers that were placed fatefully close to one another had both died in the same now-extinguished blaze. All that remained were the stains of humidity and ash that had been fused to the warped metal skeletons.

The tin can that Mike called home was tethered to the ground with vine and the upward creeping of wet earth. His little shell sat soft and unstable under the oppression of the midnight heat and it was fortified on all sides by cars that looked like war relics dug up from the battlefields of decades past. As we milled around, the mosquitoes bit at my skin, which was already agitated from the heat and the touch of the saw-grass that polluted Mike's community of one. But even more distressing than the rash that bubbled over my skin in random patches was the threat of becoming an alligator's late night treat. I knew they were watching us through the dark, and this was a fear that nagged at me continuously. With my clothes damp from sweat and my heart tense with the unease that nature brings, Mike finally stopped our trawl and tapped his fist upon the hood of an old Honda.

So this was to be the chariot that would deliver me from Florida and my rotten run of luck. What a piece of shit. It was about six different colors, the right front fender was crunched, and the passenger side mirror was shattered. A GPS system was glued to the dash and the screen was glazed from the inside with fog. Mold clung to the armrests, the air conditioner didn't work, and how's this for a fun surprise? The dying Honda had a fucking cassette deck. Yep, these things haven't been put in cars for about a million years but now I had the privilege of experiencing the wonderful feature of auto-reverse/playback. Great, now hopefully this little turd is also a time machine so that I can travel back in time to buy some tapes.

Mike could see my astonishment that this dinosaur was the *older* car that he had touted so highly. Honestly, I was more concerned that he had convinced me that it was a steal for the low price of two thousand dollars when, in fact, his entire inventory of junk would probably have struggled to reach that figure. But like any good con, he had a trick up his tattoo-sleeved arm. I watched as Mike smiled at me and slid his arm in through the driver's window. He wrapped his fingers around the keys and gave the ignition a turn. Within seconds, that immortal car started and purred like a cat. Not a young cat mind you, but a kitty-cat all the same. It was at that point that Mike turned to me with his arm outstretched and his palm open.

"See," he said through yellow teeth and chewing tobacco. "Silent...and running."

Now who can argue with that? I handed over the money and climbed inside. The seats were damp with humidity and only one headlight responded to my command. Mike graciously threw an atlas into the deal, a fucking paper atlas, just to complete my retro look, I suppose, and without any acknowledgment of his charity, I put that car into gear. To my surprise, the little Honda had a full tank of gas, and with absolute predictability, I got lost trying to escape the Everglades. I wove my way through that labyrinth of dampened greenery and darkened sky for an hour or two without seeing another human soul. I felt the sear of the black heat as it clung to me and I watched as the shadows melted and morphed themselves into ephemeral creatures as my eyes set about playing tricks on me. Sure, it took a while to escape the croak and groan of the cacophonous swamp, but it was just a temporary setback. I was leaving Florida. I was starting again.

Eighteen hundred miles, countless detours, five tanks of gas, three breakdowns, and one week later, I finally arrived at where I left you guys hanging a while back. I was most likely in the Oklahoma panhandle with my gut full of pancakes and tension and my foot on the step of a worn out tractor. Shit, this thing made my Honda look young. I didn't know what kind of truck it was, but it sure was old, I knew that much. It didn't have any of the sleek and curvaceous touches that new vehicles tend to have. It was angular and jagged, full of dents and splotches of rust. It just looked mean, with the tall grill all bent out of shape like a row of stained and crooked teeth. The truck voiced its complaint for life with every shake of its rough idle, and, like a diseased breath exhaled from hell, the dull stacks belched black smoke into the sky above.

I climbed inside and plunked down on the passenger seat that had degenerated into nothing more than a collection of dry-rotted fibers and corroded springs. Drier than the desert outside that masqueraded as Darlene's parking lot, a cloud of dust was hurled into the already stale air of the cab from my action. The windows, all stained with nicotine, were rolled up, and they trapped the particulate ghost I had awakened, but they also held in the icy breath that floated from the vents on the dashboard. Through the dust and the chill, I watched as the trucker lit a smoke, to add further pollution to our atmosphere. He offered me a cigarette and I didn't accept, to which he just shrugged his shoulders and withdrew the pack. One rough hand, full of calloused skin and yellowed nails, wrapped itself around the shifter as the trucker forced his beast into one of the gears it apparently had left. He then thrust his fingers into the air supply buttons to release the brakes of the truck and the equally ancient trailer behind us. And just like that, we were on our way.

As the truck jumped out onto the highway, I watched as a long-dead air freshener swung from a lever on the dash that had since lost its identification. The useless ornament was rectangular, one of those cheap cardboard and felt things that is chemically infused with some fake-ass scent. It was yellow with a brown border and, down the center of the creased and useless object, one word had been stamped into it: outlaw. The word struck me, the way a history book does as it relays tales which in this modern age now seem wholly unbelievable. It spoke of the past, our true nature, maybe. Whatever it was, I just couldn't set that elusive feeling down.

"Outlaw," I said. "I didn't think there was any outlaws left."

"I'm the last of them," muttered the trucker as he solemnly stared straight ahead as if glimpsing the dismal future.

We drove further west for quite a while, but neither one of us really had much to say. I enjoyed the foreign landscape of New Mexico, as it resembled nothing that I was used to seeing along the east coast. As the sun was beginning its daily retreat, the dying rays painted the land in orange along a lonesome and remote stretch of Interstate 40. The land around us was full of brown grasses and flat-topped rock formations. Patches of dull green dotted the panorama while streaks of red cut themselves into the deeper sections of the rock. The huge stones rose from the earth like the remnants of a lost civilization now reduced to a silent and petrified ruin. We hadn't seen another vehicle for what felt like an hour, but then all of a sudden fate came screaming up the highway inside a flashy new sports car.

Me and the trucker were chugging along in the left lane, as the right side was a true gauntlet of potholes and rippled asphalt. It was then that this zippy blue car came shooting up behind us. He had no intention of placing his jewel in the right lane, either, and was utterly incensed that a big, chunky truck was in his way and would not move over. He blew the horn, waved his arms in disgust and even shot us the finger a couple of times. The trucker gave no outward reaction to all of this but I swelled with a great amount of worry.

Finally, the right side of the road smoothed itself out and again resembled a proper interstate. We moved over right on queue, and that impatient prick behind us shot past like a lightning bolt thrown from the hand of Zeus himself. He moved over in front of the truck and dangerously close at that. This dude sure must have been a fan of Russian roulette, because he spiked the brake, shot us the bird again, and, at the very moment before the truck was about to eat the backend of his pricy machine, the daredevil jumped on the accelerator and disappeared in a flash of blue. The barrel was spun, the trigger was pulled, and the chamber was empty. You lucky fucker.

I looked over to my companion and to my surprise, he was unfazed. I said I was surprised, but don't mix that up with relief. I was in no way relieved. The trucker knew something that I didn't. He knew something of fate, of karma. All these years later, and I still can't explain it, but as I witnessed the little smile that hid itself in the corner of my frightening captain's lined mouth, I could tell that he was convinced that we hadn't seen the last of that little sports car and its arrogant driver. Just a little further down Interstate 40, the reckoning was coming.

The disappearing sun smashed itself out over the desert and now it utterly drenched the land in a blaze of red and burnt orange. Far into the distance before us there was a gleam, a glimmer of something that didn't belong. It was the glint of light as it bounces off glass and it flashed at us like a beacon. Its call was one of distress, but instead of relief, only darker things were called to that stilled blue sports car, its over-heated engine, and its cocky driver.

The trucker geared down the rig and allowed his beast to crawl to a stop about one hundred yards or so from the only other manmade thing in sight. As he exhausted the air from the brake systems of the tractor and its rickety companion, a plume of dust was called up from the ground, and it smoked out the scenery in all directions. Once the ephemeral body of dry earth had begun to dissipate, the trucker creaked open the cab door and climbed down. His boots smacked off the bitten soil below his step, and between his teeth, a fresh cigarette was slid. He sparked its march toward extinction with the complaint of a nearly emptied Zippo lighter and opened a tool compartment that was built into the side of the truck. I could hear the clang of metal as he fumbled for god-knows-what, but then, in an instant, all grew quiet. The trucker had apparently found what he was searching for, but he had stopped a moment, almost like he was granting this tiny tick in time the stillness, the terrible respect it deserved. Out from that dark little hole, he withdrew a winch bar and calmly started over toward the stranded driver. Oh and just in case you're not exactly sure what a winch bar is, it's a big fucking pipe.

I was frozen in place upon the passenger seat. I stared out through the glass shield and all of its yellow trails and dried water marks. As the trucker strolled away from me and into the glare of the infernal sun, he looked to be the archangel Michael sent to expunge the wicked. Only there was no virtue to be found in the bar that was his blade, and as he came slowly upon that unsuspecting buffoon with the overactive middle fingers, I was made witness to something that no other American had seen in more than a generation.

Without warning or provocation, the trucker raised his instrument and brought it down violently upon the head of the offending party. The victim was probably already dead by the third blow. This fact did nothing to calm the storm of punishment that blew through New Mexico that day. As he lay motionless on the ground, his body was nearly cleaved in two by a blunt object and I saw as half of his brain tumbled its way out to the centerline of Interstate 40. Some distance away and I could hear that mad trucker wail as he reduced to brittle fragments one of the more impressive internal skeletons that nature had ever conceived. I swear I could taste his sweat. I could taste the blood of a man I had never met. I was gripped with fright and unable to remove my eyes, not to mention my body, from the feral scene. Every fiber of my being was splintered, and in between the slices was a deeply nestled fear.

On that day, I knew the true meaning of fear. I thought I knew fear before. I didn't know shit. Being arrested, having a car repossessed, having the hottest girlfriend you ever had dump you out of the blue for a dude twice as broke as you, these aren't things to fear. Nope, those things and just about everything else are simply inconvenient. A pain in the ass, not fear. This was fear, watching a man being beaten to death out in the open, under the bright sun, this was real fear. Hey, if it happened to him, it could happen to me, it could happen to you.

Yes, even during that time in America, the specter of death still hovered all around us, but this was different. Car crashes are random, disease is unavoidable. Accidents will happen, as the saying goes. But the ways in which death visited Americans back then was just a means to an end. It wasn't malicious anymore, it wasn't evil. Murder had gone by the wayside. It was relegated to the history books. This is what children were taught and this was the lie that we all swallowed.

Come on, you can't kill murder. It has been with us since day one, it was there that day in New Mexico, and it sure as hell is here right now. Back then, it took me a while to wrap my head around such a notion, but there was one lesson that came at me fast and profound.

I now knew the meaning of life because I'd had death thrust in my face. I truly felt alive and for the first time. What I felt was primal, wholly primal, and exciting. But what I felt most of all? Life, I felt *life*! And then I experienced the second profound revelation: I had to create CrimeSpree Inc.

Rich Hayden

Chapter 2

A fateful walk down 15th Street

Gather around, kiddies, I want to tell you all a story. Okay, I know I'm already doing that but this is just a little side note. This tale serves a greater purpose. Think of it as a terrible little anecdote to the bigger picture. This yarn is about a girl. Not just any girl, a very special girl. She's not at all like the women I have already spoken about. Her name is Alice Spenski and in no way, shape or form does she bear any resemblance to crispy tits Darlene. She is nothing like Lucy Miller, either, and being as though I have never actually met young Alice, that makes her far less important to me. But to the world, to society, Alice is very important. Ignorant at the time of her position in history she may have been, but Alice was a revolutionary.

Ms. Spenski was just twenty-two years of age when she came to my attention, and by all accounts she was the perfect American girl, almost nauseatingly so. She was 5'9"—she probably still is come to think of it—and had hair the color of sunlight. She had an average build, maintained an average weight, and wore all the fashionable clothes that could be found at the mall at that time. She was a cheerleader in high school, an over-achiever in community college, and she loved horses. Young Alice drove one of those Jeeps that practically zips apart for summertime fun. She drank light beer and liked to go to dance clubs in the evening. She had a lot of friends, was well liked and had a peppy attitude that was incurably infectious. Did I also mention that Alice was bored out of her skull?

Yep, born from the white-bread suburbs of Midwestern America and raised with the comforts of a middle class life, little Alice had grown a bit restless. She wanted something to do. She wanted an adventure, a sense of excitement. Partying was fun, boys were okay, but there was a feeling that Alice longed for,

34

even though she had never even experienced it. Hell, she couldn't even describe it, but she knew it was out there, or maybe just inside her, waiting to be awakened. It was about this time that Alice heard the reports of 15th Street and the frighteningly intriguing things that were rumored to have happened there. The reports were sparse and usually found buried in the back pages of newspapers or lost among the jumble of words that creep along quietly as part of a news ticker. 15th Street wasn't very well known at the time, and what was known about it was seldom taken seriously. But Alice knew different. Something inside her told her that it was all real, and the more she thought of it, the more she obsessed over one day walking along its dimly lit path of broken asphalt and garbage.

There are countless 15th Streets all across America, but none quite like the one that Alice sought. It was placed eight hundred miles away from her, in the middle of nowhere, and none of her friends could understand why she wanted to go. She tried to explain the feelings that she was having, the craving for something more, but Alice struggled to understand this herself. As a result, she could talk no one into accompanying her on the road trip, and rather than risk added confusion, Alice kept her fantasies of 15th Street private from her conservative family. So with a week's worth of vacation, a brand-new GPS system, and some sketchy details about an even sketchier place lost in the wilderness of western New York state, Alice hit the highway.

Anticipation was a wonderful and most potent drug, and it kept Alice company during the long drive. No matter what happened, Alice was off to do something that she shouldn't. She was offering herself up to something dangerous. This was real danger that Alice was driving toward, too, not that mock bullshit white-collar danger that was so prevalent at the time that Ms. Spenski was clicking off the miles. She felt like a daredevil, or like one of those bad girls that she had only read about in history books. This sensation gave her a saccharin connection to the likes of Nancy Friday or Queen Arsinoe II or Courtney Love. This feeling swelled in her and it produced a chemical change, an evolutionary uprising of the brain. She couldn't feel it happen, exactly, but once Alice arrived at the entrance to 15th Street and reflected back on her trip, she knew she was different. Oh, how different she was soon to become.

Before she set foot down that darkened alley, Alice thought about what had taken place along the highway. Three hours in, she bought a pack of cigarettes and she didn't even smoke. At hour six, she was traveling fifteen miles per hour over the posted speed limit and blew by a waiting cop. He pulled out and set the strobe lights spinning but instead of calmly pulling over, Alice jumped on the accelerator and kept right on going into triple digits and out of sight. A short while after her mild flight from the law, she exited the highway and grabbed a quick dinner at a burger-and-fries restaurant. She had a bacon burger, cheese fries, and two diet Cokes, and walked out on the check. Eleven hours into her journey, and dusk was approaching. Alice was hazy, a little wired from her string of bad behavior, somewhat sick from nicotine, and she was also having sex with a stranger in the bathroom of a Starbucks. Prior to this tryst, Alice had only been with two other men, both boyfriends and both quite respectful young men. This dude wasn't big on the sweet stuff, but he was hot, and that was good enough for the changing Ms. Spenski at the moment.

As Alice stood under a rusted streetlight and the dented sign that marked the road as 15th Street, she paused another minute to mull over the details of her time spent on the road. The collection of remembrances made her feel jittery, dirty, and a little scared. But Alice didn't feel guilty or ashamed. She was almost proud of herself as she had done more living in thirteen short hours than in the previous twenty-two years of her young life. Alice then stared into the darkness that came pouring from the cavernous road. She heard startled cries in the distance and listened to the voices of cheap neon signs as they spoke to her in crackles.

At her back were the sounds of crickets and other wildlife, and of a breeze that danced through the leaves of the forest. Just one glance behind and everything looked so peaceful and undisturbed. But the vision of unchecked growth that crept behind Alice was natural, and she knew that the soothing exterior of the forest was just a mask that obscured the true barbarism of nature. Surely somewhere deep in those darkened woods was an animal wounded and left to die. Its company was nothing greater than the impending chill of night and the pale, indifferent stare of the moon. There it would die, alone and in agony, but just before its expiration, that beast would know what only the dying can know, the true value of life.

Bored as she had been with her calm existence, Alice didn't seek death any more than the unfortunate beast in the black. But Alice had come to 15th Street for a taste of life. She needed a reminder of its worth, a reminder that possessed the subtly of a cannonball. Alice knew that all-encompassing safety wasn't natural and, as she peered ahead into that lost urban world of uncertainty, violence and grime, Alice knew that fear had become a necessity for her. She needed a taste of it. After all, you can't eat a cake until you bake it. You can't fully appreciate life until you fear its disappearance. Alice couldn't say what might become of her by the night's end, and she loved that elusive and intangible feeling. With that fluttering unease in her gut, Alice stepped on down the road.

15th Street was more of a glorified alleyway than a proper street. Tall and decrepit buildings rose high up into the darkened sky and they walled Alice in. Very few gaps could be found between the collection of crumbling brick and brittle mortar, as nearly every building was built right up against the other. Every now and then, a sliver of open space could be found where the dumpsters and utility service boxes were usually kept. The blackness that spilled from these little wounds was even deeper than the cracked asphalt that challenged Alice's step, and the sense of foreboding that they offered hurried her pace.

Alice scurried past a closed laundromat that had its front windows smashed out by looters. There was a gun store and a pawn shop that both had their front entrances enwrapped in an expandable metal cage. A check cashing loan office sat a bit further down the road and its facade was decorated with flickering lights, yellowed glass and a dried assortment of blood spatters across the door. She anxiously checked her phone and it came as no surprise to Alice that she didn't have any reception. Even though nearly every corner of America now had cell service, Alice had known that 15th Street would be different. But what startled her a bit more was the fact that it was only twenty minutes after nine in the evening, it sure felt more like 4 o'clock in the morning. Everything was closed, dead and abandoned, and as Alice stared up to the heavy transformers and swaying telephone lines above her, she knew she was all alone. Under the roll of the clouds and the cold glare of the moon, Alice felt so small, and she knew that there was no going back now. For the path that had already been placed behind her was just as nefarious as what lay ahead.

It wasn't far behind, but Alice could no longer hear the forest, as it felt like 15th Street had now swallowed her whole. She heard the sounds of blown-out subwoofers as they belched the beats of crude rap music. The discordant hum produced by florescent lights and faulty HVAC units enwrapped her like a film. In the distance, Alice heard as a car refused to start and she was shaken by the loud string of obscenities that followed its disobedience. The angered words soon devolved into a fit of coughing that caused Alice to commence a cautious jog. But for all the noises that unsettled her, Alice's ears were most aware of the telltale clicking sounds made by her shoes, and how they practically called out to the lurking predators like a siren's wail.

Alice knew she had to steady her twitching mind. She was treading the line drawn by panic, and if any more nausea tangled her gut, Alice was convinced she would pass out. She raised her eyes up to the buildings that towered over her like a court of dissatisfied deities and stared into the countless sets of vacant eyes. Using a child's coping mechanism, she frantically counted the many windows that streaked each apartment complex like rows of scars. She tried to number them and assemble some sort of order, just to have a distraction from her present situation, but with all the broken glass and spider-webbed designs that hung inside the warped frames, a simple numerical tally was something that Alice couldn't handle. Concentration became a difficult beast to cage, and the closer that Alice looked, the more dire her surroundings became.

Most of the windows appeared to be nothing more than deadened eyes, but others bled a sickly amber glow. Some blinked at Alice as they evacuated the hues given off from flickering televisions and others produced more noise. Alice couldn't handle the noise. She tried to ignore the shouts produced by a couple mired in a heated argument, but with every shriek of the female's voice, Alice winched. She heard the undeniable sound born from the act of a fist meeting flesh, and, by the third such crack, Alice reflexively clamped her hands over her ears. Tears ran through her makeup, and once Alice found the courage to lower her hands from her head, she actively tried to locate the raging couple. Alice desperately needed to find the source of this din, because the sooner she found it, the sooner she could run as far away from it as possible. But all her searching proved meaningless, for as the screams and wails bounced off all the concrete and glass, something emerged from the black to find Alice.

It came like a scraping, and Alice knew that someone was keeping pace with her as the sounds of heavy boots as they rub against asphalt became more apparent to her. Alice's frazzled mind quickly recounted the stories of all those who had walked out of 15th Street with nothing more than a terrible fright and she prayed for safety. Her mind may have been trying to lull her into a false sense of security, but her body could not be fooled and her legs revealed their faithlessness in prayer as they sent her off in a sprint. During her flight, Alice dropped her purse and passed what seemed to be another girl slumped over dead inside the hazy glass of an old phone booth. In the brief flash that Alice viewed the girl she appeared skinny and sick, disproportionate even. Maybe Alice had just witnessed fresh death firsthand or maybe this was just an eerily placed mannequin? Alice couldn't be sure, as everything seemed unreal to her then, almost as if the whole thing had been staged. Either way, she kept on going without a thought for anyone or anything else until an upturned manhole cover bit her toes and sent her body to the ground.

Under the beams of moonlight, Alice could taste the blood on her teeth as her damaged lip spilt the warm fluid into her mouth and down her neck. The damp road under her dotted her exposed skin in filth, and the curb under her side sent a hot spear of pain into Alice's ribs. Her toes throbbed from the blunt kiss of cast iron and her calves cramped up tighter than her knotted stomach. Alice choked on the pink mucus that slid down her throat, and as she felt the paltry cling of her wrinkled clothes and the lack of protection that they offered, more tears broke from her eyes.

For a moment all was quiet. Alice just laid upon the hard ground in her agony and stared up at the skinny column of sky that the buildings permitted her to see. From this vantage, the graffiti-laden structures looked to be curved at their tops, like they were poised to come down and crush little Alice. This quiet moment of newfound fear, this unsettling silence, was at once broken by a frightening calamity as a stuffed bag of trash was hurled out from one of the black corridors that branched off of the street. It splattered upon the ground, mere feet from Alice's head, and sent all manner of debris around her in a halo of waste. The rank smell of rotten food was hers to absorb and as glass bottles rolled around and clinked off one another, they broke the focus of Alice's raw senses. It felt as though a rattle toy had been violently shaken inside her skull and, before Alice could reorganize her thoughts, she felt as two greasy hands wrapped themselves around her ankles.

Okay, I think we need to stop for a minute. I need to take a break. This isn't a story I tell very often, although I think about this instance quite a bit. When it happened, I was horrified at just how primal the whole thing had been. Which is ironic, because the search for that animalistic instinct that's buried deep inside all of us is what started all of this way back in New Mexico. Anyway, once the full impact of Alice's walk down 15th Street was being felt around the nation, I was pretty sure I had done the right thing. But now, from time to time, I question it. I'm not sure if what I did helped bring humanity back to its true nature, or if this all just served to drag humanity backward. But we'll get around to the philosophy in just a bit, alright?

It needs to be said, or maybe I just want to make myself feel better, either way, I'm not entirely comfortable about what happened next, but everyone who ever walked or worked along 15th Street knew the risks. Alice even informed me that she doesn't regret anything that happened to her that day, and this particular day has been called *important* by a number of respected societal analysts, for whatever the hell that's worth.

So, as to what happened next to perfect Alice Spenski? Well, she was dragged by the ankles down into that dank corridor that stank of body odor and standing water. Along the way, loose bits of road pulled up her shirt and coursed her back in thin, red lines of welts. Her head jumped over a curb and sent a fog into her eyes that stayed with her for the remainder of her ordeal. Once she was tucked into a dark corner of damp concrete and loose garbage, Alice was flipped onto her stomach. Hands tore at her clothing and stripped her naked in a matter of seconds amid her cacophony of screams. She couldn't be sure of just how many hands pawed at her dirtied and bruised skin, but as Alice wept with her face pressed into a plastic bag filled with the decaying remains of fast food, she felt the uninvited penetration of at least two men.

Her rape was a storm of violence, extreme even by the imbruted standards of 15th Street, that lasted mere minutes. Beyond the damage that she had already suffered, the assault left her with a black eye, a chipped tooth, a sprained ankle, and three fractured fingers, as Alice did not go quietly into the lust of her attackers. Her body was also decorated by scrapes, cuts and welts, and into her calm future, Alice could remember this moment by counting the scars that this encounter had earned her. To Alice, it felt like a lifetime had gone away since she first set foot on 15th Street, but in reality, less than forty minutes of time had elapsed. Once the violence had left her, Alice was given only seconds under the black sky and the moonlight. The sweat cooled her body and her heart slowly reined in its thunderous beat. Her mind reentered her body and Alice knew that her turn down 15th Street was over as the footsteps of her attackers faded into inaudibility. It was with this realization that Alice attempted to rise, but before her body would allow her movement, the bright rays and safety of a faux daylight poured down over her.

All the lampposts of 15th Street, even those that looked burnt out and beyond repair, now burst to life. A team of paramedics were at Alice's side with great immediacy, and they took every precaution as they gently placed her on a stretcher. She was wheeled to a waiting ambulance that was clean and pleasantly scented. Two female attendants checked Alice's overall condition and then gave her a tall bottle of icy cold water. They wrapped her in a warm robe, washed her face, dressed her wounds and offered Alice some aspirin for the pain. She was given some oxygen, and with the friendly smiles of the women and the comfort of their soft hands as they took turns holding Alice's, she felt a calm wash over her. One of the nurses, the shorter of the two, who looked not a day older than Alice, even cracked a joke that called a relieved giggle out of Alice's throat.

"So?" the effervescent nurse asked. "How do you feel?"

Alice paused a moment, as though searching for just the right word to describe the new feeling inside her. And then, through a filter of shaken breath and blood-stained teeth, she answered.

"Alive," said Alice firmly.

Chapter 3

The 8th Day Era

Alive. Did you get that? She said she felt alive. Alice Spenski was raped. She could have been killed, and she felt alive because of it. But let's get something straight before we move any further. Alice didn't want to be raped. This wasn't some sick fantasy that she harbored, and she wasn't a masochist. Remember, Alice was a normal girl. Alice merely wanted to place herself into a situation that could offer her a sensation so strong it would confirm that she was, in fact, alive, a human, an animal with instincts and emotions.

The degree to which Alice was assaulted bothered me for an extensive period of time. From the very beginning, I knew that 15th Street would be violent and controversial, but even I didn't see it going this far. The mannequin that I created had now come to life and assumed an identity all its own. The beast that I had stitched together with inanimate pieces was now a force of nature, all feral and howling. Evolution was underway again and there was nothing that I could do. But I again find myself skipping ahead. Tick-tock, you know? Anyway, back to Alice.

Alice became my biggest fan. She wrote me letters, a lot of letters, and called my office on almost a daily basis. Once she got a hold of my e-mail address, she flooded my inbox with great ideas and annoying little messages of no consequence or value. She had become a bit of a pest and a secretary of mine even suggested that I should file a restraining order against Alice. Can you imagine? I was pretty much responsible for this chick being raped, and now I was supposed to file a restraining order against her? I'm not that evil. If Alice felt the need to pester me with countless letters of adulation, fine.

As I said before, I never actually met Alice. I couldn't bring myself to do it. I didn't want to know her, I didn't want to like her. It would have only made my guilt heavier. I did, however, write Alice a lengthy and sincere letter. It was hand written, placed in an envelope and graced with a 95-cent stamp. Fucking ripoff. Anyway, I guess I just like to do things the old-fashioned way. After all, the old ways are what first spun the cogs of this mad machine all those many years ago along a bloodied stretch of Interstate 40. In my letter, I apologized, praised Alice for her courage, and thanked her for all the kind words she had sent my way. I graciously explained to her why I felt we could never meet, but I also never asked her to stop calling the office or fire-bombing my inbox. If this was something she felt that she needed to do, then so be it.

But things seem to have worked out in the end. Alice went on to become a very successful writer, and her poetry has been favorably compared to some of the most respected works in the literary arts. Honestly, I do think America is better off, too. We were too stale for too long. Once we forgot all that made us primal and savage, we also forgot all that made us truly great. We forgot the arts, we forgot what it meant to compose. We forgot our creativity, our very soul. But we have those things back now, for the better and for the worse, in some instances.

I like to think that the good outweighs the bad, but as for me, I'm not better off. This sure is some fucked up thanks I get for reawakening an entire nation.

So let's rewind the clock again. We're going to go way back before the fateful journey of Alice Spenski and long before our 15th Street was ever built. We're going back beyond the day when I watched as another guy's skull got smashed into the New Mexico pavement and even long before I was a budding con-man as a teenager. Yes, we're going all the way back to the medical labs, the constitutionality of the laws and the vaccines that followed. We're going back to the 8th Day Era of America.

The 8th Day Era. This was some fancy tag that a politician had applied to the America that most of those in my generation used to know. It was in reference to that ridiculous story about how God took seven days to create the earth. Which, by the way, might explain why so many parts of our little planet have been so crappy for so long. Seven days? That was all that God could throw at this sucker? Seems a bit hasty to me. Well, either way, this new age was seen as enlightened, at least for a while, and as such, some felt that God had again visited his divine hand upon man. What a masterstroke, let me tell you. We don't call that moment in time the 8th Day Era anymore. Would you like to know what it is referred to as now? Generation Lost. Yep, that's it. Stale, boring, and uninspired, that was Generation Lost. A generation so vapid that we failed to impart any mark on history. An entire generation of Americans, lost. That is, until me and CrimeSpree came along. But let's discuss the beginning of the 8th Day Era before we jump right to its end, shall we?

For many years and with a cost that rose into the billions of dollars, a team of scientists was charged with the task of developing a vaccine that curbed violence. It was a top-secret program that has since been uncovered, along with all the humorous and horrific side effects of their efforts. Like all simple inventions and epic breakthroughs, there was a certain amount of trial and error that had to be suffered. But in the case of this vaccine, the eventual end would justify any means, or so it was thought.

In the early days of the testing, prison inmates were used as the guinea pigs for this heady experiment. Now hold on, don't get too excited! The inmates were all fairly compensated. For their participation, many won their families large sums of money and some were even guaranteed early release. There was only one problem. Most of them died. Oops! One of the first sets of vaccines that were tested on humans completely removed aggression from these over-sized and tattooed lab rats. So far, so good. They also showed no hostility toward each other and it was nearly impossible to provoke them, yay! Oh yeah, most of them also felt the overwhelming urge to kill themselves and many of them succeeded. There was even one guy who cut off his own ponytail just to have something to hang himself with. Now that's dedication, kids.

So Solution #23 was no solution at all, but adjustments were made and progress was slow, but visible all the same. After years of tireless work from some of the brightest minds in the medical community and after years of failure, it was a common sentiment among them that Solution #237 was a winner. Like #23 and the multitude of erroneous fluids that would come later, Solution #237 passed all the animal trials and as a result, it was administered to humans. Within hours of the injections, every last one of the inmates dropped dead. Congratulations, nerds, you made poison. I have a four-dollar bottle of Drano under the sink that can do the same thing.

Solution #312 made all of those blind who were unlucky enough to suffer its test run. Shit, even some of the scientists who handled #312 lost a significant amount of eyesight. Solution #378 targeted speech and left everyone who took it permanently shackled to a foreign accent. I always loved that one. #406 did absolutely nothing, and Solution #499 drove all of its little test subjects right out of their minds. I'm talking padded-cell, helmet insane. Speaking-in-tongues, fighting-shadows, trying-to-chew-your-own-face-off insane.

Solution #499 was some creepy shit and it handed its own form of judgment down onto the heads of its creators. Decades after its failure, security recordings of the Solution #499 experiment were leaked onto the internet. In grainy, black-and-white footage with no sound, all the world watched as crazed inmates rampaged through the medical facility. With no grasp upon reality and no reaction to pain, some tried to bash their way through the thick concrete walls with their own heads as their only tool. I'll give it to those mad bastards, they tried like hell, and not until the pearly white walls were washed in blood and brain did they give up in twitching heaps upon the floor. Others, for reasons only known to the insane, attempted to eat everything in sight. Doctors, other inmates, clothes, staplers, light bulbs, chair legs, it didn't matter. The footage many have been poor, but the vision of a guy busting every tooth out of his mouth on a fire extinguisher without so much as a pause to take a breath will make you wince no matter the quality of the film.

Then there were the empty ones, the ones that just milled around real slow and stared into nothing at all. They mostly could be seen in the background of the mayhem, oblivious, it seemed, to the world as it came apart around them. With their minds flushed of anything higher than the basics needed to operate, many of the patients shuffled along awkwardly and in unsettling patterns. The poor quality and dead silence of the film made these guys look like ghosts. They might have been the hardest to take. One inmate in particular became the face of this atrocity as he took a simpleton's fascination for one of the cameras. He was probably in his seventies, heavily lined by age and prison. His head was full of wiry hair, every bit as gray as his eyes. Before he was shot in the head by the clean-up crew responsible for quelling this little nightmare, he stared unblinking into that camera lens for seventy-two minutes and fifteen seconds. I watched the thing in its entirety once, and after that, I was convinced that founding CrimeSpree was the right thing to do.

You wanna know the creepiest thing about it? In the seconds just before his head gets cleaved by a bullet, the inmate said something into that silent, electric eye. There has been plenty of study and discussion over what he said, but the truth is that we'll never actually know what brand of lunacy came tumbling out of his mouth. I like to think that he was trying to warn us. I think he was trying to give us a vision of the future. The dull, bland, dumb, mindless future. But we never listen, do we? We just go about and fuck around with nature as we see fit. The funny thing about all of this is that if these recordings had hit the internet sooner, the whole project would have been scrapped. But Solution #504 came out first, and do you know what was so special about Solution #504? It worked. Yep, somewhere in an underground lab, most likely hidden under the sands of the desert or tucked away inside a ridge of the Appalachian Mountains, they did it. A team of the most brilliant minds in medical science had formulated a vaccine that would quell our innate urge to be violent.

There were laws, more laws, congressional delays, protests, a small riot, laws, and a couple of more laws just for good measure. In other words, it took some doing, but Solution #504 was finally approved to be administered to the public. Only now they called it Porrima, after the Roman goddess of the future, how nice. So, it was decided that Porrima would be used on a trial basis in Utah, as if enough bad ideas haven't come from there already. But whatever. I guess the thinking was that controlling the collective temper of a bunch of Mormons can't be that hard. Baby steps, you know?

At the age of five, everyone who resided in the state of Utah was given an injection of Porrima once every six months. Everyone. This was a schedule that theoretically extended until the age of seventy. I guess the powers that be figured that by the time you reach seventy years old, you won't be feeling very uppity. This ambitious plan didn't go over very well at first, and a lot of people fled the state. Anti-government protests came into fashion like never before and many of Utah's own sons and daughters refused the injections. The penalties for this disobedience were severe and quick to come. For the first offence, a fine of one thousand dollars was issued. The fine for the next offence was triple that of the first, and for the third offence it was three strikes and you're out, asshole. Actually, you were sent to prison until you agreed to take Porrima. So with a big stick in the right hand of Big Brother and a scary needle in the other, eventually all of Utah acquiesced to the Porrima initiative.

Once it was confirmed that a 100% compliance rate for Porrima was reached, the clock began to run. This was to be a five-year experiment that would be graded by nothing more complex than with a branding of pass or fail. If the Porrima endeavor didn't show lofty signs of success once the allotted time expired, the whole thing was to be abandoned. Billions of dollars were invested in this project, most of it taxpayer money. Perhaps the only thing more frightening to most people than actually taking Porrima was the notion that maybe the product would one day be nothing more than a great shovel used to dig an inescapable pit of debt. But if it was successful, then a whole bunch of crap was about to change. Because in five years, all of America was slated to be put on Porrima.

When Porrima was introduced, violent crime in Utah accounted for only 7.9% of all crimes committed in the state. This was actually a couple of points higher than Utah was accustomed to dealing with, so when that number fell to 6.4% the following year, Porrima was given little credit. After year two the violent crime percentage in Utah fell again, but this time it only slipped downward by half a point. This wasn't all that impressive. After all, these small improvements could still be attributed to nothing more than luck and coincidence.

By the end of the third year, it was looking more and more likely that Porrima was destined to become nothing more than a bizarre footnote in the great big book of America's history. Violent crime had crept back up to 6.1%, and there it stayed through the end of year four. Now we were entering the homestretch and Porrima was running out of gas. It hadn't changed a goddamn thing and, as a result, a lot of the politicians that had backed the Porrima experiment were now looking for work. The twenty-four-hour news cycle was all a-buzz with scathing commentary over just who and how many of those involved should take the fall for the Porrima failure. The protests groups that were so rabid when Porrima was first made known to the public now had a fresh clip of ammunition, and they fired away at the drug and its makers at every opportunity. There were lawyers, an endless stream of lawyers, who came crawling out of the woodwork once year five got underway. They sharpened their knives and put on their Sunday best for the butcher's ball that was about to commence, but there would be no carving to come.

       The trial was over, the clock ran out, and it was time to count all the smashed windows, the home invasions, the barroom brawls. The broken and the bruised, the raped and the murdered. Violent crime still had a piece of the outlaw's pie, but apparently it had since lost its appetite, as only 1.3% of the total share had been nibbled away by its formerly fearsome teeth. This caused people to take notice and Porrima was suddenly taken very seriously, but one nice run after four years of nothing at all wasn't seen as enough to save Porrima from the gallows. After all, if a very average MLB pitcher manages to rack up twenty or more wins in one year toward the end of his career, we say *hey, man, nice season*. We don't put the guy in the hall of fucking fame.

       As it turns out, the bar of medical excellence was set pretty low in those days, and Porrima was given a big, fat stamp of approval. The justification for this was that no side effects could be traced to the prolonged use of Porrima, ergo a national trial would be a harmless, albeit expensive, experiment. That sounds so easy, doesn't it? Understandably, this caused fresh outrage, a batch of conspiracy theories out the wazoo and an avalanche of lawsuit filings. A full-scale riot was even set off in Louisiana that resulted in the deaths of forty-seven civilians and three law enforcement officers. It looked like little Goddess Porrima had some work to do. A lot of people fled to Canada to play hockey and club seals, just a guess, and nearly everybody else who stayed behind resisted the injections in an impressively broad number of ways.

The end result of Porrima was supposed to justify any means, and, as it turned out, the American people were bent on making sure that those behind the Porrima initiative had to employ all means. The peaceful types went on hunger strikes and stoically served prison time for their failure to comply. The violent ones attacked medical labs and government facilities, and the crazy ones killed themselves in an effort to *die pure*. Some places became so violent that martial law had to be declared, as was the case in St. Louis and Galveston. It was still up for debate whether or not the taking of Porrima actually curbed violence, but one thing was made certain: the idea of Porrima-nation caused some chaos. The rest of us just resisted using the tried and true methods typically used to get out of doing anything unpleasant. We whined, complained, hid, pushed and shoved, and were generally annoying to everyone involved with Porrima.

It was a nice run of disobedience, but they got to us eventually. They got to all of us eventually. Their patience was thicker, their resolve was stronger and their medicine was better. It took nearly ten years to achieve a 100% compliance rate across the nation, but to look back on that chaotic decade and the war on human instinct that was waged is a fascinating thing for sure. Consider this: the Porrima compliance rate during the first year was a laughable 0.9%. After that it nudged up to 2.3%, then 4.6%, then 9.2%, and it the fifth year it rose to 18.4%. Are you noticing a pattern here? Yep, the compliance rate for Porrima doubled every year after the second year until the very end, when it took a hell of a long time to achieve that final half of a percentage point. But they got it—you knew they would—and what does this prove? Porrima works. Every year there were fewer and fewer people willing to protest, revolt, and break stuff. Toward the end, it became monkey see, monkey do until those still not on Porrima finally gave up the fight and took their medicine as they witnessed its calming effects.

100% is a nice figure and it looks good on medical reports. It's a number that news anchors and politicians both like, and the public at large is very comfortable with 100%. It's easy to understand and it generally suggests that everything is working A-OK. But nature doesn't give a deep rat's ass for 100%, and, as such, rape, murder and an elaborate menagerie of human violence continued for years after that fancy bastard 100% showed up. Nature is a stubborn bitch, but Porrima was relentless, and nature's reign as supreme ruler was just that, a reign, an empire poised to fall, a moment in time. Good job, nature, you spent quite a while on top. Eventually, a full three decades after Porrima was introduced to every soul in the good ol' US of A, America was declared safe, as not one report of rape or murder was made for a full calendar year.

That was a trend that continued for another thirty years. Can you even imagine, growing up in an entire nation devoid of violence? Sure, it had its advantages, but there were a lot of casualties that fell under the sword of Porrima too, we were just too damn comfortable to see them until it was all over. So this was the 8th Day Era, the thirty years of utopia, the time of God and enlightenment. This was the America I grew up in. This was my generation. What were we called again? No, no, not back then. I mean, what are we referred to as now? Oh yeah, that's right, Generation Lost. Generation Lost—that's not a very flattering title now is it? We'll get to just why my generation earned itself such a tag in a bit, and, believe me, we earned it. But first, let's look at my America, the way it used to be.

If you thought that pampered suburban youth were insufferable before Porrima, you wanted to kill yourself after the drug took full effect. What I mean is, you know that snot-nosed, smart-ass kid who just needs a good ass-kicking by a nerd to straighten him out? Well, now there was no one to beat his ass. I have to admit, Porrima spared me plenty of beatings, of this I'm sure. But anyway, the greater point is that violence, even the threat of it, is enough to make most people tolerable. Only now, during the pompous 8th Day Era, many regular Americans of my generation developed a sense of entitlement that would have made a princess gag.

You see, Porrima was developed to curb violence and it did just that, mostly. Violent behavior wasn't completely expunged from America, but the small amount that had remained was barely worth counting. As I said before, rape and murder had disappeared during this time, and most other severe forms of violence followed their champions into dormancy. By the time I entered my 20s, muggings were all but a memory and even destructive vandalism underwent a steep decline. Bar fights still happened from time to time, and the occasional drunken scuffle at a ball game still took place, but things never escalated. It was like a wall had been thrown up in our minds and once our anger was about to turn to rage, we hit that wall and simply stopped. It's actually kind of creepy to think of it now.

I remember one instance in particular that I watched from the safety of my car while mired in a traffic jam. Some dude had tapped the backend of the car in front of him, and with traffic nearly stopped, as it was, both drivers got out of their vehicles and hurled obscenities at one another. The guy who was on the receiving end of the nudge, a bald-headed tubby fellow in his forties, reared back and punched the offending driver in the face. This dude hit the ground hard but he sprang up in a heartbeat. He was primed for the counterattack, and baldy was set to go on the defensive, but then all of a sudden, they both stopped, like a director had yelled cut. They both calmed quickly, politely exchanged insurance information and got back in their cars to continue waiting in traffic.

Mild displays of violence like this adorable example were rare, and that's all the more harrowing things ever became. But as I watched this play come to a close, I couldn't help but feel that it was one of the most goddamn surreal things I had ever witnessed. It was like watching water fall out of a bucket, stop in midair, and then rearrange itself so as to fall evenly, without a splash. It was wholly unnatural. Don't get me wrong, it was nice to be able to walk through a park at night or explore the streets of a formerly rough neighborhood without fear of being attacked by a hammer or another such unpleasant object. You could even safely meet someone in a dark alley, if that was your sort of thing. But something was just off. We were different and it was something that we were unable to pin down until it was all over.

So, the side effects of Porrima. But wait, you say. There are no side effects to Porrima! Well, there weren't side effects as the medical community would define them, but Porrima changed more than it was intended to, let's put it that way. But what do you have to say about a little suspense first? No? Too bad, it's my story and I'm telling it my way. Besides, I want to touch on the subject of soldiers for a bit. Ahh! You didn't think of that, did you? The whole world wasn't on Porrima, therefore we still needed a handful of our people who were willing to kill other people's people.

This task was made easier by the fact that America was in peacetime during the 8th Day Era. However, the military always has something to do and, as a result, soldiers are always necessary. The emphasis on combat drones and remote attacks was greatly increased during this time, and their heightened use was a great success. As you might have guessed, extreme violence became something of a fantasy, a form of entertainment like never before, which Hollywood and video game makers cashed in on big time. Not to be outdone, the military had its soldiers conduct as many missions as possible from computer labs that utilized combat machines and remote guns. In these scenarios, the images of the enemy that appeared on the high definition screens were digitally altered, or *softened,* as it was called. The enemy looked to be nothing more than imaginary characters in a video game that needed dispatched before the next level could be achieved. To make the killing seem even less real, as in easier, points were even awarded for the quality of each kill. I don't think there were credits awarded that could be used at a gift shop though, which was kind of a bummer.

It can't be totally avoided. Sometimes you need people to kill people. I'm talking gun in the face, knife to the heart, fingers around the throat. Old-school murder. These were the elite soldiers, the Cowboys, as they were unofficially known. Once they joined the military, they underwent an extreme detox process that was said to remove all the effects of Porrima in about two to four weeks. This process also brought on bouts of epilepsy in about 30% of the patients, and its affliction would prove to be a lifelong bother. Yay! Killy McMurder now has a shaky trigger finger. Anyway, something had to be done about these barbarians once their military careers were over, right? As you might have already surmised, once their service was complete, they were pumped to the brim with Porrima. For a period of time, sometimes as long as two years, these bravest Americans were supervised on military bases before they were deemed fit to return to decent society.

Oh, by the way, how can you be sure that a former Cowboy won't fly into a rage unexpectedly? You provoke the hell out of him until he no longer tries to beat your ass. On a daily basis these guys were basically begged by everyone around them to fly off the handle and administer justice, medieval style. For no reason and without warning, these guys were spit at, kicked in the back and punched in the balls as they slept. They had feces put in their food, their clothes were stolen, and they were humiliated in front of their peers, you can guess the ways. The unfortunate soldiers whose job it was to poke the bears wore heavy body armor, but at times a tank couldn't spare these pests from the judgment they courted. One guy, a Rodeo Clown, as these soldiers were aptly known, was beaten into a coma after he posted pictures around the base of himself having sex with a Cowboy's wife. The pictures were real, the act was militarily sanctioned and the Cowboy was deemed not yet ready for society.

Other vicious beatings were commonplace, and though the Cowboys and the Clowns were both heavily compensated for the parts they played, there was emotional damage suffered on both sides that followed these soldiers around like their own private ghosts. Once back in society, the scarred soldiers fell into a lugubrious melancholy as the effects of Porrima masked their pain and numbed their rage. The sorrow hung heavy around their shoulders, and these guys often withdrew from the rest of us and became recluses. The funny thing is that what kept us safe from them is also what prevented many of the tortured from ending their own mental symphonies of discord. Porrima wouldn't even let most people kill themselves. Now, how do you like that?

I love stealing shit! Man, that's exactly how I felt ever since my seventh full year of existence on this strange planet. I was in the 1st grade and right next to me sat Amanda Mathers. She was a plump little cherub and had an attitude that made a porcupine seem snugly. We were learning how to spell simple words that day, and up at the blackboard was chubby Amanda. She had a brittle piece of chalk gripped between the sausages that grew from her palm, and all alone and unguarded on her desk sat a candy bar. I remember seeing the candy and thinking about just how easy it would be to relocate it into my pocket. I didn't have a moral debate with myself and I didn't even come up with a plan, I just took the fucking chocolate.

Amanda was so pissed when she got back to her seat. Not only had she failed to properly spell the words charged to her, but now she couldn't even drown her sorrows in caramel, sugar, and other such sweet delights. I watched as she looked around the floor under her desk, the panic swelling all the while. Eventually, she raised her hand and raised the alarm of treachery to skinny Mrs. Weathers.

Okay, I was sweating bullets right about then. I knew what I did was wrong. After all, I had the presence of mind to stash that sucker inside a social studies book and not leave it out for all the world to see and then scorn my deed. I knew Mrs. Weathers was gonna march right over to my seat and expose me for the criminal I had become. But let's not forget, I was seven years old. I didn't know shit. Mrs. Weathers was thin as a rail, middle-aged and diabetic. She cared about spelling, not about some fat kid's chocolate. She basically told Amanda to pipe down, and that was all the more attention she paid to the missing candy. Fifteen minutes later I was in the bathroom, crushing a sugary snack, and in between every chewy bite I was made aware of just how easy it all had been. You know what's funny? I can't even remember what kind of candy bar it was. I think that's because I realized that it wasn't just a Snickers or a Twix or even an Almond Joy. It was better than that, it was stolen! Chocolate never tasted so good.

I have a feeling that events like this were unfolding all over America at right about the start time of Porrima-nation, because years later, the rate of white-collar crime exploded. Trickery and theft went off the chart. Insurance fraud, identity theft, and a whole menagerie of scams spread through the country like a can of paint carelessly booted over. All of this probably played a big part in my success as a con-man back in the early days. Think about it. The law was busy with the big fish, the guys that were hacking into bank accounts, defrauding corporations, and emptying car lots of new cars without ever spending a dime. In short, I flew under the radar. I kept it small and exploited the lack of resources that the authorities were allotted to deal with every clown who stole five hundred bucks from a senior citizen. Slow and steady wins the race for the tortoise, especially the tortoise that sticks to the shadows.

I'm pretty sure the lesson here is that we need to be bad. Porrima wouldn't allow us to smash stuff and beat each other anymore, so we found other ways of feeding that innate desire to do wrong. I'll give you a few wonderful examples of this unquenchable thirst for going against the grain. The first comes to us from the great state of Wyoming. Wyoming, you say? Yes, Wyoming, imagine that. In the capital of Cheyenne, a very curious crime wave swept over the city. People everywhere were walking out on restaurant checks. This behavior seemingly came into fashion overnight, and quickly people of all ages were caught up in the rapturous fun of eating a full meal and then bolting like a scared dog. This digestive form of thievery became so rampant that the city of Cheyenne eventually was forced to pass an ordinance that declared it only voluntary to pay for food at a restaurant. The businesses would then in turn be subsidized by the government over the lost revenue, as this was seen as cheaper than tracking down and arresting everyone who skipped out on a check. The kicker was yet to come, however, for just days after the ordinance was passed, restaurants were reporting only a 3% walkout rate. That was down from the all-time high of 61% just a week prior. It's just not as tasty when it's legal.

So why did this rash of bizarre disobedience befall Cheyenne, Wyoming? Were there a lot of hobos or hungry people at this point in time? Was the food obscenely overpriced, or was it all just so goddamn good that you had to have it? Why Cheyenne? The simple answer is that no one really knows. Wyoming's event wasn't unique either. Over the years, Porrima seemed to call up these swells of strange behavior among groups of people all over the country, and just as quickly as this weirdness arrived, so then it went away. For instance, in New York City, people began jaywalking like crazy. As you can imagine, this caused quite a problem. In Tallahassee, motorists ignored traffic signals like they didn't even exist. This rendition of bumper cars lasted for a about a week, while in Seattle, a month-long run of intense smoking in public places was all the rage.

But without any doubt, my favorite cartoonish version of organized crime had to be the Black and Blue Bandits of Raleigh, North Carolina. These dudes were probably pretty badass, huh? I mean, the Black and Blue Bandits, they must have been a fight club, right? No, not really. These clowns stole ink. To be more specific, they stole black and blue ink, a lot of it. Any pen at a bank, diner or other business that held those dark hues was fair game. The pens disappeared like the dodo bird and soon ink cartridges, ribbons, and stampers all pulled a disappearing act as well. This went on for months with very few arrests and soon tons of red and green ink were being put into use to try to quell this foolishness. It became quite comical as receipts and contracts of all kinds started to resemble Christmas cards made by a 5th grader. I'm sure by now you've asked yourself the inevitable question: *Where did all the ink go?* This was something that everybody in Raleigh wondered about for quite a while, too, until the now-historic arrival of Ink Weekend. It was a calm Saturday and Sunday set that was bookended by the chaotic and messy days of Black Friday and Blue Monday.

I liked just about everything about these criminals, but using the clever terminology of Black Friday and Blue Monday to literal effect made me love the Bandits. On that fateful Friday, they splattered black ink on just about anything it would stick to. The dark liquid was hurled from pickup trucks in buckets, painted on buildings and bridges like proper graffiti, and arranged in mild explosives to make ink bombs. This was a large and well-organized effort as nearly every corner of the city was under assault, to overstate it greatly, during the afternoon of Black Friday. The following Monday played out in much the same fashion. No real surprises there, but the impression the Bandits left was a lasting one. So just in the event that you've never chewed the artery out of a pen in school, let me tell ya, ink is really fucking hard to remove.

And that was the point. The Black and Blue Bandits disappeared back into society after that with precious few of them ever prosecuted, but they had made their mark. They announced to the rest of America that they were indeed an entity, a creative entity that had produced something of ponderable worth and then left behind bold reminders of their efforts. But I think there was more to it than that. It was about more than just us and our unquenchable desire for attention. I think it was the mind itself engaged in a rebellion against Porrima. The human mind was attempting to announce to the drug that it could not be kept down, that when one door was shut and sealed over, it would find another way to explore its limits.

I'm basically just a cheat who has experienced varying degrees of success. That is to say, I'm not a philosopher and I have never claimed to be one, but just humor me for a minute. I think that the mind and the conscience are two separate beings. Two warring beings, actually. I think that the mind wants to do all things, all the time. It wants to guide your hand to pet a puppy just as much as it wants to guide your hand in the act of murder. The mind sees no difference between the two, and it finds no good or evil in either act. These things, and all things, are simply just acts of doing to the mind, a testament to its power. The conscience, on the other hand is our inner Porrima. It is the part of us that segregates right from wrong and distinguishes good from evil. It reigns in the wildness of the mind and molds its feral power into an instrument capable of awesome creation. Conscience channels the mind down the avenues of the useful, the inspirational, the magical. Peace is made when the two sides come to a truce and work together in a union stronger than the sum of its parts.

Sure, the conscience doesn't always win. That's why we sometimes stab each other and steal other people's parking spaces. And that is my point. Even when we weren't butchering one another, we were still stealing other people's parking spaces. Ergo, Porrima hadn't improved the conscience, it had simply dulled the mind. Our brains were beset with caltrops that came in the form of Porrima injections, and our minds tripped all over them. During the 8th Day Era, we might not have killed each other—that's a plus—we should all be able to agree on that, but not all was well in the mental kingdom. We already touched on the early failures of Porrima. We've discussed the disturbing ways in which the armed forces chose to deal with Porrima, and we peered at some of the silly things we've done since its introduction, but now how about we discuss all of the things that we never did?

During the 8th Day Era, which spanned a generation and change, we Americans made movies, wrote books, painted pictures, and sang songs. However, looking back on all that now, we didn't do any of it very well. To be honest, we sucked. Under the bright lights of technology, we experienced an age of darkness. This was a different type of dark ages. It didn't host much violence obviously, the mortality rate was low and disease was something that worried very few of us. It was creativity, inspiration, and artistic expression that ended up smothered by the blackness of the 8th Day Era.

So, did we give out Grammys and movie awards during that time? You bet your ass we did. Awards, prizes, trophies, all that shit. It went on uninterrupted. This is because we didn't realize just how bad it all had been until after the fact. Metaphorically speaking, we threw white paint on a blank canvas and called it beautiful. This is how it was across the spectrum of the arts and entertainment during that era of vapid gray. I was about to refer to the 8th Day Era as black or dark again, but that would be doing a disservice to those things. At least the darkness is interesting, mysterious. It has something to offer. When mankind explores the dark we sometimes discover incredible things and at other times we get bit by monsters. But for fuck's sake, at least something happens.

During the 8th Day Era nothing happened, and believe me, the rest of the world took notice. The records being made by U.S. musicians were all but completely ignored by the world beyond our borders. Our movies were universally panned by foreign critics who used to trip over one another to praise anything American, and our book sales to other nations were laughable. We were also so arrogant during that time that we held fast to the notion that the rest of the world just couldn't grasp our higher understanding. *If only they were on Porrima too,* we so foolishly thought.

I propose a challenge if you still doubt the wasteland of trash that we produced during the time of Porrima. Watch an independent film from the 8th Day Era and see it all the way to the credits without killing yourself for want of something better to do. Write a will, that's all I gotta say.

But seriously, it's a shame, if you really think about it. Consider the fact that since the advent of the printing press, the paint brush, the moving picture, and the electric guitar, no area of the arts has ever experienced a thirty-year run of complete worthlessness. That is, until Generation Lost came along and all of these mediums waded into an unprecedented mire of shit at exactly the same time. It's sad. Not one movie, not one single song, not one little poem from my generation is worth preserving or remembering. Can you even imagine such a dearth of inspiration? And that is why we are called Generation Lost. We might remember time by the violence or the struggles that we endure, but time remembers us by the things we leave behind. We didn't leave anything behind, anything of value, anyway, and so we, those of my banal generation, are just a hole in time, a vacant slot in history.

But mercifully, the 8th Day Era is over. We are all rediscovering the artistic triumphs of our past and those just in their creative infancy are free to feed upon true inspiration. I have hope for the future. Sure, there's gonna be crime and murder and rape, but there's gonna be all the good stuff again, too. The stuff that makes us forget about all the crime, the murder, and the rape for a while. The stuff that makes us forget about death and instead marvel at life and the arts!

You have me to thank for the resurrection of the arts, you know that, right? You sanctimonious fuckers. A lot of people have told me a lot of things about what I do wrong and I can say with confidence that the only one among all of my critics who was unquestionably right was the dead and lovely Lucy. She always used to say that I curse too much, and, yeah, I do, I won't argue that. But the value and the damage of everything else I've done is up for debate, although the time for discussion is just about over. Let's just take my founding of CrimeSpree, for instance. My business liberated all of America from the clutches of Porrima and returned it back to the bosom of reality. That's how I see it, anyway. A great number of other people do, too, the majority of Americans, in fact. Science doesn't lie. But here I remain, judged, scorned, and punished.

We'll continue with that later—much later I hope. For now, let's ride the time machine again. After all, the last time we discussed the topic of me, I was frozen with fear, staring out the hazy window of a tractor and watching some dude get his brain smashed into the hot New Mexico pavement.

Chapter 4

Coconut, artificial flavoring, and an epiphany

For just a moment, the whole world stood perfectly still. Once the trucker had finished swinging the hammer of god, he just stood there. He didn't move as he stared down at the splattered mess that was once a man. I don't even remember any wind at that moment. It was like I was just gazing into a very large and graphic picture of our lawless and violent past. Everything was soaked in the deep orange of the fleeing sun, and all was deathly quiet, too. That is, until the trucker allowed his pipe to drop to the ground. The sound it made could have rivaled the furious impact of a meteor as it collides with earth, but it was the aftermath of this initial collision that was the most terrifying. As the bar bounced and rang off the ground, each end taking its turn in shaking off the gore, the sharp pings sliced their ominous song into my ears and the light that was refracted off the steel shot right at me. Those rays of darkened amber were hurled straight at me like spears, and as I gazed out at the arid desolation that surrounded me, I knew there was nowhere to run.

I said there was nowhere to run, I never said anything about no longer having the ability, and so run I did. I sprang open the passenger side door of the tractor and nearly flung it right off the hinges in my panic. I took a rough tumble down to the dusty highway and I managed to concentrate the brunt of my clumsy landing onto my right shoulder. I didn't know if it was broke, bruised, or smashed, but it fucking hurt. In the very second that the asphalt kissed my shoulder with its brutal lips, I felt a spark of agony as my nerves rippled a shockwave up through my neck and deep into my skull. The immediate headache I suffered narrowed my vision and drove a wrenching nausea deep into my gut. I felt as a mild splash of puke hit the back of my clenched teeth and I think I might have pissed myself, but there was no time for that, no time for me to collect myself. I had to go.

As I lay on my back with my brain sloshed and my gut tumbling, it seemed to me as though someone from a higher plane drove by and hosed me down with a truckload of misery. All I wanted to do was run, just to get up and run, but a new pain grabbed my attention. My left leg was hung up and stuck on the bent bottom step of the truck, and the expanded metal had its teeth sunk obscenely far into my ankle. I tried to twist and move ever so slightly and I tried to delicately extract my flesh from the dirty metal, but I was quickly alerted to the fact that my emancipation was going to be neither pretty nor easy.

Everyone has moments like these in their lives where there are only two choices to be made, two outcomes to be had. One bad, the other bad. I call these times fuck-it moments, because sooner or later, you just gotta say fuck it and pick one. Option #1 for me went a little like this: I could allow my leg to remain pinched and wait for the trucker to return. Undoubtedly he would've been displeased with the rough treatment I had showed to the door, and he couldn't be happy with all the blood that my ankle had so carelessly spat onto the exterior of the cab. That's when it would become my turn to make out with the winch bar, or maybe he would just get back in the truck and let the highway scrub the flesh from my bones, my bones from my other bones and my soul from my being. No, thanks, let's have a peek behind door #2.

Not any better in here, and yep, I still might die. But even with this knowledge, I find myself with my fists balled tight and my right leg braced up against the step. My knee is bent and I know it's only gonna take one quick thrust, one quick, painful motion and I'm gone. The desert has me slicked in sweat and sprinkled with its dust. Even the fading sun feels like its burning me. I watch my blood as it pools in the creases of the step, and I follow its trails as it courses away from the wound on my ankle. There is no time left to think or feel. It's now or never, a paltry guarantee of at least a few more minutes of life or a certain death. With a palpitating heart, I focused all my strength into my right knee, and with a stare into the darkness formed by my eyelids, I pushed away.

As my leg was cruelly freed, I felt the tears that opened over my flesh and across the things that are meant to remain under the skin. A pressurized spurting of blood flew into the air and arched over me like a rainbow ripped from the atmosphere of hell. The force of my shove was so great that I managed to somersault myself a few feet backward, but not even that was far enough to escape the rain of red. As the hot blood splashed down across my face and my chest it felt like the sun itself had liquefied and fallen to earth.

As I lay in the dirt with scraps of dry and brittle grass greedily sucking at the sweat that covered my body, the gravity of the situation began to settle over me. I was speckled in so much blood that it was impossible to tell just how many wounds I had, and how many were serious. I thought of my shoulder and I wondered just how many bones were lying broken and jagged beneath my skin. Were they going to carve me up from the inside? Was a splintered rib going to find its way into my heart? As I dragged myself up to stagger and limp away, all of my attention was understandably driven back to the flayed clump of skin and bones I so erroneously referred to as an ankle. From the intense heat, my blood already possessed the consistency of water, and I was growing concerned over how much of it was trailing behind me. I didn't really have any medical knowledge back then, still don't, but I am familiar with elastic. I thought of the tendons around my ankle and tried desperately not to dwell on the image of one of those cords unwinding itself inside my leg.

That's when I looked back toward the road. Considering the condition I was in, I had put an impressive distance between myself and the truck, and it now looked as though nightfall was soon to become my traveling companion. I watched as a few pairs of headlights cut through the creeping darkness, but I never entertained the notion of going back. This wasn't help, this wasn't the return of civilization, this was just more death. If they were smart, they would just keep right on driving, fast and far away as they could. But I helplessly watched as one of the cars pulled over and as soon as it came to rest the headlights went out. It was like life was dimming. There was nothing left for me to see, there was no more need for me to linger close to the killing ground that had overtaken Interstate 40 that day. I turned and faced the moon, I stared up at the stars with my bleary eyes, and I thought of all the other ways in which death might come to claim me.

At some point in time there exists the chance that an idiot might read this. Just to cover all my bases, let me make you aware of something: the desert is unpleasant. When most people think of a desert, they tend to imagine a great expanse full of nothing but sand and the occasional tumbleweed. There's a lot more, believe me. This bodes well for variety, I guess, but I wasn't there to sightsee or explore. I was there because I was running for my life, and running for your life in a desert is like jumping off a bridge to escape a traffic accident. In short, it's a bad idea. It sucks.

Oh yes, the desert is full of things you'd rather not encounter. First of all, let me remind you that it's dark at this point, and the absence of light has a way of making any situation more threatening. I can't see the coyotes, but I can hear them howl in the distance, and I wonder if they can smell the blood as it trails behind me in warm pools of human vulnerability. I've never seen a scorpion before, never wanted to, either, and now I find myself in a habitat that supports nearly three dozen species of the ornery little bastards. There are snakes out here, too. Some are poisonous and some aren't, but who really cares? I can't tell the difference anyway. Tarantulas live in the desert and I don't have to tell you just how unsettling this fact is to a person who quivers with unease at the mere sight of a common house spider.

So in case you're keeping score at home, the desert has a plethora of nasty beasts, an abundance of sand, and a near complete lack of water. Of all the things we take for granted, clean water has to be number one on that list of luxuries we now view as ordinary. I never gave it a second's thought. In fact, I even had the nerve to drink bottled water my whole life because the liquid that flowed freely from my tap just wasn't good enough. How could any American be expected to ingest such dreck? What an asshole. I probably would have set fire to an animal shelter that night if it meant I could have just one cup of warm tap water. And speaking of warmth, there wasn't any of that out there either. But it's the desert, you say, the desert is hot. Yep, it sure is—during the day. At night it can be downright freezing. Of course, I was still wearing just my faggy orange shirt and my thin shorts all bedazzled with blood and dirt. They sure didn't do a good job of keeping me safe from the cold, and as I felt the goose bumps crawl over my skin I looked up to the frigid sky that hung above me.

Here's a little PSA, a freebie from me to you. If you're ever disoriented, short on blood and water and just feeling rather lousy, don't look up. When I craned my neck to look to the sky, that bowl of stars swirled around me like the whole world had been put in a blender. I remember feeling dizzy, but it was just a fleeting sensation. I'm pretty sure I passed out cold before I even hit the ground.

How much crap can one dude be expected to shovel in one day? When I woke up, my tongue was tender and it immediately relayed to me the news that two of my teeth had been aggressively harvested from the bone farm inside my mouth. They were front ones, too. I'm looking better every day. But it wasn't all bad, after all, I woke up.

He is risen! I heard someone say. It was a joke and it garnered some laughter, but as my ears collected the voices around me and as my face absorbed the touch of a new sun, I knew I wasn't alone. This relieved me and it scared me anew all at the same time. By this point, I had surmised that someone had taken some measure of care with me, but I also knew that I was still in the desert. I hadn't opened my eyes yet, but I could feel the dust in the air and I could feel the raw rays of the sun as it cascaded, unfiltered, down from its position to mine. I also heard the twang of a slightly out-of-tune banjo as it gave a rhythm to the dirty limericks that were being sung. This kinda tipped me off that I wasn't in the hospital.

As it turned out, a group of hippies decided it would be cool to camp out in the desert that night. They had arrived in a creepy-looking van that appeared to have been built for the sole purpose of pedophilia and had parked it not far from where I was passed out in a heap. Sometime during the night, when the campfire and the joints were blazing heartily, a lanky fellow named Chuck wandered off to take in the desert and to take a piss. He was close enough to notice me in the dark, which unfortunately means that I was probably in the splash zone, but hey, at least he didn't have to shit.

Apparently Chuck thought the best plan of action was to freak out and announce to his friends that he had just stumbled upon a dead guy. He was damn convinced of this fact too, and as a result, I laid there not knowing any kindness or care for another hour and a half. At first no one would even believe him. I guess people with soul-patch beards and hemp necklaces aren't the most reliable sources of information. But he was insistent that a dead guy was lying in the dirt and so, after some time went by, the five friends formed a circle around me and debated what to do next as their minds swam in a soup of beer, pot, and shock. It was a lucky thing that my mouth produced something that approximated a cough with them all standing over me, because Chuck could finally put down the theory of me being dead. My being alive was a revelation that gave Chuck a fresh reason to freak out all over again, but at least it gave the others a reason to help me.

Lying on the rocky ground with my eyes half closed, something kind happened, but not right away. I'll get to that. Something cruel and brief was to come first. As I tossed my eyes slowly around the circle of five, I couldn't make out any of their faces. Well, almost, there was one familiar vision. There above me I saw her again. Lucy Miller was gazing down at me. She was there to dress my wounds, to wash my dirty face. She had come to save me, to take me home. I didn't feel dead in that moment, I felt very much alive. This wasn't some ghost or angel sent to collect me, this was actually Lucy. I must have heard wrong, there must have been some mistake. Lucy wasn't dead! She was right there in front of me! I knew my speech was going to be slow and slurred, but I wanted to talk to her, to say hello, to ask to hear the humorous tale of how her death was falsely reported. I felt vigor in my body, I felt happiness, I felt hope, and then I heard a voice fall from those familiar lips that was as foreign to me as life is to the moon.

A poppy cadence delivered words from a dry throat that was rendered rough by the effects of smoke, and, as this voice carried on, my eyes were forced completely open. Lucy's face melted away and under this mask was a girl named Tori. Young Tori was your typical hippie chick. She had a few braids tangled among her otherwise frizzy, auburn hair, she wasn't wearing a stroke of makeup, and her clothes were drab and baggy. All in all, I guess she was cute, and definitely well built, but the short story was simply that a shower and a bra would have gone a long way to pretty up earthy Tori. But hey, back to the kind stuff, right?

The three guys helped me up and set me in the back of their van. It was a lot cleaner than I would have ever thought, although now the putrid stench of patchouli was added to my offensive aroma. Tori then set about fixing me. She used what little water they had left to wash my face and clean out my

71

wounds as best she could. She wrapped my ankle in strips of cloth that were no doubt the remnants of a dirty shirt, but, hell, it was better than nothing. She fed me some granola crap that tasted like organic ass and pulled the last of their cheap beers from the cooler. Once I washed that gravelly shit down, Tori dabbed the sweat off my face and stepped back as if to examine me.

There was another girl who stayed with me and Tori in the van, although she didn't seem too interested in what was going on. Once Tori seemed convinced that I wasn't gonna die, the other chick bailed. Her name was Orchid or Tulip. I can't really remember, but she had a flower's name, I know that much, and I'm quite sure it was a nickname she had bestowed upon herself. She looked more like a Melissa or a Tiffany to me. Either way, I'm sure she hated the name her parents had given her. She just seemed difficult like that. The guys, they couldn't have cared less about what was happening in their van, as they were more interested in playing hacky-sack, and sucking at it, I might add. Petunia, or whatever the fuck she called herself, took to sitting all alone on a rock. She didn't do much and it looked to me as if she was impatient with the whole situation. These people who probably weren't really even her friends, everything. I think Dandelion had a drug problem that she was itching to sate.

But Tori was different. For all the peace-loving hippie crap that surrounded me, she seemed to be the only one of the bunch who actually could be bothered to aid her fellow man. She talked to me for a while, not really about anything in particular. She just kept me company. It felt pretty good, especially after what I had just witnessed the day before. And speaking of the winch bar massacre from yesterday, not a damn one of them believed me, not even Tori. They all thought I was suffering from the heat, and the general consensus seemed to be that I had been lost out in the desert for quite a while. I was so adamant and graphically descriptive that an air of unease settled over the cramped van as we drove out of the desert. They all really started to believe that I was just a crazy person and flower-bitch even suggested that they throw me out.

Fortunately, I wasn't cast back into the desert, but I think they were quick to unload me. Tori was more or less sweet to me the entire time—she even gave me a hug when we departed— but I could sense that even she was relieved just a bit to see me go. They dropped me off at a town big enough to support bus service, and then drove off into the distance with a story they would tell for the rest of their lives.

That's when it hit me, just how profound and important the whole experience had been. Because now life had become more real for me, more alive. I was shown the fragility of my own existence. I was flooded with emotions and sensations. Most of them were terrifying, but that didn't matter, my own feelings were outside the bigger picture. I was flooded with emotions and sensations that I had never felt before. Never, not once, not ever. And though my time with the trucker was frightening, it awakened an area of my brain that Porrima had put to sleep. My senses felt heightened. My observations were more sharp. The world looked bigger, deeper, and full of more color than it had before.

I imagine that those hippies shared in a little of my awakening, because fear and doubt had been put back into them. Before they found me, not one of them ever entertained the thought that they might stumble across a madman in the desert. Not one of them ever had an inkling that murder was an act that might descend upon them. But from now on, for the rest of their lives, each one of them will feel just a prick of unease, just a blink of hesitation every time they look down a barren stretch of highway or peer into the creeping dark. The ravings of my lunacy gave them just a small view into the range of feelings that Porrima had stolen away from them. The unknown was given back to them.

Rich Hayden

That was the answer, I said to myself as I sucked on some Zingers inside the lobby of a dirty and sparsely populated bus station. I finally figured out Porrima. We should have never shed our fears of violence or our hesitations about the darker side of mankind. After all, these things still flourished in other countries. Sure, our borders were fortified and entrance into America by any means was a difficult, brief, and often supervised thing, but these unpleasant things were still a possibility. They were all around us in some sense. We didn't fear violence and murder anymore not because they ceased to exist, but rather because we were already dead. Porrima had beaten us to death. We were walking corpses, unimaginative, uninspired. We had become robotic and boring. The poet William Morris probably put it best when he said this.

I am a boor and the son of a boor...how often it consoles me to think of barbarism once more flooding the world and real feelings and passions, however rudimentary, taking the place of our hypocrisies.

Sure, that sounds a little hoity-toity today, but it fit. In fact, that observation of a time that existed centuries before mine defined Generation Lost perfectly without another word being needed. But I had a solution to this problem, for our collective malaise, we just needed a little amusement.

Chapter 5

CrimeSpree

We're not superheroes. That's why we make movies about Spiderman, Batman, and their ilk. We dream about outer space, write songs about knights, dragons, and the bottom of the sea. We paint pictures of things that have never existed and write books about things that never will. We cheer on our favorite sports teams as they hit all the home runs and score all the touchdowns that we all used to pretend to do as children. It is this imagination, this make-believe, that sustains all of us. We all have the inborn need to imagine ourselves doing fantastic things without the pain and labor of work, just as we all imagine ourselves doing wicked things without the bother of consequence. We play cowboys and indians because pretend death is interesting and enjoyable. We ride roller coasters because we like to be scared, so long as safety is waiting for us at the end of the ride. Bingo.

Can you guess what lies between Jamestown and Binghamton, New York? Oh, don't even try! The answer is not a goddamn thing. Okay, okay, there are some small towns along the way, cornfields, cows, and such, but for the most part, not much else. But for just a brief stretch of time, a tiny portion of this no-man's land was home to CrimeSpree. So what was CrimeSpree exactly? I'm sure you're dying to know by now, and this feels like the proper time. CrimeSpree was...wait for it, wait for it! An amusement park.

I've been accused of being a lot of things: the leader of an underground crime syndicate, a new-age Don. This is rubbish. Those things, I have never been. I'm an entrepreneur, a businessman, a person with vision. I was a guy with a good idea, there was a public with a need, and there was money to be made. I've even been called a drug dealer for these reasons, which is complete crap. We didn't even sell cigarettes at CrimeSpree, for Christ's sake.

So CrimeSpree, my wild idea given form, it was quite a sight to see. The small portion of land that I purchased for next to nothing was cleared, leveled and prepped for construction. Up from the ground then rose a replica of seventeen city blocks, and not just any city blocks. They were some of the most sordid, dirty, and squalid streets you could imagine. Nothing so new ever looked so damn bad, that's for sure.

The whole area was paved first, and we took special care to make sure that it didn't come out perfectly level. Once that thin coat had dried, me and the hired hands had some fun decorating that massive black square in tire tracks and divots. After that came the lumber, the construction equipment, and the buildings. Man, were they a mess, but you certainly couldn't accuse me of being wasteful. We used every kind of worn out, used, and inferior material that could be found for cheap. Many of the phony buildings were just empty shells, while still others were nothing more than old movie sets. Some of the warehouses and apartments that we threw up were real, though. Real enough I should say. Some had electricity and running water for the obvious reasons, while some of the more involved buildings had entire floors that were habitable. The employees of CrimeSpree used these spaces to help run the park, and often times this is where we staged our actors to put on fake fights and screaming matches. I kept an office in one such building, and we even lodged some of the employees on CrimeSpree property, as ours was a pretty remote location.

Once the buildings had been put up in rows that resembled seventeen narrow alleyways, we took to the task of assembling the finer details. We put up rickety lampposts, some real and some not, street signs, mailboxes, phone booths, parking meters and billboard signs. We strung traffic lights and miles of assorted cables, most of which carried absolutely nothing. We parked junk cars along the curbs and left them there to rot away. Plywood was nailed up and anything that came out looking too nice was beaten down. Store fronts were set up, rather haphazardly, and most were made to resemble establishments that had been looted or robbed. We even burned a few for some jollies. You gotta keep morale up, right?

Then came the tedium. Summer was in full roar at this point and we now were faced with the task of hanging signs and torn curtains in windows and painting hours of operation onto the fronts of our faux businesses. Since you could see into the many establishments that were at ground level, we had to put glasses on the bars, cigarette butts in the ashtrays and we had to dress the mannequins that posed inside the boutiques. We strung lines between the buildings and hung out dirty clothes that we never planned on retrieving. Stereos were set up and light bulbs had to be screwed into the fixtures that were wired. There were plumbing issues that needed addressed and manhole covers that needed to be laid over sewers that didn't even exist. Look, the list goes on and on. I can give you a copy of the expense and planning report from the setting up of CrimeSpree. Few things are as boring, trust me.

But as autumn arrived, all of our collective aggravation was about to be rewarded. It was time to set about spreading the icing over this rancid cake, which, by the by, was a blast. It took weeks, but not a soul complained as everyone took vigorously to the task of trashing our fake village. We littered the streets, smashed in windows, bent the signs and the poles and sloshed the whole damn town in graffiti. Mannequins were hidden in dumpsters and slumped over the steering wheels of cars. We staged these inanimate people in any dark corner that might bring a fright to a patron and had makeup artists complete the look of our imposter corpses. Water was pumped into a few chosen buildings until its touch softened the structures and offered a nice, musty funk to the sky. A lot of gunfire filled the air that fall, too, as just about everyone involved with CrimeSpree took their turn in blasting holes through just about everything. Ahh, good times.

Well, it took months, but finally the sounds of hammers and back-up alarms ceased. Fourteen scummy replicas of filthy urban life had been erected, and then it was finally time to give a portion of CrimeSpree that inviting atmosphere that every proper amusement park has. The first three streets of our unique little town looked a bit dangerous, too, but in that alluring, city-chic sort of way. Most of the lights worked, and the music that was pumped out of the brand-new speakers sounded good. A customer could venture into most of the shops in this three-block stretch and enjoy a cheeseburger or have a drink. There were a couple of arcades set up, a gift shop, and plenty of customer service centers just to remind everybody that in this area of CrimeSpree there was nothing to worry about.

The mouth of 1st Street looked directly out into the parking lot and the wildness of rural New York. This is where we set up the turnstiles, took the tickets and stamped the hands of those old enough to purchase alcohol. All of our food vendors lined 1st Street and offered the usual fare of funnel cake, corndogs, cotton candy, and a bounty of sugary soda pop. If you took a turn down 2nd Street, you would find all the games and the weirdos that ran them. Most of my employees were rather normal, boring people but I encouraged them to dirty up and act the part of proper carnies when they were working the money wheel, the dart toss, or any other street-fair favorite. 2nd Street was the busiest section of CrimeSpree, as most people apparently like to gamble, play games, and snack just on the other side of harm. I always thought this was funny. Some people drove halfway across the country to visit CrimeSpree and most never wandered any deeper into it than 2nd Street. Thanks fools, you forked over coin to see nothing more than a common bazaar.

But this was the charm of CrimeSpree, that intangible *It* factor that even I failed to predict. We opened our doors in March and unsurprisingly, business was slow. It was cold, no one had ever heard of CrimeSpree, and we were placed in the middle of nowhere. But by the end of spring, everything changed. We became the toast of pop culture, and just a visit to CrimeSpree bought bragging rights impressive enough to make any ordinary dork into the man. We sold souvenir flyers that listed how many streets a customer was brave enough to explore and we offered photo opportunities in any area of the park. You just had to arrive early and lay down a ten spot. The bottom line was that CrimeSpree was cool and it became a cool place to be. We even had regulars who would come on a weekly basis and never leave the amusement and relative safety of the first three streets.

Which brings me to 3rd Street. It was like that thin wall that stands between your apartment and the wife-beating, meth-head who lives next door. It was the fragile barrier that strains to keep the violence out while letting all of its feral shrieks in. As you might have gathered, CrimeSpree was only open at night, and with a walk down 3rd Street, one was made immediately aware of just how unsettling the dark can be. 3rd Street held all the bars and nightclubs, we even put up a small strip joint just to increase the sleaze factor. It was patronized by people of shaky morality, and with all the stimulus of bright neon, loud music, and the carryover of screams from the roads beyond, 3rd Street could feel quite intimidating.

No one under the age of eighteen was admitted into CrimeSpree, and everyone who did get in had to sign a waiver that absolved the whole shebang of any responsibility. As a result, we were pretty liberal about what was allowed to take place. The first two streets were kept in order, the final fourteen were purposely made dangerous, but 3rd Street was a fantasy land, and as long as things didn't get carried away, we kept the policing to a minimum. It was the devil's playpen, if you will. People drank too much, had sex with strangers in dark corners, and generally behaved loudly. That was kinda strange to witness. It was a primal exhibit of us, not us our best, mind you, but a part of us that had been locked away.

There was one part of 3rd Street that possessed a quiet though. It was a strange quiet, one that was unsettling, and one that rang of uncertainty. A diner was put at the end of 3rd Street, which was also the entrance into the final fourteen alleyways of CrimeSpree. Here some people gathered to have a cheap meal before exploring into the unknown, but often times, they talked themselves out of venturing into actual danger. It was interesting to watch as people silently contemplated the benefits and consequences of voluntarily walking down roads which could lead to any number of violent assaults or violations. These diner people were different than those who came to CrimeSpree simply to misbehave with their friends. The quiet ones who stared into their coffee, never really finding the nerve to step into the unknown—they were the ones that CrimeSpree was built for.

I used to be one of them. Porrima was sunk so deep into our minds that we became frightened and indecisive about every aspect of life. Danger—the smell of fear, the threat of harm—no matter how small, was enough to make us useless. We could do and create nothing of worth because we were just too damn scared. This was the ultimate failure of Porrima. Sure, it removed violence from our being, but it could never fully remove fear and doubt. Why do you think I shuffled from state to state my whole life? Why do you think I could never hold a job? Why do you think I always cheated and stole just to get by? Huh? I was always scared, I was a runner, but one evening in New Mexico I was shown something actually worth fearing. That's what these people needed, they needed just a taste of what I saw. They needed a glimpse of the end so they could appreciate the here and now. But most of them never went in. I just wasn't given a choice along Interstate 40.

And then there were the ones who had just come out. Even though every street had its own exit, the diner at the end of 3rd became something of a hangout and a place to recover. Some people would leave the park right after a trip down one of the final fourteen streets, but these people were rare. Most preferred to stick around for a while. It was a surreal thing to see, the look of these people. They were different from everyone else and they knew it. They wore the looks of bravery, determination, and pride right on their faces for all to see. They became momentary celebrities, as everyone at the diner wanted to hear their tales. As soon as one of the survivors walked through the door with their shuffled clothes and that unmistakable look of fear in their eyes, the whole place would get quiet and wait. Most of the survivors would order a meal, or maybe some coffee, but others could barely sit down, as they needed to get it all out right then and there.

They all had their own way of telling stories and they all had their own flair about them, but every story taught the same lesson. These people had experienced something profound that most everyone seated around them couldn't even fully imagine. They excitedly described the horrible filth of the streets and the stench it created. They quietly spoke of the assailants that were met in the shadows as if these criminals still lurked just inches behind. They held everyone in a taut state of attention as the survivors feverishly rambled on about what it was like to flee from the villains who closed in all around. They rolled up their sleeves and unbuttoned their shirts to show off the bruises and cuts that were earned from the journey. The bruises and cuts that were *earned* from the *journey.*

Just one trip down any of these fabled fourteen streets of CrimeSpree was a journey indeed for these people. It was their own personal *Odyssey.* Sure, the path of Odysseus spanned decades and this was nothing more than a half-hour or so spent inside an amusement park, but it was life-changing all the same. When it was over, when these people came out the

81

other side, they were different. They were damaged and made new because of it. This is how far we had fallen as a species. A visit to CrimeSpree now qualified as daring adventure. Hey, it made me a ton of money, so I won't bitch too much, but you have to acknowledge just how ridiculous that is.

So, as for the adventure, the harrowing interlude found between the beginning and the end, the frightening unknown that stirs between point A and point B. Here it is. At CrimeSpree we recreated criminal situations that once existed in America and charged people to play the victims. Simple assault was featured on 4th Street. Here you could expect to be mildly tussled or maybe punched at the worst. You could bring along a friend or go in a group. This led to most people running out of 4th Street without even a scratch. 5th Street offered the same unpleasantries, only 5th Street was a one-at-a-time ride. You had to go alone. In the event that you were a real tough guy, we upped the ante on 11th and 12th Streets. They were operated by the same rules as their counterparts, 4th Street and 5th, only here the violence was increased. Even in a group, you probably weren't leaving 11th or 12th Street without a bloody nose or a chipped tooth. We even had a few instances of broken bones. Oh, the cost of being entertained.

Here's a hint, don't bring your valuable shit with you if you plan on sauntering down 6th or 7th Street. Down these dirty avenues you could very much expect to be robbed, in a group or by yourself, respectively. 9th and 16th were big money-makers for CrimeSpree, too. You wanna know why? No overhead! Not a goddamn thing took place on these streets. They were completely unmanned except for the necessary medical personal who hid just out of sight. We listed 9th and 16th Street as mystery streets on our menu of violations and everybody clamored to get in line. There were even stories about the crazy shit that took place along these forgotten roads, but our cameras and employees proved that these wild tales of

82

criminality were in fact just that, fables. People sure do love to exaggerate.

8th and 13th were quite bizarre and they added an unsettling ambiance to the neighboring streets. These were the harassment streets. Sounds preposterous, right? Well, it kinda was. As you might imagine on 8th Street our employees hurled insults and vulgarities at those who passed by, all in an effort to put our customers on edge. The raving lunatics of 8th Street mostly stuck to the shadows and were rarely seen in plain view, but this was not the case on 13th. The 13th street of CrimeSpree was a malcontent monster. Yes its bark was worse than its bite, but the bark of 13th Street was still pretty fucking mean. We had a lot of people manning this street, more than any other, as we gave it a gangland atmosphere. Bottles and other light debris were hurled out of the windows down at those who passed by below, while on street level, an intimidating mob milled about.

The screaming was constant, truly overwhelming, and it spilled into the air of the surrounding blocks. As the guys shuffled past, they were endlessly reminded that they were faggots or pussies. They were peppered with disparaging remarks about how their dicks were little and about how they pissed the bed as grown men. The girls fared no better. Their breasts drew constant attention and malicious scorn. They were called whores and junkies, and if they had to endure the threat of rape once during a flight down 13th Street, they probably suffered it one hundred times more. Rank water was tossed at these punishment gluttons. They were spit at and speared with unspeakable obscenities. 13th Street was a mind-bender, that was for sure. It was an emotional beating. More people ran crying and in a panic from this street than any other, and most were never even touched. The power of suggestion can be a wicked bitch.

Without the inclusion of the next four streets, CrimeSpree would have still been a hit. It would have been prosperous and fun, it would have still been dangerous, and, most likely, it would still be open. But that's not the point. Without the inclusion of the next four streets, CrimeSpree would not have changed the common American, and they in turn would have not changed America. Sometimes the best ideas aren't fully appreciated until they're dead and gone.

Dead and gone, now that's a chilling thought.

10th Street, otherwise known as murder row. With those seven words I bet you're convinced of the reason that CrimeSpree no longer exists, well guess what, slappy? You're wrong. 10th Street was advertised as murder row, but no one ever actually died there. It was nothing more malicious than brilliant marketing. We told people that they were gambling with their lives if they fancied themselves brave enough to traverse the grimy stretch of 10th Street, and, man, did we sell the lie hard. A special waiver was drawn up just for this road and it was comically stuffed with enough legal jargon to drown an entire courtroom full of lawyers. The document was so full of twists, turns and nonsense that we actually got people to believe that we could kill them and suffer no repercussions for it. Listen up, now, because I want to say this as clearly and succinctly as possible. People are fucking stupid.

The truth about 10th Street was that it was nothing more than a dishonest version of 12th Street. Sure we attacked those who walked the road, got into some nasty fights and spilt enough blood to earn the street a fierce reputation, but we never killed anybody and we never tried. However, everyone who purchased a ticket for this ride was under the impression that they might be killed, and that made it real enough. The illusion was so real that rumors persisted about those that had met their end here and names were even attached to the ones who supposedly left 10th Street in body bags. You couldn't type the word CrimeSpree into a Google search without the word murder trailing too far behind in the search results. Predictably, the menagerie of misinformation, half-truths and blatant lies that is the internet was utterly striped with horror stories about the parade of death that occurred at CrimeSpree. There's a reason we rarely advertised.

I want to take this opportunity to thank just about every American politician and just about every group that even loosely associates themselves with a guy that we think might have been named Jesus. You guys made me a lot of money. Which is funny, because as CrimeSpree rose in popularity, it came to my attention that these very people probably missed violence and crime more than anybody else. Railing against such things is good for approval ratings and donations, if you follow.

I gave those in government and those mired in archaic ceremonial practices a new pedestal to stand on, and it was just as high and mighty as any they ever had. I didn't receive much thanks for this favor though, did I? Hell no, I didn't! CrimeSpree was boycotted by those who never had any intention of visiting anyway, and demonstrations were held just on the other side of my property line. My car was vandalized, my employees were harassed and even the front facade of CrimeSpree was decorated with quaint messages about how God thinks I'm an A-hole. How warm and fuzzy. Just a note to the graffiti artists, next time send me a fax. I don't like spending my mornings painting out Bible verses.

Believe it or not, I like to spend my Sundays watching football, enjoying some snacks, and lazing on the couch. I don't wanna think about work, and I sure as hell don't want some dude knocking on my door trying to save my soul with the Word. Long story short, the religious types were annoying, relentless, at times, but the politicians were even worse any time an election of even trivial importance was looming on the horizon. These guys made the shuttering of CrimeSpree top topic, and they made sure that my fine establishment was thoroughly investigated numerous times. They always begrudgingly reached the same conclusion, though: I was doing nothing wrong, and CrimeSpree was run by the letter of the law. We had a lot of accountants, a handsome collection of lawyers, and all of our customers entered our gates by their own volition. We provided medical care to the injured, and, as absurd as this sounds, we maintained a safe environment.

No one could get it through their heads that CrimeSpree was a great illusion. It was fake. It was less dangerous than bungee jumping, hang gliding, surfing, skiing, rock climbing, and chess. Chess? Yes, chess. I'm sure somewhere in the annals of history somebody has died while playing chess. Nobody ever died while inside the gates of CrimeSpree. Outside the gates is a different story, but I'll get to that in just a bit. Which leads me to the point that these and other leisure activities are commonplace and often encouraged. Some people just wanted to attend CrimeSpree once in a while to get a lasting fright. What's so bad about that? People go to 3-D horror movies all the time. I just allowed them into the 3-D horror movie.

Hey, we have three more streets to visit on our tour de CrimeSpree, so let's get a-going. 17th Street, the last alleyway in the smallest and most dangerous city in America, was a voyeurs paradise. We gave this place a special name. We called it *Witness to the Crime*. All along 17th Street a whole plethora of illegal activities were put on display for all to witness and marvel at. Everybody slows down to stare at a car accident, right? This was the only street in our twisted little town that kept the customers out of the action, and only the most skilled of our actors got to work on 17th Street and enjoy the hefty wage it bestowed.

In the darker corners of 17th Street, we had our actors participate in mock assaults that ran the gamut of intensity. I use the word mock because we weren't going to beat our own asses. That just wouldn't have made good sense. We made the fights look real and used the cover of darkness to our advantage. We pretended to rob the employees who we had planted in the audience, snatched purses, and that sort of thing.

And, yes, we gave everyone who walked 17th Street a front row view of what rape kinda looks like. As you might imagine, we used actual couples, and mostly the ones that got a thrill from having sex in front of strangers. This went off fairly well, but if you looked close enough, you could uncover the farce. Some of our exhibitionists seemed to enjoy themselves a little too much. Remember, people, this is supposed to be a bad thing! Others had a hard time getting through the ruse without cracking a smile, but we did have those couples that took their jobs very seriously. From beginning to end, these actors were all business, and with all the rest of the uncomfortable stimuli that came with a visit to CrimeSpree, these imitation rapes were unnerving at best.

I'll admit it: this aspect of CrimeSpree was immoral and disgusting. There are some things that you can't unsee, and for this reason, I didn't spend very much off-time on 17th Street. I heard stories about those who were plagued by nightmares after a visit to *Witness to the Crime*, and I'm not at all surprised. It was a horrible place and it was meant to be so. We were a living, breathing museum of deplorable human behavior and we did our best to be convincing. I'm not proud of everything that took place at CrimeSpree, and I'll be the first to admit that it did get out of hand. I made a monster, and monsters are hard to control. But it can't be overstated that everything at CrimeSpree was voluntary, and, to some extent, enjoyable for our customers. Hey, if you order a rare steak, sometimes you get blood in your mouth.

Aside from those visual sights of savagery, we made sure to pay close attention to just how terrifying it is to hear a crime that unfolds just out of sight, just around the corner. We set up people in the upper floors of the surrounding buildings and encouraged them to raise every variety of hell. Out of sight, these employees would shout all sorts of obscenities at each other while the most shrill-throated of our girls would scream at the top of their lungs. Way up above the frightened patrons, the actors would fire off blanks, bang pots and pans, and slap hunks of meat around in an attempt to mimic the sound of someone being severely beaten. We used these tactics on most of our streets, but on 17th and the harassment avenues, we really ratcheted up the ferocity. It all sounded damn scary, too, and eerily real, but to actually see how this magic was made was anything but frightful. A bunch of adults were regressed back to children as they giggled quietly in front of their friends while yelling the F-word and breaking shit. Funny stuff, for sure.

Those who bought a ticket for 17th Street were led down the center of the road by a carnival barker of sorts. This colorful character would act as a tour guide as he drew attention to all the despicable behavior that was taking place. With a fractured cadence and a sharp voice, our MC loudly described what was put on display. All the while reminding the audience of just how vulnerable they were. At any moment they might suffer a multitude of violations, he warned, as he cackled with mad delight at every sight of violence and barbarism.

His name was Clint Ruin, and I'm certain that this wasn't his given name, but it appeared on three different forms of his identification and so Clint Ruin he was. Clint was one of our first and most loyal customers, and, man, I'll never forget the day I met him on 2nd Street under the heat and the dusk of a late spring evening. Way back then nobody knew who I was. The fans of CrimeSpree and its biggest detractors might have known my name, but no one really knew who I was. I was a common nobody, but not to Mr. Ruin. He knew exactly who I was. To this day I don't know how he knew as much about me as he did, and to be honest, it still kinda gives me the creeps.

I was leaning over the counter of a game we called Poke, Pop, Prize! It was nothing more than our version of the classic carnival game that features rows of balloons taped to the back wall of the game stand. A couple of bucks bought a handful of darts, and if the thrower was able to burst one, two or three of the balloons, a prize was won. Pretty simple stuff but I was sucking at it something terrible. It's a good thing that CrimeSpree didn't get much business back then because I was quite an embarrassment. After all, if I couldn't win this stupid game, how could I expect my customers to shell over cash to play this obviously tilted amusement? Anyway, there I was with a bundle of cotton candy in my left hand, the last bleeding of the sun at my back, and frustration on my face. I had just tossed three darts into three different balloons and each time those sharp, steel needles bounced right off the thin skin of those inflated rubber tits. What a load of shit, but then there was Clint.

He was standing right beside me, but his entire figure looked pure black, like a hole carved in space and time, as the sun outlined him in blazing orange. He wore a ridiculous green top-hat that was heavily creased in the middle with a ring of black fabric around the base. Oh, and just in case you're itching to know Clint's personality, feel free to skip ahead because I'm just getting started with my man's wardrobe. If we start now from the bottom of this wiry figure, we find a pair of heavily worn combat boots, one dull purple, the other colored to an approximate match with a magic marker. A pair of baggy black slacks were tucked into the boots and as they rose up the man, they flared out, which gave Clint an even more exaggerated stride when he moved. A belt of bull-rope and iron rings wrapped itself around his waist, and above this border of metal and frayed fiber was a crisp silk shirt that was every bit as green as the hat. A flaming pink tie decorated with the images of dollar bills split the center of his chest and gaudy rings of imitation gold hung heavy from every finger. To complete this madman's ensemble, Clint held a cane in one hand that was nothing more functional than a clever decoration. It was a crooked stick that had been generously clear-coated to an obnoxious shine and it had a small animal's skull for a topper. I'm not sure what kind of critter it once was, but I'm pretty certain that it was real.

The inimitable Clint Ruin looked to own a share of just about every nationality you could think of, but he most noticeably didn't own a toothbrush. Aside from the yellowing and the creeping rot, Clint's teeth were set in rows as crooked as his absurd hat. Both his eyes were pale, like they were without any color at all, and his nose was probably sharp enough to cut glass. His limbs looked to be a bit too long for his body and his head hung forward like that of a large bird. Maybe it was from the weight of the hat, I don't know. He had a strange way of talking, too, imagine that. He had suffered some type of seizure as a kid, and now his lower jaw twitched when he spoke and the words came out in erratic spurts. His machine-gun tongue would be randomly interrupted by a cacophony of gurgling sounds that stuck in his throat, but once he cleared them out, it was back to firing away. Hearing Clint choke on his own insides was kinda disturbing, and it seemed rather unpleasant. I'm guessing that is why he talked so fast.

To employ an overused expression, you can't judge a book by its cover. That was the message of Clint Ruin the man. He was one of the nicest, most genuine people you could ever hope to meet. For all the weirdness that draped his exterior, Clint was almost alarmingly practical, and he was quite the thinker. He seemed to know a little something about everything. The poor bastard probably didn't have a lot of friends growing up, I would guess, but he made up for this by reading more books than many small libraries stock. He loved to impress people with the endless supply of trivial facts and historical anecdotes that he had crammed into his skull, and, sadly, I have to admit that Clint was built for a purpose higher than CrimeSpree. I bet he could have built a spaceship in his garage if he wanted to, but what Clint really wanted to do was to be an entertainer, a showman. And what a showman he was.

Witness to the Crime existed before Clint came along but what it eventually became was owed mostly to him. Aside from the Master of Ceremonies, he was the acting manager of

17th Street and I mostly stayed out of his way. He handpicked the actors that worked that dirty road, and staged the assaults that would take place each night. Clint's title was that of a tour guide, but he was more of the band leader of the underworld, and he took his job seriously. He kept it fresh and new, revamping his game plan everyday just in case there was a semi-regular in his audience. He appreciated every dollar he earned and never wanted anybody to pay to see a rerun. With his kind heart it was really surprising, unbelievable, almost, that every night he gleefully led the masses down the rabbit hole of torture and depravity.

When he performed, which is how Clint viewed it, he was transformed, possessed. The odd qualities of his voice were amplified, but the really weird thing was that he spoke better at those times. He would laugh and point at what was seen, and gesture wildly with his oversized appendages. His eyes bulged and the veins that rimmed his sockets would swell and throb. As he hoarsely described the attractions of 17th Street, his lips would recede into his mouth and expose the rotten tombstones that rose from his inflamed gums. His body moved in a jerky rhythm, and Clint often removed his hat in order to bow before his followers, like he was the omnipotent puppet master of 17th Street who kept them all scarcely shrouded in a fragile safety. He spun his cane as he moved, and whistled to the sounds of domestic violence and pseudo-rape. And you know what? When the trip was over, Clint would personally thank every guest that attended. He raucously engaged those who were flooded with adrenaline, and he would comfort the frightened.

Clint even went as far as to set up a counseling center just outside the entrance gate. He reminded me that even the worst of worlds houses a sanctuary or two. Okay, Clint. All were welcome in Clint's center, and he often stayed there long into the mornings, talking to anybody who wanted his company. His energy seemed inexhaustible and he really did make CrimeSpree as positive a place as it could hope to be. As I said before, Clint was built for a higher purpose. I suppose the seizure that rocked him in boyhood just must have knocked a few screws loose. I think it was CrimeSpree that finished the job though. Maybe it was me that ruined him. Maybe Clint saw it coming.

Just two weeks before the doors of CrimeSpree were beaten in and the agents arrested every employee of mine that they could snag, crazy Clint Ruin vanished. Into thin air, too. Poof, gone, just like that. In this day and age in America it is nearly impossible to disappear and it's been this way for some time. But that's what Clint did. We have cameras hung from every goddamn utility pole in the country, satellites in outer space that can peer into anybody's bedroom window, and we even have overprotected children that have been fitted with chips under their skin that can be tracked with GPS. Did you ever think it would come to that? So much for the milk carton, huh? But as for one of Mother Nature's more eccentric children, nothing, not a trace. Like a puff of cigarette smoke into a tornado, Clint was gone, never to return to the world of man.

I'll never forget the last day that I saw Clint. It was an unseasonably cool day, the kind that sees a fresh sun carve minute rivers into the frost leftover from an icy night. It was early afternoon, and we were busy in the park getting things ready. The games were being setup, food was being cooked, and the actors were running through their bits. Me and Clint were walking down 17th Street and he was showing me a couple of changes he had made to up the creepy factor of *Witness to the Crime*. It was the damnedest thing. Right in the middle of enthusiastically drawing my attention to an incredibly convincing mannequin that dangled from a noose tied to an old streetlight, Clint stopped. He looked me dead in the eye with disquiet all over his face, as though the voices in his head were in full roar. He trembled just the faintest bit and, for the first time in probably his entire life, Clint spoke slowly and softly.

"Heyya boss, do ya think I could get today off? Not feeling so hot," he said.

That's what he said to me, although I'm sure he called me boss a few more times. He did it constantly, even though I always asked him not to. Anyway, I told him that it was fine. One of the actors who had worked 17th Street since its inception worshiped Clint, and I knew he would jump at the chance to stand in for him, so it was no deal if Clint needed a break. That was probably only the second time in the course of two years that Clint ever looked tired to me—really tired, exhausted. I was going to ask him about it and offer him some more time off, but before I could, Clint quietly thanked me and patted me on the shoulder as he turned away. He walked away from me in a stride that resembled the gait of a normal human being, and just as he reached the end of the street, Clint removed his hat and delicately placed it on the ground. I watched him get smaller and smaller until he disappeared into the thickness of the woods that crept all around CrimeSpree, and that was the last trace of Clint Ruin that anybody ever saw.

I get the sense now that something in Clint's brain changed in an instant, CrimeSpree had that effect on people, I've come to find out. For Clint, though the carnival was over, good yielded to bad and what was once fun and games had now put out the proverbial eye. The pieces were broken and Clint didn't want to play anymore. For all his madness, he saw the consequences and he saw the end before any of us did. Here's to you my friend, wherever you are.

Fifteen down, just two to go. If you remember the tale of bold Alice Spenski, then you know what's coming. On 14th and 15th Streets, being raped was the risk. 14th was rape-lite. Sorry, that probably wasn't very funny. What I meant to say was that multiple people were allowed to travel down 14th Street at one time. This, of course, greatly reduced the risk of being

93

assaulted, and as a result, I can't recall anyone ever actually being raped on 14th Street. We kept the attacks pretty tame on this road, which gave the friends of the chosen victim a fairly easy task of maintaining safety. They would fight off our thugs and then run in a panic until they crossed over that invisible line that segregated danger from total harmlessness. Someone would get the daylights scared right out of them, someone would get to play hero, I would make money and everyone involved was given a story to tell. All good, lecherous fun and nobody had to bleed. The implied risk was enough to satisfy most anyone and that's why we should have stopped there. CrimeSpree would have done just fine with 15th Street omitted.

But we went ahead and built it anyway. Alice Spenski decided she needed the real deal and a few of our employees forgot they were actors and became the parts they played. It was the perfect storm. By the way, why do we include the word *perfect* when we describe horrible events? It's just our flawed nature, isn't it? It's why we killed, raped, and beat each other for thousands of years, it's why I built CrimeSpree when we stopped doing those things, and it is why we are killing, raping, and beating each other again. We just can't help ourselves.

What happened to Alice along 15th Street wasn't common. In fact, it was unique. Yes, it's true, a few others had been raped there, but none like this, and certainly there had never been a gang-rape at CrimeSpree. Usually things went down in a much less realistic fashion. Our victims were groped, tussled, and tossed around, but they were always given ample opportunity to escape and 15th Street was explicitly designed this way. Most of the instances that did involve sexual intercourse were more on the side of dirty one-night stands than actual rape. Truthfully, the great majority of those that were fucked, for lack of a more eloquent phrase, on 15th Street had this done to them to fulfill a debauched fantasy that they could not sate anywhere else. This didn't make 15th Street any less disturbing, mind you. I had seven employees transfer away from 15th and I had three others quit CrimeSpree altogether. There was also one employee that committed suicide after playing the part of rapist. We mourned his death, but kept this news hush-hush for as long as we could. I'm sure you've done something that you'll forever keep from the light of day if you can, so withhold your judgments.

Before he superseded the will of Porrima and put a gun down his throat, we called the departed Adam Markson. Adam was a regular guy, a lot like Alice Spenski, come to think of it, in that middle-America kind of way. If he and Alice had met inside the narrow confines of a 1950s teen flick, they probably would have nurtured a sweet romance at the malt shop before fading into happily ever after. Different place, different time, same people, different result. Oh, how times change. Oh, how time changes us. But back to Adam. He was normal by all measures and unremarkable at best. He was that guy whose face looks back at you from an old high school yearbook and as you look at him, you are perplexed as to just who in the hell this dude was. He wasn't great at anything and he wasn't an idiot. Adam wasn't all that funny, but he wasn't a dork, either. He liked cars and girls and sports, and his dress was always casual. He was just a nice, regular guy and he painted the inside of the rear windshield of his car with his brains.

The shot was so goddamn loud it probably got the attention of people in Canada. That's the way it seemed anyway. It wasn't just a great, jarring noise, it was brutal. Everybody has heard gunshots for one reason or another and to the untrained ear, they all sound pretty much the same. Not this one, it was different. The way it broke the air, this bullet was meant for a man. There was no mistaking that.

It was early in the day, probably around ten in the morning near the start of what would eventually be our last spring and summer of operation. There weren't very many people on the property of CrimeSpree. In fact it was just me, a few crew members, and some maintenance workers. We all heard it though, even as we were all spread out around different areas of the park. Like ships pulled to the call of a siren, we all ignored whatever it was that we were doing and sailed out of CrimeSpree and toward the death knell of Adam Markson. It was incredibly surreal. The others and I all seemed to spill out into the parking lot at exactly the same time and everybody froze at the sight of each other. I guess we were all waiting for someone else to take the first step. Whatever it was, we just all silently shifted our eyes back and forth between one another as the sun swept out over the asphalt and reflected off the cars.

I don't remember the walk to Adam's car, and I don't recall how we all knew just what car to go to. Adam's usual shift didn't start until 8 o'clock at night, and this fateful day was even a day off for him. What the hell was he even doing there? Maybe he never went home from the night before. Maybe he just spent all night in his car with a gun in his hands thinking about death and sin and guilt and whatever else the incredibly despondent tend to think about. Whatever those things are, I'm betting they're not the stuff of unicorns and rainbows. Who knows? Maybe he thought of nothing at all. I'll never know and neither will anybody else because Adam didn't bother to write a note to try and explain or justify his actions. Maybe it was just too personal.

You would probably think that this was the worst part of the whole ordeal. I mean, we had just found one of our friends shot to death in the backseat of his car. Yeah, pretty bad times indeed. Adam certainly had killed himself. The only problem was that he didn't kill himself instantly. The driver's side rear window was rolled down and I could hear this gurgling sound. I can't even tell you for sure what part of Adam was responsible for this noise. It was just awful. It didn't matter where it came from. I saw his eyes shake in their sockets and they looked frantic, but I'm almost certain that he couldn't see any of us. It was either that or he could see something that we couldn't, something that only the dying are permitted to view. Whatever it was, his vision went somewhere else.

The hole that was blown out of the back of his head was enormous, and I arrived just in time to watch as a piece of scalp slid down the back window. It had been forced there from the blast, and that chunk of wet skin and hair clung to the glass like snot flung onto a napkin. But the bright sun seared through the window and it thinned the blood that had acted like a paste. As it heated, the fluid lost its grip and all those itty-bitty pieces of brain and head started a slow descent to the rear dashboard. And Adam was alive the whole time. Barely, but he was alive. Whether that can be blamed on God, nature, fate, or plain cruel coincidence, I don't care. It was fucked up all the same.

I heard somebody behind me throw up, and I heard the footsteps of someone else as they ran away. In between those events is when Adam died. The funny thing is, I don't think any one of us actually saw him die. With all the puking, the running, and the shared shock, we all seemed to look away or to each other in the very instant that Adam expired. It was only then that I even noticed who exactly was with me. That's not really important though, is it? Those people know who they are and they'll never forget what they saw. We were common acquaintances, co-workers and on that day we were forever bound to each other by a moment that we would never discuss with one another again.

There were two people who interested me, though. They were a couple in their fifties, the hippie type. They loved nature and all things that depended on the bare minimum of technology. They were local, from that rural area of New York state, and came to CrimeSpree with a great enthusiasm. They said they were drawn to the park because it showcased the primal nature of the human animal. I bring this up only because the female end of this duo, a thin thing with a wave of grain for hair, tore into me something vicious. She called me all sorts of disgusting names and slapped me in the chest a number of times until her husband restrained her. She even directly blamed me for Adam's suicide. In a roundabout way, maybe I was responsible. But I just planted a seed, a seed that could have grown into any number of things. After all, you don't accuse a farmer of raising weeds just because a few linger among the corn, do you? Getting people to kill themselves wasn't ever my intention and it wasn't a goal of mine. I just returned to them the right to do so. Hey, bitch, you wanted nature, you wanted the primeval. You got it, all pock-marked and flawed.

This is fucking depressing. I was kinda enjoying myself when I was telling you about all my misadventures and crime capers. Reminiscing about my Lucy was bittersweet but cathartic. It seemed appropriate. Looking back on it all, I had a pretty interesting life. I had variety and spontaneity. I've lived all over the country. And I've kept company with some of the weirdest characters anyone could ever hope to meet or avoid, depending on your perspective. The short explanation of it all is that I had the experiences that are necessary to fully shape a human being, and I did it all while on Porrima.

Yep, I was on Porrima the whole time, just like everybody else was back then. Sure, I moved around and preferred the shadows, but I made damn sure to go and get my injections right on time. There is such a thing as hiding in plain sight, and during the 8th Day Era nothing aroused greater suspicion than a Porrima card that wasn't up to date. Which begs the inevitable question; why would a guy like me, someone who lived a colorful life exactly as they wanted while on Porrima the whole time, need more? Why? I'll tell ya why. Because all the interesting things that I did and all the sights that I saw never made me feel a damn thing. I was a dull, dead puppet tugged along by Porrima. We all were. I'll agree that Porrima was good in theory, it just broke down somewhere along the way, that's all.

That day in New Mexico, come on, you know which one I'm talking about, a veil was torn away. I was given a peek behind the curtain, I saw the land of Oz. I witnessed a future without Porrima, and yes, it was frightening, but it was more real than anything I had ever experienced before. It was the minefield of life that we were all meant to walk. Some of us were gonna make it across and some of us were gonna blow up, but it least it would be authentic. I had to get there. I did this all for me. CrimeSpree just had a way of taking everybody else along for the ride.

Which brings me to my employees, who were all also pumped full of the 8th Day Era's miracle. Many of them were instructed to beat and rape and perform all sorts of nasty tasks which, if you've been paying attention, were supposedly impossible while taking Porrima. And they were, at least back then. My people were actors, that's how we approached it. We had to. It was the only way to even approximate the real deal. I should probably mention this also, my people were horrendous actors. Man, were they bad. CrimeSpree was so lame in the early days, it's no wonder that we couldn't even buy bad press. If Mary Poppins decided to open a horror-themed amusement park, this would have been it. We weren't convincing in any aspect, any of us. CrimeSpree was downright pathetic and I soon came to realize that there is no such thing as recreating fear. It couldn't be staged, it couldn't be faked. My vision had failed.

But against all odds, CrimeSpree remained open. We had just enough customers to keep the utilities turned on, and most of my employees continued to show up for work. And why not? For the first six months that the park was open nobody did shit, I was a free paycheck. But the seasons shift, that shiny new car will one day rot in a junkyard and winter will always strip away every last leaf that the sun and the summer had worked so hard to grow. The point is, that change is inevitable. It's gonna go one way or the other, good or bad. Change doesn't care to linger in-between. But for me, at least for a while, that's exactly what it did. CrimeSpree got better, the people came through the turnstiles, and the cash rolled in with them. My actors got better and sharpened their acts. For some, the job started to become easier. The violent charade started to come to them more naturally.

Let's stop right here for just a moment. I just said that violence had become *natural* again. That's not to say that my people became violent. Their brains were just reintroduced to the option of violence and aggression. This is about the time that the pendulum of change was hanging right smack-dab in the middle. What CrimeSpree was quietly doing to those who worked there and those who paid the price of admission was unwinding the hooks of Porrima. And in that moment in time, this small minority of Americans were balanced. We all had our full range of emotions and abilities at our disposal again, but we also still had our sense of right and wrong. But the conscience had grown soft and lazy. Porrima had been doing all the work for years, and, back then, nobody saw it coming, but that's when the spiral began.

Chapter 6

Burn it down

Hello, my name is Mickey Moore and I'm an alcoholic. Okay, that statement is only half true, but I've never been that good at introducing myself. I suppose I should have told you my name earlier, but the right time just never seemed to show up. Well, here it is, finally, and now you all have my name. Nothing really has changed, has it? Nope. What real difference does it make anyway? Time will eventually forget me. Sure, I might be hot shit right now, but someday, one day, all of this will be lost.

Forever is a word that we toss around way too much. If you ever really stop and think about it, forever doesn't actually exist. It's just a made up-concept. Did you know that in about a trillion years or so, every single galaxy will be as far away from each other as the universe is presently wide? In simpler terms, everything will one day be so far apart that not one little star will twinkle in the skies above. Not even light is forever. So, now that the science lessen is over, let me say again that time will eventually forget about me. It will forget about you, too, and everyone you have ever known. A time will come when everything that has ever been done by everyone who has ever lived will no longer matter. When you think about it in those terms, this whole charade feels a bit empty doesn't it? Yes, it does, the answer is yes. I know this fact won't delay the inevitable but it at least gives me a small measure of solace.

Here I go again. I told you I was bad at introductions. This was supposed to be the part when we exchange mild pleasantries, but instead I tugged at the wheel and plunged our conversation into the arena of inescapable nothingness. I think about death a lot these days. That's a sad statement, really. At my age I should be squeezing every last memory out of my mind to quietly relive the good times before there are no times at all. C'est la vie.

Okay, we'll try this again. Hello, my name is Mickey Moore. There, that wasn't so hard. I guess one of the reasons that I never told you my name before is because a lot of expectations come shackled to a name. Especially a ridiculous name like Mickey Moore. What the hell kind of name is that anyway? With a name like Mickey Moore I should have spent my life robbing trains or building motorcycles. Mickey Moore was even the name of a boogeyman who supposedly trolled the darkened woods of Johnstown, Pennsylvania looking for little children to murder. Remaining anonymous is underrated.

Whew, the formalities are out of the way. Better late than never, right? Well, I'm not sure if that cleared anything up, but maybe now I've made myself a bit more personable. Either way, there is sure to be plenty about me that is still erroneously assumed, but train-robber, bike-builder, and kiddie-slasher can be scratched from the list. And with that, class, pack your stuff, because Mr. Moore is taking all of you on a field trip back to New Mexico.

As you might recall, I was stuffing my face with tasty imitation pastry snacks inside the lobby of a bus station after those hippies plucked me from the dry desert soil. As you might also imagine, I was looking to high-tail it out of there. Like an animal spooked by a loud bang, I just wanted to run away. I didn't have a direction or a location in mind, I was just looking to dart off. But I'm not an animal, no, no, no, I'm a human. And what do humans do? We think. And as I stood there with coconut and red dye of my fingers, I thought of murder.

Not one day ago, I had watched a guy get his brain splattered all across the highway. That meant that somewhere along Interstate 40, there was an abandoned car and a dead body. These are the sorts of things that, when paired together, tend to draw attention. This grizzly scene also took place along a major highway, and in a country where the act of murder was thought to have gone extinct a generation ago. We as a nation were about to be reintroduced to a beast from our past. A vicious one, too, that was thought to have gone the way of the mighty mastodon and the nasty smallpox. This was gonna make news, this was gonna be huge. Some dude was such a bad motherfucker that he had superseded the will of Porrima and caved in another man's skull. This was gonna shake the public to their core.

If a tree falls in the forest and no one is around to hear it, does it make a sound? I'm gonna say yes. That just makes sense to me, although I'm not sure if science has ever bothered to explore this question. What I do know, however, is that if a human being gets beaten to death in front of another human being under the bright rays of the sun, it makes an undeniable sound, and a whole lot more at that. My point is that it happened, I know it happened, but nobody else seemed to notice or care.

I decided to hang around New Mexico a while and gather the news. This was ground zero. I shacked up for about a week inside a horribly filthy motel room—I was quite poor—remember, and kept my eyes and ears on high alert the entire time. I obsessively watched every news channel and dredged the internet for even the smallest tidbit of information. I hung around the local gas stations trying to overhear some gossip and I closely inspected the pictures on every missing person report. I even went as far as to procure a police scanner which I kept at an audible volume as I scoured all the newspapers for word of the murder I knew I had witnessed. Nothing, not a whisper.

I didn't just imagine this. Don't fucking tell me I imagined this! I rarely even dream, and on that fateful day, I was wide awake. Sure, I was a little dehydrated, I was stressed, and just generally out of sorts, but that was all. I wasn't out of reality. It was absurd to suggest that I was on drugs, I couldn't have afforded even the cheapest variety back then. Yes, it's true that Darlene's cooking was ferocious, and I'm sure her kitchen wasn't the cleanest, but this was no food-borne hallucination. This was absolutely real and it was being covered up.

Since I'm an upstanding member of society, I went to the local police station to report what had happened. Okay, I might have waited a week or so to do this, but that poor sucker who got slathered all over the asphalt of old 40 was in no rush. Time wasn't of the essence, because that nameless fellow ran fresh out of his. He was dead. My procrastination could be criticized, I suppose, but it should be celebrated. Every last citizen who was living in or around New Mexico back then should personally thank me. My laziness, my fear, my shock, whatever it was, it keep me quiet for a week and, as a result, I let that monster get away. Hopefully he drove that rig straight back through the gates of hell. You're welcome.

The cops weren't of any real use anyway. The first two officers that I spoke with barely said three words to me between the both of them. The first guy I spoke with was some hot-headed esé. He was in his mid-twenties and probably a pinch too short to ride most of the rides at any common amusement park. Though he was diminutive in height, he was no lightweight. He was built like a fireplug, all chunky and made of iron. His name was Eric but I'm guessing that it used to be Enrique. He was American, barely, but he was American all the same. The problem with this guy was that he wanted to be a lot more American than he actually was. This asshole wanted to be G.I. Joe. Through dark sunglasses and with his arms folded across his chiseled chest, he just stared at me as I frantically rambled. He shifted his jaw, cracked his gum and exhaled impatiently. Finally, he muttered something about junkies and then brushed me aside with one of his thickened paws. Thanks for your help, prick.

I think that the next guy honestly believed me. He was an older guy, no, scratch that, this dude was ancient. He looked to be a good ten years past normal retirement age and he looked tired. It was 9:30 in the morning and he looked exhausted. I'm guessing that he desperately needed the paycheck and that was all he was there to do, collect some funds, punch out and go home. At his age, I couldn't blame the guy, and I could tell that once upon a time he would have jumped all over this case. I just arrived about three decades too late.

As I said before, this guy did believe me. I know he did. There was something in his eyes that told me as much. It was a fear that I recognized, it was a fear that I had, too. Porrima had kept our primal nature in check for thirty odd years or so, and even before that America was one of the safest nations in the world, but at least it was real. A real world with real threats. This is the world that the old cop came from. All during his childhood, his adolescence and his subsequent maturation into adulthood, he was told of violent crime. He read the papers and heard the news reports. Maybe he had been held up while working at a gas station as a teenager, or maybe a much more virulent form of animalistic behavior made itself known to him. Maybe a relative had been shot, or maybe an ex-girlfriend had been assaulted. Maybe none of this shit happened. It doesn't really matter. What matters, what the point is, is that he grew up with the fear of these things. He knew to be wary of bad neighborhoods, he knew to withdraw from the sounds of gunfire. He knew to fear the dark, and, as a result, this tired old man still recognized the aftermath of crime when it looked him dead in the eye.

He led me into a small side room not far from the entrance of the station. It was obviously a break area, complete with some vending machines and a couple of coffee makers. There were bulletins on the wall, and a most wanted list that featured ten guys with ten different faces, although somehow they all looked like me. What I mean is that none of these men appeared at all threatening. And this motley bunch of fresh-faced pussies was the ten baddest dudes in all of New Mexico? There was something sad about that. It was just another pathetic example of the devolution of the modern American. We weren't even good at being bad anymore.

The arthritic cop cranked open a valve on the faucet and the rush of water that came forth pulled my attention away from the flyer and back to him. He swirled the water in his cup and then splashed the light brown liquid into the sink. He filled his mug with coffee anew and took a sip of the steaming brew. Just like a man, too. No cream, no sugar, just straight black and bitter to the gut. Porrima hadn't dulled his every edge. Maybe the burnt, unrefined coffee was all he had left. Either way, he went ahead and poured me a share of that caffeinated water into one of those cheap paper cups that practically disintegrates before you can even finish your drink. Without asking, he plopped a couple spoonfuls of sugar into the blackness and then lightened it up with a generous pouring of milk. It was like he knew. We were two different beings, he and I, right down to how we took our coffee. It was two overlapping moments in time that separated us, but the distance was as wide as the known universe, and Officer Nostradamus knew this well.

He didn't say anything, because there was nothing to say between the two of us. He was a dinosaur that had survived the meteor, and all that was left to do was to wait for the extinction. I represented the new wave of the American world and he was the fading stain of the past. He slowly walked by me but stopped just as he reached a step or two behind. He placed one of his worn, wrinkled hands on my shoulder and spoke firmly into my ear. *Forget about it,* he said. And he wasn't referencing the coffee. I had seen Bigfoot, an alien, an anomaly, the unexplained, and I was instructed to let it go. Fuck that.

I extended the old dude the courtesy of not making a scene with him still in the building. I watched him walk out the door, fold himself into his squad car and drive off like any common grandfather. I took a few more sips of my coffee and then commenced the freak-out. I started yelping about how I had witnessed a murder and that no one believed me. My sharp words accused the collective police force of being lazy, and I threatened to take my tale to the local news. There were a handful of people in the building, citizens and law enforcement alike, who heard the whole tirade. As you might imagine, this garnered me the undivided attention that I thought I had sought. Wrong, wrong, wrong. As it turns out, cops don't like it when a stranger gets all uppity in their house.

Faster than you could say *Boss Hogg*, I was grabbed by the arm and whisked away into what was most likely the single most clichéd interrogation room in the United States. The floor was covered with a thin, brown carpet and the walls were painted a dull gray that exposed every imperfection in the plaster. There was a small camera mounted in the upper left-hand corner of the room, and a shadeless 60-watt bulb hung from the center of the ceiling. One of those rugged folding tables that churches tend to use at banquets was placed crookedly near the center of the room, and behind it was a bony chair. It was the type constructed of cheap plastic with a rounded framework of stainless steel. In other words, it was one of those god-awful things that you spent four years of your life killing your ass upon in high school. Oh goody, there are only two items in the room and each one reminds me of an institution that makes my skin crawl.

I'm not sure how much of it was planned intent or just pure laziness that kept me in the room all alone for a stretch of time, but either way, I was left to my own company for about an hour. Well almost. You see as violence had ebbed away during the 8th Day Era, the cops were forced to get creative with their interrogation techniques. Long gone were the days of rough slaps to the face or aggressive shoves into concrete walls. The violence had left but the misery stuck around.

Once my escorts had left, the first five minutes of my solitude passed without incident, but then came the pinpricks and the tightening of the screws. Out from a speaker I couldn't see, a high-pitched tone crept into the room. It was barely audible at first but it rose in ferocity quite quickly. It was reminiscent of the ringing that floods your eardrums after they have been assaulted by a loud and sudden bang. It twisted a mild headache into my temples and then it just shut off, just like that. I held my breath and tried to figure out if it was in fact truly gone. After a long minute had elapsed, its ghost was still in my ears but I was starting to ease up. Big mistake. I knew they were watching me, and, goddamn it, they saw as I grew slightly comfortable. A smell floated down from the ventilation duct that had surely been born from the pungent union of methane and burning diesel. There was no smoke or other visible source to this odor, but it was there and it clung to the membranes inside my face like a film.

This was my punishment for telling the truth. I had made a scene and now the cops were making a statement. This is how they did it back then. This is how they made you comply. Uncomfortable stimuli was hurled at the brain and the longer a visitor behaved in a disagreeable manner, the more of the mental knifing they received. I was gonna be good and speak calmly, I was ready to acquiesce. The cops saw all of this, too, because just as the rancid smell dissipated back into the plain air, the knob on the door began to rattle.

This next part gets filed under *going from bad to worse*. This is because I was sitting in the plastic ass-eater and with me inside this glorified closet were two of the largest human beings I had ever seen. Tweedle-scum stood in the corner all corpulent and uncomfortable. He sucked on the insides of his cheeks and rested his chubby hands across his monstrous gut. He shuffled his feet regularly, as it was clearly distressing on his bones to be placed upright for any stretch of time. He never said a word, but he also never removed his stare from me. This was meant to be intimidating, and it was, but not for the effect that fatty was trying to impose. I'm guessing that as his beady eyes pierced into me, he was attempting to force upon me the idea that I might be criminally punished or in some way even physically assaulted. These things didn't concern me all that much, but what scared me silent was the idea that I might be eaten. Sure it sounds absurd, but it felt wholly possible at the time. This dude was a loose ball of shifting skin and sweat and he liked to keep that belly full. At that very moment, I was keeping him from snacking, and as a result, I was in danger of becoming the mid-morning treat. I might have been skinny, but I was gonna have to do. Wonderful. I strayed into New Mexico, witnessed a murder, and now I was about to be devoured by cannibals.

That's how I remember it anyway. Maybe I was out of it back then or maybe my mind is just failing me now. Both things are equally possible, but what hasn't changed is the fact that a murder was committed, I saw it with my own two, wide eyes and nobody believed me. Some people still contend that I made the whole thing up. Fine, let them lie to themselves, let them deny the obvious—that Porrima wasn't so much a wonder drug as it was a mask.

Oh New Mexico, you are really having a rough go of it in my tale, aren't you? There's been an arrogant hot-shot, a murderer, some annoying hippies, a handful of useless cops and I haven't even made it to Tweedle-glee yet. Okay, I'm sure that the collective citizenry of the Land of Enchantment are fine, upstanding examples of humanity, both in times past and now, but bear with me as I disparage yet another of your own.

Tweedle-glee was built explicitly for the American Southwest, and the nickname that I bestowed upon him was ironic. He was not very pleasant. As you probably have surmised by now, he was a giant fat fucker, too. Ah! You are so very sharp. Anyway, he wore a pair of jeans whose upper circumference surely topped out in the neighborhood of sixty inches. This denim abyss was held up by a pair of crisscrossing suspenders, big surprise there, and underneath his unbuttoned uniform shirt was a white tank-top. Awesome. His chunky feet kicked around a pair of boots that were a size or two too big, no doubt to accommodate the swelling that inflamed those hooves by the end of each day. I say *kicked around* too because using the word *walk* to describe his clumsy gait would have been a disservice to language and to proper movement. During his spells of waddling about, the oversized cowboy hat that he donned would bounce on his clammy head that was short on hair but heavy with perspiration.

Just like his mongoloid friend in the corner, Tweedle-glee stared into me. A pair of large sunglasses were tucked into his shirt pocket, and it was a wonder that he needed them at all as his eyeballs were barely visible. He had those folds of fat above his eyes that droop down the way excess glue does after it has dried. In addition to this lovely image, his cheeks were set high and they were as red as a harvest moon. The bulbous flesh on his forehead and those chubby cheeks conspired to form scant crevices that, upon the closest inspection, housed his eyes. They were small, dark and devoid of anything all that interesting. If the eyes are truly the windows to the soul, then this man's eternal being was an empty garage. Dull and dusty, this space offered little of value and even less in the way of hospitality or virtue.

Appearances aren't everything, are they? No, absolutely not, but they're a pretty good indicator of what you're in for from any given subject. For example, if you purchase a pickup truck that is twenty years old and seven different colors, there's a better than average chance that the old beast might break down the very first time that you drive it. Also, let's say that you find a sandwich in the fridge that has gone neglected. You might check it for mold and inspect the coloring of the meat, and maybe it seems alright, but if the dog won't eat it, therein lies the likelihood that it will taste like doo-doo. How about one more, just for kicks? Here's the scene: it's 1:30 AM, you're in a dark, country bar that's situated on the edge of town and you're chatting up a drunk stripper with a cocaine dependency. Let me prognosticate about what would happen next. You're gonna take this chick home for the evening and savor every last fractional second of it, and after that, you're gonna hope and pray to never see this crazy girl ever again. This I know for a fact. And so class, how did we learn all this? From appearances.

Earlier I warned against not heeding the old adage about the book and its cover, blah, blah, blah. As it turns out, Clint Ruin was the exception to the rule, and yet they still say that you can't judge a book by its cover. This is false. You shouldn't judge a book by its cover but you can absolutely judge away. This impatient approach shouldn't be used in place of scientific methodology, but sometimes with just a fleeting glimpse of the binding, you can nail that sucker down. I wouldn't say that I had old Tweedle-glee measured down to his finest details, in fact, he didn't have any. At first glance I thought this guy was a disgusting hog fart belched from the wet anus of an ogre, and I'll be damned, I was giving him too much credit.

Tweedle-glee leaned on the table and cast a great shadow over me. He shuffled a toothpick back and forth between his engorged lips and I could hear the breath as it struggled to push its way out of his lungs. He curled his swollen fingers into his palm, leaving only the pointer out which he petulantly shoved in my direction. He then removed his hat and allowed it to rest on the table. In an instant, his free hand shot behind me and grabbed a handful of my hair. I honestly never would have thought that he was capable of such quick movement, but in a flash, he had my head jerked back and that fat finger pressed into my nose.

"There ain't no murder in New Mexico," he said slowly with a predictable drawl to which I just made a choking sound.

"There ain't no murder in New Mexico," he said again. "Ain't been one in decades, and there ain't one now. Now I don't make much nevermind over what you're doing here or what you plan on doing once you get to getting, but let me instruct you on something, son. Porrima ain't perfect."

That was enough for me. A smile came over his face when he finished and I took in every minute aspect of his wordless warning. He might have been an oaf that wandered off the evolutionary path, but there was a wisdom to be gained from his ignorance. I knew then that severe violence had not gone extinct, it was just exceedingly rare. This revelation is a story in itself which I'll revisit once we get back closer to the Atlantic, but across the table from Tweedle-glee, I had other things on my mind. He had threatened me and I knew he would deliver to the fullest. I didn't know what he would or could do to me and he didn't elaborate, but he was a man of his word. For all I knew, that trucker might have been an employee of his that was just earning the day's pay. Either way, it was time for me to move on and the Tweedles made this quite clear, just in case any doubt remained.

"Officer Hooper, would you kindly show our friend to the door?" he asked as his left hand practically engulfed my bicep in a death grip.

"Now remember boy," he whispered to me as I was being led away. "Get."

That was fun wasn't it? Nope, not even a little, just in the event that you're keeping score at home. I didn't get what I wanted when I walked in that police station but I didn't leave empty handed, either. I left with the knowledge that Porrima didn't work as well as the whole of America had been told. It seemed to me that murders and other violent crimes still took place, and probably all across the country. They were scattered incidents, anomalies that didn't warrant inclusion into the bigger picture. Sure, maybe murder had become one in a million, maybe it was even less. That didn't matter. What mattered was that it still took place and it was being swept away with political brooms. I didn't have all the facts then, still don't, but it was coming into view. Think about it. If an alien visitation could be proven or if religion could be wholly debunked and only the government knew about this, would we ever know? Oh, don't be so naïve. The simple answer is no. Sure, the failure of Porrima wasn't on the scale of the first two I mentioned. But it was close. You have to understand what it was like in the 8th Day Era. The talk of murder or a return to our animalistic past could have thrown the nation into a panic. The role of government is to shield the people, and in turn itself, from panic. Sometimes this means looking the common man in the eye and giving it to him straight, and it sometimes means turning out all the lights and assuring everyone that everything is A-OK.

I didn't have a car and I had only the clothes that I was wearing. I bought a new pair of shoes and bribed a motel clerk into letting me use one of the rooms just to use the shower. He stood outside the bathroom door the entire time, which was a bit creepy, but I was just happy to feel hot water and soap. I still had my debit card but that wasn't worth the plastic that went into its construction. There were still a few dollars in my pocket, but what good were they gonna do? And so with my new shoes, my clean hair, and a brief glimpse at a map of the state, I hit the road. I found my way to Route 60, took a few steps east, and stuck out my thumb.

What in the hell was I thinking? Taking a ride from a total stranger is what got me into this mess in the first place. Maybe that's not entirely true. Maybe I was always in this mess in some form or another. Bad people do bad things, and bad things have a way of finding bad people. I thought I was low when I had left Florida. That was nothing. Even the day that I had heard about Lucy's death was a better day than this. Yeah, I felt devastated when I hung up the phone, but as I trod over Route 60, I knew that this day was indeed worse. I had less money, less opportunity, less security, and even more loneliness. It felt like the end. The road had gotten so goddamn long and dirty, and there wasn't an oasis in sight.

The darkness and the moon fell over me and the cold chill of the desert at night became my only companion. I had been walking for miles, but it was hard to mark the time. Every minute felt like an hour, anyway, as my convalescing ankle still loudly complained with each step. There wasn't much to look at, or maybe everything just appeared so desolate because of the expanding emptiness that had rooted itself in my gut. It didn't matter. Time would defeat me, and it was only a matter of a few small hours before I would be beaten into sleep on the side of the road.

Two headlights seared through the black, and being as this was the first car I had seen in about an hour, I stuck my thumb out as noticeably as I could. Understandably, the car passed me by but the brake lights lit up like two demonic eyes. The car came to a stop and those irritated eyes studied me some more. I felt my heart jump up into my throat and I swear I nearly choked on the fucking thing. Something else was about to happen, and it was impossible to predict. My life could be changed immeasurably, my life could end. My brain rode a carousel of uncertainties and I began to feel sick. The image of the trucker beating that poor man to death replayed in my mind, and it was a scene so vivid it nearly dropped me to my knees. It was in this weakened state that I saw the reverse lights of the car as they flashed awake. The blinding white brightness that punctured through the black expanse that enveloped me was the last shred of uncomfortable stimuli that I could endure. I felt vomit crawl up my throat, and before I could even properly open my mouth, a splash of that acidic liquid crashed against the back of my teeth.

Earlier I was ranting on about how a lot can be gained from appearances. I touted the merits of judging a book by its cover. I even encouraged it. At this moment in time, I was really hoping that the driver of the car didn't fall in line with my way of thinking. Sure, I looked like a weak little fleck of a human being, but I also looked like a dude who you didn't want to invite into your car. At the very least, I had puke breath. This wasn't going to go well.

Oh, New Mexico, you clever girl! During my stay in the Land of Enchantment, I had a shitty time that was punctuated by crappy experiences, and it all was slathered in feces. But much akin to the surprise of winning the Powerball after purchasing just one ticket, something pleasant finally happened to me.

The car was a newer model compact that had cheesy chrome wheels, something lame written across the windshield and a plethora of bumper stickers pasted on the back. It was bright red, the windows were the color of charcoal, and I could hear as a nauseating pop beat bounced around the interior. For all this car's cuteness and mock sport appeal, only one thing could be ascertained. This was a girl's car. And what do you know? As the darkened driver's window lowered like a sunset in reverse I was treated to the image of fair, female skin and a straight, white row of teeth.

"Where ya goin'?" she chirped as she gnawed at a piece of gum.

"East," was all I said.

"Okay, get in. But I'm only going as far as Clovis."

I didn't know where Clovis was and I could only assume that it was a town. For all I knew, it might have been a nightclub or a college, but none of that mattered to me. If it was only as far as the next exit, well, that was a few less miles that I had to walk. Clovis could have been a fancy name for the entranceway to hell and that would have been good enough for me. As it turns out Clovis is a proper town, and it's one of those Southwestern places that people like me tend to think only exists in make-believe. Was it the last patch of land left that Native Americans still ruled? Was it an integral cog in military operations on this side of the country? Was it something of a sacred place to aspiring rock musicians and fans alike, or was it simply a place for mega-department store chains to set stakes? Who the hell knows? The only thing that I could conclude was that Clovis seemed to have something of an identity crisis. Then again I was fed this information by a caffeinated girl who was barely out of her teens.

Maybe it was the zany descriptions of the place, or maybe I was just feeling a bit better and adventurous, but something made me want to explore Clovis. I also felt the growing desire to do a little exploring on bubbly Brittany, but, sadly, neither took place. Which leads me to the wonderful memory of the amusement park that was the body of Brittany something-or-other. She had shiny golden hair, big sparkling eyes, and a set of plump lips that owned a slick sheen brought on by the charity of youth. Her facial features were the perfect nascence of adulthood, and they were all unmarked by the creases and cracks that time inevitably deals out. If her face was divinity, then her body was pure vulgarity in all its fresh, hormonal glory.

Oh, god, where does an old man begin? The mind is frequently not able to unsee terrible events, and it is equally deficient in forgetting the image of a beautiful girl. Like many American girls, Brittany's diet consisted of fast food, elaborate coffee drinks, and sweet snacks. I'm sure her thighs are paying the price now, but back then all the fat, the hollow calories and the engineered meat products had Brittany thick in all the right places, and youth kept her thin and tight in all the places that women kill themselves trying to keep thin and tight. Her ankles were small and her colorful toes were nestled loosely inside a pair of flip-flops. Her calves bulged and her thighs were swollen with sexuality, but the skin that contained them was so taut that it kept them separated and shapely. Her ass was the rounded jewel that dotted the heart-shaped crown of her hips, and it appeared firm enough to crack an egg upon. Her partially exposed stomach was as flat as the highway and her breasts were waging a war with the threads of her shirt. Brittany struck me as a late bloomer, and, as a result, I think it was safe to guess that those titties were only about three years old at the time. They were new, exciting and she was downright tickled to be showing them off. I'm certain that her inflated cleavage earned her plenty of free drinks and impure comments, but it had stolen all variety away from my thought process. There was one train and one track and I was happier than a ghost in a graveyard.

As it turned out, we weren't all that far from Clovis. I saw that the exit was slated to appear in about two miles and the sign jarred my attention just enough to fracture the spell I was under. I realized then that we hadn't done much talking. Well I hadn't anyway. Brittany chattered on about this and that and bobbed her head to the garbage that was spewed from the speakers. I had barely reciprocated anything to her and offered even less in the way of intelligent conversation. She didn't seem to mind, though. Girls her age aren't looking for intelligent conversation anyway. And that's when it hit me, the gravity, the reality, the farce. I had been in this girl's car for about two hours. I had taken only wavering interest in what she had to say, said little myself and stared at her tits nearly the entire time. I was acting creepy, guilty as charged. But for her part, Brittany had freely offered a ride to a stranger she happened upon on a darkening and lonesome stretch of highway. And she did this dressed like some sort of teen fantasy stripper that guys like me tend to order for bachelor parties.

"What in the hell were you thinking?" I blurted out as the Clovis exit sign rose over the horizon.

"What? You mean right now?" she asked, genuinely oblivious to the source of my question.

"No, no, no. what were you thinking picking me up? I'm some dude you never met, obviously broke, probably desperate and it's nighttime for fuck's sake."

"Okay, you're a little weird but what could happen? I just wanted some company," she said, with still not a trace of alarm in her voice.

I had Brittany drop me off at the end of the exit ramp and thanked her for the ride. The music from inside the car swelled almost as soon as I shut the door, and as I watched her disappear, I couldn't help but shake my head. Porrima had to be stopped. It was now killing common sense. Women were no longer afraid to invite strange men they found in the middle of nowhere into their cars. What was next? Hey, fish that bread out of the toaster with a fork, what's the worst that can happen? Did you just take a dump and you're running late for work? Why bother to wash your hands? After all, it's not like there's any risk of an infectious disease getting passed around the kitchen. Was I the only one with the presence of mind to realize that not every situation was made invincibly safe by Porrima?

It has been said that history repeats itself and I can assure you that when you're broke, it is a bleak history that reprises itself with alarming regularity. Every day, every hour is the same. There is no reprieve from destitution. You're always hungry and uncomfortable. The body never feels warm, it never feels good. It's always too cold or too hot. The bones of the poor man always ache, his stomach is wrapped in a permanent knot, and his mind is always afflicted by an unrelenting trouble.

I didn't know where to go or what to do. I had just crossed over the New Mexico border into Texas and I was walking a forgotten stretch of bad road. The stars dripped light down from the sky that blanketed my surroundings in a haunting ambiance. The grass around me was tall, but it had been bent crooked and low from a lack of attention and nourishment. The exact same assessment could have been made of me. I peered into some manner of building which sat unevenly a few hundred feet off the side of the road, and it looked as though its purpose had grown irrelevant long ago. Its body was white, not from paint, but from washed stone as it begins to disintegrate. It had four square windows across the front that all had their innards smashed out, and it supported a flat roof that most certainly leaked. Plywood had been nailed up over the door and an army of twisted trees grew right up through the walkway and the rotten boards of the porch. Why do people just up and leave things? There are over seven billion people on earth, and apparently not a damn one of them wanted that place. Or maybe they all just did like I did. That is, maybe they all failed to see the future potential in something old and just kept right on moving.

The asphalt under my tired feet smoothed out and I could see modern lights in the far-off distance. I could just barely detect the outline of a couple of remote houses that strayed from the town ahead as they slept under the blanket of the night. About a quarter of a mile down the road, there was a small gas station that had closed for the evening, and, as its image sank into my eyes, it filled me with the kind of hope that only the despondent can feel.

I was so tired and hungry, I was starting to see the world as it wasn't. The darkness was folding itself into shapes that would shadow and torment me. The light above and the light beyond were conspiring to distort my perception and illuminate just enough of the foreign landscape to flutter my heart. The cold breeze ripped at my skin and, with every rash of goose bumps, the headache that battered the inside of my skull was intensified. But I still had my despondent hope, the hope that can only be realized by causing sorrow to another.

In a less colorful and abstract way of speaking, I took my hope and put it into the form of a brick. I smashed my way into that gas station and stuffed my gut with snacks and stuffed my pocket with all the cash that I could pry from the register. I reintroduced fluid to the dried-up waterways of my insides by flooding them with soda, sports drinks, and alcohol. I flipped my way through a couple of the dirty magazines that were kept behind the counter, and tore open more packs of cigarettes than I could possibly smoke. I was riding a thief's high inside the relative warmth of the store with my stomach satiated, my lungs corrupted, and my wallet thickened. In that scant moment of making anything that I touched my own, I could have felt that way forever.

After the initial whirlwind of vandalism subsided, I plunked down on the linoleum floor with a can of cheap beer in my hand. I allowed myself to fall back into a display rack and nestled my head into a pile of potato chip bags. With my eyes closed, I poured another gulp of Jaguarundi Black down my throat. Man, did that stuff taste like shit. I listened to the sounds of the night as they poured in through the broken glass and I allowed myself to think. The events of my life swirled around in my memory, and they all started to feel like throwaway events from the lives of others. Nothing I had done to this point had really mattered. None of it had any real impact. For good or for bad, I had changed nothing. I was just plodding through the days, inconveniencing others along the way and routinely failing to make myself comfortable. The crash was upon me and I could feel it. That's when I thought of Lucy. She was dead, but I found myself thinking about, well, myself. Things could be better for me, things could even be good, but Lucy had to go and die. How could she do this to me?

That was the thinking that brought me down to the bottom, because every high has a low, every drug has an itch, every crime has a punishment, and everyone has something left to lose. I was going to put this theory to the test. With the ground-up remains of a candy bar in my teeth, I stepped out of the store with a hand siphon in my grip and a bad idea in my head. I placed one of the tubes down the throat of an old car that was parked outside and filled an empty bottle with gasoline. I stuffed a wad of paper towels into the bottle and lit a cigarette. I took a few drags and stared into the blackened cavity of the pillaged store before me. This motherfucker could use some color.

I damn near blew my own hand off in the process, but I managed to launch that nasty little explosive just in time. It somersaulted through the air like an angel smacked out of heaven by the furious hand of god. I watched as it sailed through the hole I had opened in the glass, and my eyes grew big as it disturbed a rack of sunglasses. The fire spread out over the floor and crawled somewhat lethargically toward every corner of the mini-mart. The conquering orange tide ate its way up the walls and birthed pillars of black smoke as it expanded. It seemed like this was gonna be a predictable decimation. Everything was going to be scorched away, inch by scalding inch, until only a pile of smoldering ash would remain. Shame on me for doubting the mercurial nature of fire. Like a married man into the arms of a mistress, those creeping flames found their way to some form of accelerant and my destructive act declared war on the night.

The explosion knocked me to the ground, and a sideways rain of shredded metal, plaster and glass skimmed over me. A rush of energy flattened the grass around the building and expelled a great powdery cloud of dust and other such particles. A tower of fire was cast up into the sky, and it burnt the underside of heaven itself. The whole of the night glowed amber with heat, and all of the finer details that were once swallowed by darkness were now put back on display as the sun rose early in Texas that day.

I don't remember the fire department showing up. I don't remember as they doused my masterpiece in water and foam. I don't remember the ambulance and all its sirens. I don't remember the EMTs as they checked me over to make sure that I was healthy enough to properly arrest. I don't remember the cops, the handcuffs, the Miranda Rights, and I certainly can't recall declaring myself the God-man Fire King of Texas. Although I really wish I had that memory and not just a second-hand account of the matter. That must have been hysterical.

It took me about six steady hours to sober up, and a full day's time before I genuinely felt bad about what I had done. It took a week or two before I could properly be described as a healthy person, and it was a full seven months before I could rotate my left ankle without feeling any prick of pain. It also required five years, eighty-eight days, and eleven minutes for me to be released from prison. This is the story of the longest five years, eighty-eight days, and eleven minutes of my entire life.

Chapter 7

2,754,731 minutes

Five years, eighty-eight days, and eleven minutes. What's the problem? Are you doubting my math? I had plenty of time, see above, to figure that all out. Okay, there was probably a leap year in there somewhere, and the quarter-day bullshit, so I might not have it exactly right, but the point is well taken. I learned plenty of interesting things in prison. For instance, I discovered the names of every plant that grew along the prison property, I taught myself to tell the time just by the position of the sun, and I even learned how to sew. I brewed a gallon of toilet wine. Look, if you're gonna be in prison, you might as well learn how to make alcohol. I unearthed the true value of candy, cigarettes, and toothpaste and I was made to realize that paper money doesn't actually hold any tangible value. I mastered the art of passing notes from one floor to another using just fishing line, mirrors and matchbook covers. I could throw my voice through duct work, and I adopted a stray cat that wandered into the rec yard. But my time in prison wasn't all parlor tricks, amateur magic and snuggle time with wild animals. Oh, no, it was much more. It was a means to CrimeSpree.

More on that in a while, what do ya say? No need to rush things, not just yet. I wanna start instead with my mug-shot and the unlikely piece of treasured pop culture that it has become. What a sight. My eyes were bleary, my skin was gray, and, like everyone else who has ever been arrested, my hair was a mess. Due to the pain that had nestled itself in my shoulder back then, my posture was noticeably tilted and my lips were pursed somewhere in between a child-molester's smirk and a proper grimace. Through the gap of my cracked lips, my damaged teeth could be seen, as could the holes where bone and enamel should have been. I looked like a reject junkie from the planet Amphetamine who had fallen to earth during a bender of galactic proportions.

So, pop-culture icon, huh? That's right. In time, after the fall of CrimeSpree, the image of my face was copied onto bumper stickers and sewn into the jackets worn by disenfranchised punk kids. It was common to see my two-dimensional render staring deathly back at you from inside a tattoo parlor or a hipster bar, and my noggin was inflated to absurd sizes to accommodate the large signs carried by protesters. I could be viewed among the crowds who gathered to denounce corporate greed and political riff-raff. I was used to articulate some sort of point by those who rallied for constitutional rights and by college brats who wanted nothing more than a reason to gather around each other and burn shit. I was mostly okay with all of that, but I wish they would have chosen a better picture.

So, I was on my way to becoming Che Guevara, Malcolm X, and Marilyn Monroe. You know, I was on my way to becoming one of those people whose image is plastered on all sorts of things, even though the public at large knows next to nothing about them. I suppose that after CrimeSpree, I was destined to become one of the anonymous immortals. I think I'm okay with all of that, too, but first, I had some time to serve.

I was sent to a brand-new prison that had been built in Lubbock, Texas. It was a new-age, progressive prison that had been especially built for the modern breed of American inmate. From the outside, it didn't appear all that different from the prisons of old. It was a massive stone building that was situated on a patch of field that was flat, square, and located a comfortable distance away from decent society. The perimeter was enwrapped in three rows of mildly electrified fencing that rose twenty-feet into the air up from a concrete base that was sunk a grave's depth into the ground. A thick coil of razor-wire iced this nefarious cake, which was striped by shadows as the guard towers loomed high above.

This entire space that surrounded the prison was our rec yard, and we were free to roam it fourteen hours out of each day. We were supposed to spend eight hours in our cells asleep and the remaining two hours were reserved for personal reflection. The time that was left was our time. It was as much freedom as you could hope to have while being locked away. The Righted Mind Lubbock Correctional Facility was the latest thinking in prisons, and it was also a pretentious mouthful. So, how about a peek inside my Texas vacation home?

Here we go and, please, try to keep up. When someone is first admitted into The Righted Mind, they are given a series of personality and aptitude tests. This part isn't so bad. After all, you get to talk about yourself for two days, which is a pastime that most people tend to enjoy. All of this was also done in front of fresh-faced counselors who did their damnedest to feign interest in everything that was said. Once this process was complete, each inmate was assigned a wing of the prison that housed like-minded individuals. This was supposed to promote friend-building and social skills, but I'll be perfectly honest with ya. Putting people like me around a bunch of other people like me is rarely a good idea.

I was put up in the northwestern-most wing of the prison. The Righted Mind had four total wings, which gave the building an X shape when viewed from above. These four tentacles all met at a circular hub that was referred to as The Second Chance Commons. How queer. This is where the cafeteria and the library were housed. The Commons was a vast open area that also held areas for ping-pong, chess and billiards. There were some TVs that showed sports and sanitized programs about good moral behavior and other sunny stuff. There was an inviting lounge area that was stocked with fluffy couches and reclining chairs. We even had a café that was open all day except for the hours carved out for sleepy-time.

If you didn't fancy indoor activity, or if you just wanted to eat your rather plain lunch outside, you could leave the

Commons and roam about the rec yard. We had a baseball field, a basketball court, and a whole ton of picnic tables. Not much else was really there, but a wide variety of plant life was cultivated all along the outside of the fence. This was done in an attempt to encourage the inmates to reconnect with nature, and this was the only thing about The Righted Mind that felt wholly correct. It was a natural display of lush beauty in all its assorted forms. This border gave us color, and it gave us an aroma that shifted and danced with the breeze, but it was still a border. As the flora grew just on the other side of the fence, it reminded us that we had done wrong, and, as a punishment, we were segregated from things more delicate and vulnerable than ourselves. To walk the fence was a poignant lesson—and it was also an accident. You see, it was a grounds keeper who had the idea for the most peaceful and successful aspect of the prison. Of course, all the college-educated buffoons that ran the place never gave the gardener his due, but the lesson here is the same as the one being taught in my story. It was *nature,* the *natural,* that was correct.

My section of the prison looked just like the others, and each was crafted to emulate a dorm-style way of life. Each wing more or less resembled a really long two-story hallway that was eternally lit by soft, amber bulbs. The stretch was wide enough that even the most claustrophobic inmate would feel comfortable, and the floor was layered with a hearty, cushy carpet. Happy feet make happy cons, I guess. Our cells lined each side of this deep blue tongue, and they, too, had their edges dulled to accommodate the 8th Day Era's pussy brand of criminals. Yes, our cells had bars, but these weren't your average run-of-the-mill plain old steel bars. No, sir, these were fancy. The bars were artistically formed and mildly decorated the same way that overpriced patio furniture tends to be. The patterns varied so that no two cells looked exactly the same and the skeletons of these steel cages had their bones painted in the soothing hues of blue, green, and sunset orange.

Each floor had a small, generic chapel that was supposed to serve the needs of multiple faiths. The numbers of the faithful had declined during the 8th Day Era, and among convicts like me, deep-rooted religious belief was a rare beast. I mean, we didn't concern ourselves with the laws and punishments of our fellow man, so why the hell were we gonna bother with the regulations of some ghost-god floating around in outer space? These areas were actually okay though. Most of the guys in my wing just used the chapel as a place to hang out and kill time. We'd go there to trade candy or magazines and shoot the shit, making up stories about chicks we never banged and all sorts of impressive stuff that we never actually did.

The chapels were different from the Commons. Spending time in the Commons was like palling around with all the people that you see every day but don't really know. The girl who serves you coffee in the morning, the guy who jogs the same trail as you, those types. But the people you saw in the chapels were the people that you really knew, and, what was more, these people knew you. There was no fooling anybody in the chapels, especially if you had served any significant time in a given wing. It was a reprise of high school, minus the freshly developed girls. That was a drag, but the rest of it was alright. The guys in the chapel became tight because we knew all the stupid shit that each other had done. It can be pretty boring in prison, and believe me, you'll reveal some seriously embarrassing anecdotes just to melt the time away. I went to prison, came to church, and found truth. Too bad it wasn't the holy kind.

The cells weren't all that bad either. They were marginally larger than the cages found in ordinary prisons and each had an oval window that stared out into the Texas countryside. We were encouraged to hang things on the walls as a means to express ourselves in about the same way that a fifteen-year-old pledges allegiance to a rock band. We were allowed to keep a wide variety of personal items, and our beds were of a quality higher than those found in some motel chains. As I mentioned before, we were only locked away for ten hours a day. The lights went out every day at 10 o'clock at night and then they all sparked back to life promptly at six in the morning. A good-morning announcement came over the loud speaker, followed by a short piece of classical music that was played low. Then, after the daily salutations and the culture, came our time to reflect. The cells would remain locked until 8 A.M. and we were encouraged to look within ourselves and evaluate our lives for two hours each day. Most of the guys just used this time to brush their teeth, drop a deuce or read a book.

Just like a proper dorm, The Righted Mind had communal shower facilities on each wing as well. As you well know I've never been a very big fan of Porrima, but every day for almost six years, I worshiped its existence. Prison rape was no longer a threat, is what I'm saying, just in case you're lagging behind. The stalls were semi-private and clean, and we had access to a small compliment of hypo-allergenic soaps. There were always new shaving razors in stock and never once did I see one used as a weapon. Things never got any hairier than locker room hijinks. Towel snapping, an occasional ball-tap, and crap like that.

Yeah, it wasn't so bad there in Lubbock, Texas. I ate better and certainly more nutritiously than at any other time in my life, and I went to bed every night on a soft bed with a regularity that I had never known. I was given plenty of time to read, and I watched football every Sunday on spectacular televisions. I never missed a single game of the baseball playoffs during my stay, and I worked rather infrequently. We were offered work, and there were plenty of jobs available around the campus, as the officials liked to call it, but I never stayed on at any one for too long. There was no need. We weren't pushed one way or the other. We were only encouraged to do what made us most happy. If we found ourselves on the inside we could find our way when we got out.

I'm sure that snugly, sappy approach worked for some guys, but that doesn't exclude the method from being a load of shit, either. The bottom line was that at The Righted Mind, hard time didn't exist. I'm fairly confident that difficult time didn't even exist there. It was just time, a space between then and now. But don't misunderstand me, serving time is always a punishment. A punishment can be relatively comfortable, but it is a punishment all the same. There is absolutely nothing, *nothing*, like freedom. To do whatever you want, whenever you want is what constitutes the very state of living. When that is taken from you, you adapt, you change, you lower your expectations, and every day you dream about again breathing a free man's breath.

When I wasn't in the Commons, I liked to roam the grounds. I took in the finer details of the massive complex and made mental notes of any area of the prison that exhibited vulnerability. I was that quiet mouse that methodically plods along inside the walls of a house inspecting every crack, every loose bit of plaster, and every separated piece of duct work. But I never tried to escape. I never even put together a workable plan. The risks were too great. The leniency of The Righted Mind came with a caveat: escape, and pay dearly. An escape attempt, no matter how minor or bungled, was enough to add five more years to anybody's sentence. End of story, no room for argument. Oh, and if somebody made it all the way into free society? That was a ten spot. Pay up, asshole.

By the time that I had the complete layout of The Righted Mind copied onto my brain, I had already served three years. I could wait out the final two and change. After all, flying under the radar was the system that always got me by. I'll try to remember that the next time I feel the urge to burn down a gas station.

One night I was out walking the perimeter, just enjoying my own company and the low melody of *Rotten Apple* as it came trickling out of the prison speaker system. After dinner was served, a classic-rock radio station was played for us until lights out. Most of the time the music was barely audible and the DJ played a lot of crap, but it was better than dead silence interspersed with the sounds of bolt locks and door buzzers. So there I was with the music in my ears and the light of the moon above me. It struggled to navigate its way through the thick cloud cover, the air was warm and the insects that stalk the shadows were in full throat.

My fingers drooped through the spaces in the fence as I passed slowly along. I liked to feel the touch of the plants that grew just on the other side, and I liked how they looked under the distant lights that hung from the towers. I thought it was funny that the more aggressive forms wove their way through the fencing and crawled onto prison property. It didn't feel like they were trying to get in, it just seemed to me that certain types of things are just drawn to certain types of places. They can't help it, that's just the way they're wired. Maybe man, with all his gadgets and fancy phrases, is no more complex than an ordinary vine.

I'm gonna go over here...

That's the flawed instinctual thinking that puts us where we end up. Not because we want to, not because it's the right thing to do, not because it's profitable. Hell, it probably isn't even safe, but that's where we're going. I guess that's how I wound up in prison. I was headed there all along. It got me to thinking about escape again and to where I would next be inevitably pulled.

I suppose that I have bounced back and forth on fate and the matter of its existence. I still don't know which way I should call it, but if fate does exist, I will tell you what it is. Fate is that good little boy who ends up in prison for life for something he never did. Fate is that insensitive motherfucker winning the lottery. Fate is the warehouse worker who is nailing the wealthy model, and fate is a ten-year-old who is dying of some rare disease. Fate is an unbiased roll of the dice, one way or the other. Some people get lucky, some get screwed and many others never even step up to the table.

So there I was with my hands in the fence, the moon on my back, and a quiet soundtrack whirring among the warm air. There was also a hole cut into the fence. Draped in shadows, it wasn't highly noticeable as the shrubbery had been carefully tucked into the wound, but it was there all the same. Right there in front of me and just the right size, too. To my great surprise, I walked in my bedroom to find a heavy-chested hooker sprawled out naked and holding a fistful of cash. Maybe she had syphilis, maybe I would get stung, but I would never know the good without risking the bad.

And this moment brings me back to fate. Fate had no part to play that evening. I was simply confronted with an opportunity, a decision to make. I could bet big and come out a winner, or I could fold the hand and bide my time until a sure thing came tumbling my way. The only problem with that math is that a sure thing is never a guarantee. Now how do you like that irony? What I mean is, you could bang the hooker and get syphilis, which would suck, but to pass on this opportunity also lets in the possibility that you might never get laid again. I was due to be released in a couple of years, but that was also based on the assumption that I would live to see the day. Sure, I was a young man then, but cancer doesn't give a fuck if you have plans or not. I could hit my head in the shower and drown. I could choke on my state-issued breakfast. I could suffer a heart attack for no reason at all. How many seconds do you think busy Lucy Miller dedicated to the contemplation of death from the first day of her life until the very hour that the doctor gave her the news? My guess would be about a minute and a half. You never know what tomorrow might bring, so why not take what you want if it's in your face today?

That's a very good question and it's one with no answer, or maybe it's one so complex that it has infinite answers. You could say it's a question that won me a lot of the good and a lot of the bad that had wandered into my life. But on that Texas night, it was a question that was as ephemeral as fate and no more forceful than a morning breeze, because that day's final tally was Porrima - 1, Mickey - 0.

There was a siren that screamed every night at 9:45. It let everyone know it was time to get into their cells for lights-out and it wasn't scheduled to go off for another two hours. That meant that I had one-hundred and twenty minutes to stare at the open mouth of early release. It meant that nobody was gonna come looking for me for quite a while, and goddamn it, it meant that I would have a two-hour head start on the law. I had always held a certain affection for staying a click or two in front of the authorities, and I always enjoyed doing things that I wasn't supposed to do. The more I stared at this opportunity, the bigger the tits got on this hooker. Oh, and just in case you're gay or you're a chick who is out of touch with the unchanged thinking of the upright male, I'm trying to articulate that the situation before me became more tempting.

I placed my palms flat against the fence, one hand on each side of the hole, and curled my fingers through the links. I stuck my head through to the other side and inhaled the largest quantity of oxygen that my lungs would hold. I bet you think that the quality of the air was no different from one side of the fence to the other. Well guess what? You're dead fucking wrong, as wrong as you'll ever be about anything. The taste was honey and milk to a man that only knew the flavors of motor oil and dust. It was one of the most moving and pleasurable experiences of my entire life, and I left it there in the darkness of the swollen evening.

It took me about six hours to fall asleep that night. I stared up at the ceiling in a dumbstruck daze of numbness. I didn't run through different scenarios in my mind, I didn't

132

entertain the what-ifs and the what-might-have-beens. I didn't think at all. I just laid there wide-eyed and empty, like the victim of a botched lobotomy, as if successful lobotomies produce results any different. My inaction out in the rec yard had stunned me so very deeply. It seemed altogether possible that I might just expire there and then upon my prison mattress. My organs were just gonna follow suit with the rest of me and do nothing. One switch was gonna be turned off, and then another, and then another, systematically until the end arrived. What a chump I would have been then, huh? That sure would have been some vulgar version of fate.

Hey, look, more words. I must have survived the night after all. And to think, you were growing so very concerned for the wellbeing of Mickey Moore. Okay, that's probably just a dump truck's worth of wishful thinking, but the plain truth of the matter was that my body and my brain finally gave in to normality. I fell asleep and, a tiddly bit later, I woke up.

Did I mention that when I woke up, I was crying like a blubbering infant? Yeah, thought not. Well I was, and my pathetic sobbing lasted straight through the Stravinsky and the bullcrap self-evaluation period that kicked off each day. I must have sounded truly obnoxious—I even started to annoy myself—but the pity parade that I was grand marshaling had not yet reached the end of the route. And to think, if I had pulled a stunt like that in a prison of days-gone-past, someone would have busted into my cell within minutes and beat my ass into silence. That probably would have been appropriate.

I went to the chapel right around midday. I didn't go to pray and I wasn't looking for guidance or clarity, I just wanted to be alone and I was sick of tossing my eyeballs around my cell. Around noontime the chapels were almost always deserted. Most inmates were settling down for lunch by then, or putting together a game out in the yard. It was an idyllic day, too, weather-wise, as no day is truly idyllic *inside* a prison, but it was all the more reason for me to expect a lengthy stretch of peace and quiet.

I walked down the dull, gray concrete that supported a half-dozen rows of pews and passed on by the rather unimpressive and generic altar. There was a large, tear-drop shaped window sunk into the outer wall of the chapel. Sitting behind a barrier of bars, it was made of stained glass and offered no preference of faith. The sun melted through the prismatic glass and it warmed the bench that was stretched out below. It was just a stained collection of 2 x 4s with a beaten-down cushion that had a variety of frays and small rips, but it was where I decided to place my ass. I remember closing my eyes, even though sleep wasn't my intention, but with the lack of it from the night before, I hastily fell into dreamland.

Did you ever have a dream so real that when you woke up, you had to do something to test the validity of the vision? Maybe you dreamt about a new car and then rushed to the window to have a peek at the driveway. Maybe you once dreamed about being robbed, and in the still of the night, you went room to room just to make sure that everything was in its place. Or maybe you watched as a loved one was lowered into the ground, and then, upon waking, you felt it necessary to call them repeatedly at 3 o'clock in the morning just to hear them wearily tell you that it was just a dream. Something like that happened to me while snoozing inside one of the chapels of The Righted Mind.

I was standing up at the altar and I was giving some sort of sermon, although I don't remember anything that I said. I looked out over the small congregation and I saw a lot of familiar faces. The evil trucker was down in front, staring at me through his thick sunglasses, his sinewy arms folded across his chest. Mike the mechanic was there, and so was thick-thighs Darlene. She was leaning up against the wall and sharing a cigarette with young Brittany. I remember not liking this. I couldn't help but think that Darlene had nothing positive to offer the sweet and somewhat stupid girl who had given me a lift to Clovis. The hippie crew from the desert was there, although the druggy chick with the flowery name wasn't with them. It was never mentioned or plainly put in the dream, but somehow I knew that Daffodil was dead. Tweedle-glee and Tweedle-scum were there, with all their fat rolls and sweat, and an old couple that I had conned with one of my asphalt schemes so many years ago were seated in the pews as well. They seemed rather forgettable to me at the time. Apparently not.

And then there was Lucy. She was seated in the furthest pew from the altar and she was all by herself. The others looked around and talked quietly to one another, but not Lucy. She was as still as ancient stone and she stared at me with her eyes widened to a slightly unbelievable degree. It was horribly unsettling and violently obvious that Lucy was terrified. Aside from the fear that streaked her face, Lucy looked good and healthy, but she rose from the pew like a frail old woman wracked with arthritis. Her limbs were rigid and stiff as she made for the exit before disappearing into the darkness of the hallway before her.

My sermon stopped and I was frozen in place. The motley collection of parishioners directed their attention to me and impatiently demanded that I continue. This was impossible. All I could do was to think of Lucy. I knew she had died, I knew she was gone, but what was this that I had just seen? I wondered if she was a ghost, or if by some miracle she was returned to life. I even contemplated the likelihood that this whole bizarre scene was just a dream, but there was no way, it was all too real.

I stepped down from the pulpit and ran into the blackness that had just consumed Lucy. When I emerged on the other side, I was out in the rec yard, but the fences were gone and the massive building behind me was reduced to nothing more than a quaint church ripped from the American Baptist south of yesteryear. The grass under my feet was dead, and it was blown from the ground in dry, brown clumps. The sky above was red with the shades of a far-off fire and all the magnificent plant life that once encircled the prison grounds were now reduced to barren stems and a knotted collection of brittle vines. Among all this decay, I witnessed as Lucy's image darted between the trees in the distance. I ran for her and screamed her name, but I couldn't get a firm hold on just where to look. Every time I thought I had reached within a close distance of her, I would see as Lucy slipped away behind another tree, and almost always in the direction opposite of mine. Although she was far away, a clear image of her face never eluded me. She looked so scared to me, so desperate, and her expressions grew increasingly frantic with my every failure to find her. And that's just how it ended, like all dreams do, so abruptly. But I never did find lost Lucy. I never found her.

I've never been a religious man and I never put much stock in the things that we see in our dreams. It all just sounds like the same nonsense to me. But this dream was different, it shook me and it has stayed with me. I only had it once, but the visuals are still so vivid to me, it's as though I have that damned dream every night. Which brings me to two separate points. First, if God does exist and I was given a peek into what Lucy Miller is forced to endure in the afterlife whether it be for her sins or mine, I will personally crack the sky open and wring her salvation from the hands of the divine. The second is this. If what I saw in my dream was a glimpse into just a possibility of the things that await us after death, then the finite and atheistic thought of simply rotting in the ground when we're gone is a much less chilling proposition.

When I opened my eyes, I saw a man who was unknown to me. I knew he wasn't a guard because of the clothes that he wore. This would seem like the most logical and obvious clue, but it wasn't. No, I knew he wasn't a guard because it looked to me as though a child could have beaten this dude into a weeping pulp of human putty. And not just any child, either. A ten-year-old with a bum leg and some personal experience with chemotherapy could have easily laid this stranger out. Hence, he would have made for a crappy guard.

So, a long-winded explanation later leads us to the fact that the man above me was an inmate and a fresh one at that. He stood uncomfortably tall with a body that strained to push the scale over one-hundred and twenty pounds. His nose was thin and fragile, his lips practically didn't exist and his eyes were nearly as pale as his skin. He had short, receding hair, and his hands sported freakishly long fingers that were tipped by ten jagged and chewed nails. He fidgeted above me, almost like the nerves in his body misfired like an engine that had lost its time, and he looked positively spooked that I had opened my eyes. Hey, that tends to be what happens when you roust someone from sleep, asshole.

Once I righted myself and settled back into reality, me and the lanky stranger exchanged clumsy greetings. This took longer than was necessary, and for whatever reason he felt compelled to apologize about eighty times for waking me up. Goddamn you, Porrima, even prison had become polite and sensitive.

Well as it turned out, sticks and bones had a proper name, and it was Edgar Stapleton. Now, do I really need to tell you all that Eddie was locked up for embezzlement, racketeering, and just general white-collar misbehavior, or does the name Edgar Stapleton scream Ponzi scheme loud enough for ya? If that wasn't enough, his middle name was Archibald. Yep, Edgar Archibald Stapleton. Can't you just see all the broken dreams and lost investments now? Eddie was a proper piece of shit, and he made me look awesome, if I may employ a word overused by people ages thirteen to about twenty-five. He ripped off friends, relatives, even his own grandparents were forced to sell their house and move into a crumby apartment complex after whiz-kid Edgar drained the last of their retirement savings directly into his pocket. He sank over seventy middle-class families into financial ruin, and torpedoed four businesses that employed over one thousand people, all told, once the damage was all said and done. He slithered his way through two proper marriages, a laundry list of call girls and three trophy wives, all in that order.

If you're thinking of writing a thank-you note to all the hardworking folks at the FBI and the many other law enforcement agencies that were involved in bringing old Mr. Stapleton to justice, put down the pen. As usual, this man's undoing was the power of pussy. Sorry, girls, at least I didn't use the C-word. The second of the three trophy wives was a stout blond in her early twenties with no brain, fake tits, and a real big mouth. This may have been the initial source of the attraction but let this act as a warning. If there's nothing in a yapper that big, a secret or two is bound to tumble out.

Right after the split of Edgar and the plaything who was born right about the same time that he started to lose his hair, things were quiet. This was normal. The women got paid, kept it zipped and fast Eddie went on to the next thing with tighter skin. But all was not well in the kingdom. Bunny Madison, yes— that's her given name—apparently thought she was entitled to more, a lot more. Edgar had more money than God. He should have just paid her, but the shrewd businessman was cheap and the sprite wasn't as dumb as she made out. Don't misunderstand me, she was no Einstein, but Bunny wanted money, and, like a dog that rips open a trash bag in search of food, bubbly Bunny knew where to look.

This chick sold her story and blabbed her mouth to anyone who would listen, or to anybody that was within earshot. She popped up on morning radio programs that poke a stick at the FCC, and she had cozy, sit-down interviews with respected journalists. Bunny flopped around the tabloid circuit, and she also made countless internet videos in which she spelled out old Edgar's nefarious dealings. And by *spelled out,* I of course mean that she ranted somewhat incoherently and tripped over words that were far above her vocabulary level. It was for this reason and assorted others that not much of anybody took Bunny too seriously. After all, Edgar Stapleton was a respected member of the community and he kept impeccable records that he was always willing to share.

But the squeaky wheel gets the grease, right? They waited for a rainy day, but soon enough the FBI took Bunny's words with half a heart and started to nose around Edgar's Holding and the myriad companies that he owned and funded. As I said before, Edgar kept impeccable records. The problem was, was that not everybody that worked for Edgar shared his passion for attention to detail. It took a few years, and I'm sure the Feds wore out a few shovels as they upturned all the shit, but they got to the bottom of it eventually. Stapleton's lawyers threw up every block that they could along the way, and money was shuffled this way and that, but the dam was broken and it was only a matter of time before the flood washed everything away.

Like the shadowy tycoons and sideways CEOs that had come before him, Edgar had an ego even larger than his bank account. This, of course, obscured the fact that he was a spineless worm who couldn't face proper criticism, let alone a federal investigation. So what happened next? Come on, you know the next act of this play! I'll toss ya a few hints. There was a rope, a shower curtain rod, and an embarrassment of failure. Almost on cue, as the walls were tumbling in on him, Edgar opted to pay the only check that he could. This, too, did not go as planned. Within the palatial environs of his master bathroom, the agents were supposed to find Edgar cold and swinging from a rod of jewel-encrusted silver, and they would have, if hapless Edgar had known how to tie a knot. Instead they found a skinny man of middle age who had cracked his head on the marble floor. There he lay, comatose and in a puddle of blood.

Maybe this is why Edgar flinched when I opened my eyes. After all, he opened his eyes one day and found a rather nasty surprise. But like any distinguished con, Edgar quickly moved on to plan B once the whole suicide aspect of plan A went awry. He turned rat on anyone he could. God help you if you had so much as jaywalked in front of Eddie Arch. He was gonna parlay your misstep into his early release. He aided the Feds at every turn and helped to expose the very loopholes that he once so zealously exploited. I gotta hand it to him, fast Eddie drew ten years, that was all, for doing incalculable damage.

Eddie Arch, that's what I knew him as, that's what he was going by once prison enveloped him inside its stone embrace. It didn't make him any less despicable, but he knew he had to shed the name that became synonymous with the very worst that any American had to offer during the 8th Day Era. At the very least, he now sounded like some guy who probably drove a forklift for a living.

I talked to Eddie Arch for about three hours that day in the chapel. He asked me a lot of meaningless and trivial bullshit about The Righted Mind. I ignored most of what he said and just kept my side of the conversation to simple *yes* or *no* responses. This seemed okay by Ed, he really just wanted to hear himself talk and he was looking to impress somebody that he thought was a loser. And ain't that the sad truth of it all? I was nothing more than a less successful version of Edgar Stapleton. Which is funny, because he was the gold standard of the con trade, and we were both mere feet apart inside the same prison. I tried to balance this out by telling myself that I was a better person, but why put up the ruse? We were cut from the same cloth, no denying it. Sure his side of the cloth was a little filthier, but did it matter? If you get dog shit on the left sleeve of your shirt you don't rationalize that the rest of it is comparatively clean and wear the sucker anyway.

That's when I knew I had to change. Oh, believe me, I had every intention of getting by on the misfortunes of others once I was released, but not anymore. I was staring at the very pinnacle of what my line of work could produce, and it was a sad and sobering sight. I was going to be something that mattered for the very first time in my life.

Ever since that day in New Mexico, I had a disjointed idea about what CrimeSpree should be. But it was just an idea, a fairytale, really. I didn't have the means to put something like that together. Admittedly, it was bigger than me. I even felt a bit foolish as I told Eddie about my idea for an amusement park of crime. I heard the words as they spilled out of my mouth and their sum just sounded like a worthless reaction to an event that supposedly didn't even take place. But to my surprise, Eddie was hooked. Like a piece of meat on a hook, he could do nothing but dangle there, helpless before the power of my idea. Oh, I guess I should mention this, too. Eddie still had money.

By the time that Eddie had been transferred to The Righted Mind, I had only two years and some change left to serve. He was due to be released about a year after I was expected to hit the streets, and so we struck a deal. He owned a small country's worth of acreage in rural New York state and I was familiar enough with the East Coast to settle in rather quickly. Once free, it was my responsibility to put the gears in motion, and to start the rudimentary planning for the park and what it should offer. Edgar was gonna catch up with me once he was put back into decent society, and then we were really gonna get cracking. He swore to me that he had a war chest full of untold cash, but let's get back to the bones later.

We discussed using the undeveloped land for the park and agreed on some of the broader terms of our arrangement. Edgar was gonna rake in 70% of the profits while I was left with the other 30%. This was his first offer and I didn't even flinch. I

141

might have been a con and a cheat, but I wasn't an idiot. As far as I could tell, CrimeSpree was probably gonna fail and 30% of what we took in was gonna be 100% more than I was set up to make otherwise. It was a no-brainer. The most ironic thing about the deal made by me and Eddie was that there was no contract and nothing was in writing. We didn't even shake hands, as he was quite the germaphobe. I could have ripped him off at any turn from the starting gun to the very end, and he could have done the same to me. But this deal was different. I believed in what I had seen and Eddie believed me.

In a testament to just how much Eddie trusted me, he gave me clear and explicit instructions on where to find the money that would launch our operation. That crafty bastard had buried roughly a million dollars in cash in some fucking field. My god, he thought of everything. Eddie even had planned for prison. He knew the government and the lawsuits would seize his assets and drain every traceable penny that he had which is why he threw shovelfuls of dirt onto a plain box that contained a horde of small bills. The man was a genius and a success at every step. I gotta admit, I was wrong about Eddie. He wasn't a failure. He couldn't fail, and for the first time, I had an uneasy feeling that CrimeSpree might actually work.

Which brings us to my last day inside the walls of The Righted Mind. What? You thought Eddie was gonna give me information like that and trust me not to fuck it up for the next couple of years? Hell no. On the morning of my release, he put a little note inside a little sealed bag that was attached to a thin little string and he made me swallow it in front of him. He patted me on the back and smiled but he didn't say a word. It was kinda creepy, which was normal. Eddie was a creep. But there was something about his look that was ominous, like I carried within me some dark and powerful secret. I guess he was right in the end, because like I said, he thought of everything.

Five years, eighty-eight days, and eleven minutes. That doesn't seem very tidy, does it? That's because I was sentenced to six years but was granted early release for good behavior and because I'm a pussy. That seems a bit harsh, but it's absolutely true. You see, when I came up for parole, it was revealed to me that on the night I discovered that perfect hole in the fence, I was being tested. Yep, they, as in the shadowy, all-knowing *They,* came to know my routines and habits and decided to dangle a carrot in front of my face. They were watching me the whole time and they got to watch as I denied myself the very essence of what it means to be alive, they were witness to my voluntary denial of freedom. I'm sure that's when they knew that the system had won. My remaining time at The Righted Mind was just a formality. I was sanitized and of no threat to anyone or any judicial commandment. I was a prepackaged human being. I was generic and because of Porrima, I was predictable. At least that's what they thought. Take it from me, they're wrong from time to time.

Chapter 8

Dig, Mickey, dig!

It was early spring in Texas, which was good. I had earned three hundred and four dollars while in prison, and I had not a penny more to my name, which was bad. I had around seventeen hundred miles to cover with no means of transportation, which was worse. But all hope was not yet lost, because I had a tickle in my throat and a million-dollar gag reflex.

I had the prison shuttle drop me off on the side on the road. It was a flat stretch of rural pavement that connected the city of Lubbock to the small town of Idalou. This asphalt vein ran for just ten miles, but it felt like it could have flowed out forever. The land was undeveloped other than the smattering of homemade signs that advertised fresh apples or other such produce that could be found at a nearby farm stand. Fields of low grasses and fields flush with crops flanked me as I walked. Ancient barns and other indiscernible outbuildings hung in the distance, as did the taillights of the bus as it disappeared out of sight.

It was against the policies of The Righted Mind to simply leave former inmates off at wherever they damn well pleased, but, as we have learned, I could always talk my way into an extra piece of candy. I had the driver convinced that I wanted nothing more than to walk among the freedom of wide country and fresh air. This sappy line worked, but it wasn't entirely untrue either. I did enjoy my walk more than I had ever enjoyed a common stroll before, but there was more to it than just the admiration of nature.

About a mile before the elderly driver bid me adieu, I noticed a ratty old gas station and knew immediately that was where I needed to be. I just allowed some distance to be put between us, as I wanted desperately to fall completely off the map for a while. I had received my latest Porrima injection three days before I was released, which meant I had about six months to disappear into obscurity. And so, after I watched the shuttle fade from my field of vision, I turned my back and made for the Old Highway service station.

The small parking lot was a minefield of rigid asphalt, and only two gas pumps rose from this blackened garden of tar. They were the ancient kind, too, with mechanical counters that spun around as you filled your car. Old shit like this can fetch a nice dollar from collectors of Americana or from hip restaurants that are going for the retro look. But here in west Texas, these archaic beasts were still puking out petro. I gotta admit, I slowed my pace, for just a moment, to admire this example of an America that people of my generation can scarcely even imagine. Everything was big and heavy and mean way back when these pumps were still riding the cutting edge of technology. That must have been an incredible time. There was no flash, no glitter to these machines. You could look right inside at their heavy metal guts, you could smell the stink of gasoline and you could see and touch the grime as it accumulated along the hose. It was dirty and real, authentic and true.

The service station itself was nothing more than a double-bay garage built from aging cinderblock. Nearly every stone was chipped, and most of the paint that surely had this place gleaming white in days gone past now curled away from the block and flaked off to the ground. A flat, rubber roof topped the building, and, judging from the bowed ceiling panels above me, it was pretty clear that water found its way into the garage on a regular basis. Even the bathrooms were located around the side of the building—very old-school. But that's where I needed to be, I had a string tickling my throat and it was high time to hack up a fortune.

I had disturbed a tiny set of hanging bells when I walked inside, but no one seemed to notice. I milled around the cramped lobby and poured myself some coffee into a disposable cup. There was no cream or sugar to be found, the gurgling machine was quite filthy, and, yes, the coffee tasted like it had been filtered through a mesh of ass hair. I didn't mind, though. How could I? After all, much like I was, back then, the coffee was absolutely free. I nosed around at some old maps and classic car calendars that were taped to the walls, and admired the random assortment of pinup girls that were tacked up upon pages of tattered paper now devoid of their sheen. I tapped my finger over a bell that was placed on the messy counter and craned my neck to see into the shop. Still nothing. Apparently the owners of the Old Highway didn't know just who they were dealing with considering that the last time I was in a gas station, I burned the motherfucker down.

I strolled into the service area like I owned the place and found a grumpy mechanic wedged under a late-model sedan. He was about twenty years my senior, uncomfortably large, and red with aggravation. He briskly waddled over to the back wall that held a wide array of wrenches and plucked a dented hubcap from off a steel workbench. At this point, I was unaware that the hubcap had a part to play in my tale, but before I could form another thought, this cranky troll winged it at me like it was a ninja star. I caught the flimsy piece of aluminum about an inch from my face and felt as a key pinged off my chest a time or two. It was tethered to the wheel cover with a tangle of bailing wire and was mildly bent from years of being forced into the mouth of a temperamental lock.

My prison cell was a palace when compared to this shitting hole. It couldn't be called a bathroom, that would have been wildly inaccurate. It wasn't wide enough to extend your arms in any direction, and the walls were covered with stains, crude illustrations of genitals, and the phone numbers of seemingly every whore that had ever resided in the Lone Star State. There was a toilet with no seat and no tank lid, a crooked sink with a chipped bowl, no mirror, no soap, and no paper

146

towels. To borrow a phrase from old Tweedle-glee back in New Mexico, none of this made any nevermind to me.

I jammed my fingers as far down my throat as they would go, gagged, choked and spit up on my knuckles ever so slightly. I coughed, caught my breath, and blinked the water out of my eyes before having another go at it. Round two produced the same result, and the third time wasn't a charm either, but I got that sucker eventually. I fished up my treasure map amid a mild effusion of vomit and did my best to wash the muck from my fingers. I dried my hands on my clothes and took great care to peel away the layers of cellophane from my note. I could barely breathe as I unfolded the paper across the rickety sink, and I don't think that I blinked for about ten straight minutes. I just stared at my objective, my reward, my severance pay from prison. I folded my paper neatly and tucked it away into my pocket, although this wasn't necessary, as I had its directions burned onto my memory by then.

I was given an interstate, an exit number, a mile marker and a starting point. I was to walk a specific number of steps in one direction and then travel in another for so long, and so on and so forth until I fully retraced Eddie's steps. He had clued me in to the landscape and just what landmarks I should be on the lookout for and left me with one final instruction: dig. Thanks, Ed, I never would have thought to look for buried money in the ground.

Okay, after a stop for some snacks, a few essentials for the journey ahead, and a visit to a thrift store for some new clothes, I was ready to depart Texas. Lubbock isn't all that big of a city, and Jamestown, New York is barely a speck on the map. It's also pretty goddamn far away and so it took some doing before I had a course chartered that was going to place me even relatively near to my target. That was close enough, though. I wanted to make the last leg of the trip on my own anyway.

Transit buses are such miserable inventions. They're like escape pods that were built for the sole purpose of carrying the exhausted and the despondent. Every now and again some young hipster with wanderlust or some old couple kicking off the last hurrah will hop aboard, but they're mere tagalongs. Yes, long-haul buses were built for people like me, people who have no home and nowhere to go. They transport dismal hopes for the future and rotten luck from one area of the country to another. But a change of scenery has never really changed a thing, has it? Sure, it can be exciting at first, rejuvenating, almost, but in the end, you're still the same miserable asshole that you always were.

I took inventory of the sixty or so odd souls that surrounded me. Nobody really stood out. We were all just a collective mass of blandness, and we all had the same look draped over our faces. In silence, we all shared the same belief that somehow, the next stop was gonna be different. And that's when I started to think about just what it was that I was doing. And the more I thought of it, the more it sounded like a fairytale. Here I was, fresh out of prison, and I was chasing rainbows again. A part of me knew that this was gonna be just another empty adventure, a mild distraction before the con game pulled me back in, or, rather, before I jumped headlong back into it. I already knew my future. All I had to do was to examine my past. Me, those like me, the things we're made of, we never change. It's just lather, rinse, repeat until we follow the soap down the drain.

Those sure were some snugly thoughts that tucked me in, but I can't really complain. After all, I dozed off and on all the way to Atlanta. We had a bit of a layover here, which was a blessing. I needed to stretch my legs and, more importantly, I needed to use the toilet. I have made it no secret that the best decisions in life haven't always walked hand in hand with me, so I'll just heap this one onto my already substantial idiocy pile. I ate prison food every day for five years, and before I boarded the bus, I hammered down a steaming plate of barbeque.

Thanks to Texas short ribs, I almost missed the connecter to Jamestown.

Whew! With that unnecessary tidbit out of the way, I was back on track and heading north. This bus was only at about half capacity, but what it lacked in quantity, it certainly made up for in quality. There was some crappy punk-rock band that took over the back of the bus. They were a bunch of nobodies, but each one of them was convinced that they were on the shuttle to stardom. They all had obnoxious haircuts that were colored with every hue except the blonde, brown, red and black of the mainstream. A cannonball could have been made from all the metal in their faces, and they all wore stockings on their arms. The guys were wearing plastic skirts, and the token chick was dressed like some sort of mercenary from a porn film. Not a good porn film, mind you. No, the kind that features girls with back fat and bad teeth. I'm sure the genre exists.

They were fun and provided the greatest entertainment value, but the rest of my companions deserve a mention as well. There was a lesbian couple who bickered incessantly, a nerdy kid with a unibrow and a nose bleed that put at least two books of Sudoku to shame, and an old guy that whistle-snored. Another gentleman that was draped in a yellow suit had smuggled a tiny dog on board in some manner of purse. He cooed at the thing and doted over it in hilarious fashion. Even the driver was amused enough to ignore the little stowaway and its mild violation of bus policy. Two white kids who assuredly had never touched a boob or smoked a cigarette were having a clumsy rap battle while a middle-aged guy a few rows behind backed them up with a bass beat. An ancient woman who was the epitome of walking death was busy filling out a stack of Christmas cards, even though it was April. There was a pair of identical twins who never said a word, and there was a blind man that was drawing pictures. His work was impressive, too.

There was more amusement and nonsense, but you all get the point. I was on the weirdo express. Which inevitably brings me back to Porrima. All of us on that bus, we were all different. Some of us were scary, or at least should have been, but nobody bothered anybody, no one was made uncomfortable. Okay, I'll concede that this was a good thing, it made the trip pleasurable and safe, but it was unnatural. Like a dream, it was unreal. Events took place, characters showed up, but it never felt real, it never felt like anything. Nothing had any real, strong feeling, and everything amounted to nothing. I was so sick of it, sick of the numbness. I wanted to be surrounded by thugs and feel the overwhelming fear that they command. I wanted to be surrounded by sex and feel the excitement as it shook out of me. I wanted to ingest a cocktail of drugs and feel as my heart strained to hold down the explosion. I just wanted to feel alive. Goddamn you, Porrima.

It was this stage of my life that I reflected on first once my mind was fully freed of Porrima. I thought about those hours spent on that bus and what they really meant. At that time, I was a vagabond untethered by responsibility, or even sound judgment. I had been placed there by a series of events that weren't a day late or even a single dollar cheap of spectacular. In no special order, I had lived on the beach, seduced a woman of mature years, and traveled the back roads of the Everglades. I had indulged a thirst for crime and I knew what it meant to be caged. I had explored the nation, laid low, kept company with eccentrics and run desperately from a scene that could have been the backdrop for my murder. And I had to wait years just to fully experience any of it.

Like a drunk who was drying out, my past returned to me with a clarity that Porrima never allowed me to properly view. I'll never forget what it was like feeling Porrima leave my body. It was similar to the split second of alarm that you experience just before throwing up. It was scary, visceral, and it was a purge. My mind ejected all the toxins that had flooded it in the name of advanced medicine, and my body burned with the fever of withdrawal. I was free, finally free. I won't even bother to tell you where I was when I felt this absolute wash of emancipation—it's just too sad—but I was free all the same.

I spent the quiet hours of that night awake and reliving all the events of my life that had been softened and dulled. Only then did I feel like I had lived, only then did my life seem interesting. Yes, the absence of Porrima had returned to me what should have been mine all along, but it wasn't enough. My life had been stolen from me because everything I had done while on Porrima had meant nothing. Sure, there were consequences and reactions, but to me, none of it had meant a goddamn thing because I never fucking felt it at the time. And I knew I wasn't alone. We were a nation of slaves back then, but as I laid there in the dark of that enlightened night, I knew it was finally over. It was all finally going to be over.

But back to the bus, right? We pulled into Jamestown during the waning hours of the afternoon and unloaded ourselves like a group of zombies set loose into parts unknown. Some of us wished the others well while most of us just broke off into different directions. Once together, now apart, never to interfere or interact with each other's lives again. It's kinda weird, if you really think about it. Anyway, there I was in Jamestown with the dipping sun at my back. It was a weekday, and the hometown of Lucille Ball was getting ready to roll up the carpets. It was cold, too. Having spent five years cooped up in a southern pen has a way of thinning the blood. I wandered the empty streets with only shivers and the fresh illumination of lamppost light for company. It was a charming slice of America that technology tends to erase, but I found myself unable to enjoy the serenity that comes with a sleepy town. I was too cold, too hungry, and, again, I was way too homeless.

151

After having stuffed myself with six muffins and a jug of coffee from an artsy café, I checked into a crumby motel. It was one of those single-level joints with narrow doorways and thin walls, but it was all I could afford. The carpet of my room was faded and worn, the bathroom kinda smelled like mold, and the bed was so uncomfortable I elected to sleep on the floor in a pile of blankets.

The next morning, I brushed my teeth and treated myself to a clean shave. Back in Lubbock, they had asked me if I wanted a shave and a haircut before boarding the prison shuttle. What twisted type of question is that? I would have said no to a blowjob at that point. I was free. I wanted to get the fuck out of prison. Ahh, fresh and clean. I even ran some pomade through my hair and ironed my clothes. My clothes were shit. This wasn't necessary but there was an iron in the room. You'd be amazed at the mundane tasks you'll perform simply because you can. I made sure to fill my pack with little toiletries and anything else that I could lift from the room, and on the way out the front door, I asked the clerk to point me in the direction of the nearest hardware store.

Of all the advancements man has made, the one thing that we *think* we have not yet invented is the time machine. This thinking is incorrect. The hardware store is a beast impervious to the hammers of time, and it ignores the persuasions of technology. Nails are nails, bolts and screws are still made of metal, and rakes and picks still look crude and unrefined. The past is alive and well next to the key-cutting machine, and it slumbers in contentment among pipe fittings and cans of oil. I wandered the aisles and passed things that have never had the word *smart* put in front of them, and ran my fingers over devices that will never have apps. And there it was, in the back of the cluttered store just where I knew it would be: the shovel. Yes, *the* shovel, the one that was gonna dig me up a million dollars, and the one that would eventually dig Porrima out of every American skull.

It was beautiful. The blade was steel, the handle was lacquered wood decorated by the heads of sunken fasteners, and the grip was blunt and uncomfortable to hold. No ergonomic pussy shit here, this was a shovel. A mean, regular old shovel designed to puncture the earth and exhume its contents. I pulled it from a barrel that held about thirty others just like it and made for the register. It cost me eighteen dollars and forty-nine cents, and I gleefully slid my last twenty across the counter. I'd never been happier to have less than two whole bucks to my name.

Buy a shovel, steal a car. That wasn't the plan, but when a cupcake materializes, I suggest that you eat said tasty snack. As I walked out of the hardware store with the shovel resting against my right shoulder, I scanned the parking lot of the plaza. I wasn't really looking for anything in particular, old habits just die hard. There were a few dozen cars scattered around the lot of the little strip mall, but there was one that stood out from all the others. It was special. It was like that woman who is adored from afar while she is shackled to a marriage of neglect. In other words, the driver of this car didn't appreciate its potential. In plain-ass English, it was a rental.

It had minor scuffs, dull hubcaps, and no sense of personality strewn about the floor of the interior. There was only one tiny sticker slapped across the rear windshield, and it didn't advertise rock and roll or some feel-good motto. Nope, it was just twice the size of a stamp and all the more it had to say was LD5. That's Lucky Day car rental, class number five to you and me. Class one held the cars that might as well have been miniature limousines, classes two, three and four degenerated predictably, and by the time you got to class five, no one gave a steaming pile. Most of these cars didn't even have tracking devices and the ones that did were rarely updated or maintained.

It was a gamble, but I was a gambling man. The windows were down, the keys were in the cup holder and the morning was quiet. Did this guy just run into the donut shop to buy some coffee? Did he walk into the hair salon for a new cut, or did he just clock into work an hour ago at the shoe store? I had no way of knowing, but one thing was a given; the longer I stood there and thought about it, the more likely it was that he was gonna come strolling out. Whoosh, zing, gone! That was the sound of me flinging open the door, tossing my shovel in the backseat and drifting out of the parking lot with a grin on my face.

Okay, I'm on Interstate 86 at this point, going east in a stolen car with no insurance, an expired license and a shovel for company. If it wasn't for Porrima, it could be inferred that I was up to something rather nefarious. Hey, what the hell else was I gonna do? How the hell was I supposed to get to the middle of nowhere with just a crinkled dollar and some loose change? It was too far to walk. I was out of shape, broke and desperate again. I went all in. It was fortune or bust. I felt like a pioneer pushing west for gold and genocide, only I was just interested in the money. See? I'm not so bad, just materialistic, is all.

I drove 86 for what felt like a day and tried not to wreck, as the image of anything that even resembled a police car sent me into a panic. I didn't turn on the radio. I kept my hands at ten and two and obeyed the speed limit. I stared straight ahead and just thought. I was alive and well and my whole life passed before my eyes. Not flashed, passed, and slowly at that. I thought about how long it had been since I had been among the chill and hilly terrain of the Northeast. I thought about school, and the smarmy prick that I used to be. I cringed at the remembrance of Florida and tried to forget Texas altogether. I recalled old cons and trivial events that I hadn't thought about in years, and as the asphalt rolled away under me, I trembled as that day in New Mexico came back to haunt me. But you all know what I really thought about, don't you? You know what commanded the majority of my thinking.

It was Lucy. Of course it was Lucy. In a perfect world, we would have stayed together and she still would have died twenty years before me. I would have been right around retirement age and all alone again, but I would have traded it all just to have that opportunity. No CrimeSpree, no iconic status, no notoriety, just a lifetime of Porrima and Lucy. The world didn't need me that bad. After all, somebody else would have come along to change America sooner or later. It's inevitable. Nature has a way of correcting herself and correcting us. She doesn't have much patience for being fucked with.

Yes, I'm human. I have emotions, I'm weak and vulnerable. I can't be snarky all the time. But I can be that way most of the time in an effort to mask the things that trouble me just before I fall asleep. So with that being put out into the clear, go fuck yourselves, because I see Route 15 up ahead. The time for thinking is over.

I picked up 15 south and kept my eyes peeled as the road swelled and slimmed between a proper highway and a country road. I read every mile marker sign as many times as possible before they were put in my rear view, and I studied every farm house, barn, and fence post that I could. And then I saw it. I had to do a double-take. I wasn't all that far from the interstate, I wasn't lost and hungry. And then, there it was. It was just a rectangular metal sign, green like all the rest, white numbers like all the rest, but for me, it was special.

I put a few miles of separation between me and the second leg of my journey just for the sake of throwing up a ruse. I nosed the car off to the side of some dirt driveway that seemed to lead to nowhere and got out. I rolled up the windows, straightened the floor mats, grabbed my shovel, tossed the keys back in the cup holder, and locked the door behind me. The cops would find the car soon enough, and, being able to return it to Lucky Day car rental unscathed, they would chalk up the misplacement to rowdy teens just going for a joyride. They wouldn't come looking for me. Lucky day, indeed.

I strolled back to my mile marker. Yes, that bastard was mine. I hopped the guardrail, felt the crunch of leaves leftover from the scourge of winter under my step, and plunged into the woods. Before taking another step, I unfolded the piece of paper in my pocket, which had spent every waking moment with me since I exited The Righted Mind. God, this part was awful. I had figured that it would be. I was being asked to retrace the steps that another man had taken over wild terrain almost a decade ago, but I never *really* thought about it, you know? After all, how hard could it be? It was just walking. That's like asking someone to scale Mount Everest and then comforting them by saying that it's just climbing, or demanding that they perform surgery without any prior experience. What's the problem? It's just cutting.

I had on a pair of second-rate sneakers, a thin button-down that I was gonna regret wearing by nightfall and a pair of jeans that wasn't designed for hiking. Other than my trusty shovel, I had packed three candy bars, two bottles of water, and a compass from the dollar store. I also brought along a flashlight, a small knife that probably couldn't have punctured a balloon, a lighter, and a cigar. I wasn't exactly the picture of preparedness, but hey, I had to amass most of this shit by means of thievery and deception along my travels. If I had devoted a little more brain time to all of this, I probably could have made things easier, but I didn't feel bad about skipping out on the Boy Scouts as a kid, either. News flash: teaching a ten-year-old how to tie a knot and build a fire doesn't ready him for the real world. It just teaches him how to tie a knot and build a fire, both of which he will forget how to do once he discovers boobs or a flare for interior design. Either way, end of story.

The ground shifts, the land changes, trees fall, and water places itself wherever it damn well pleases. To the untrained eye, the woods just appear to be a tiny pattern that never stops repeating. Dirt, leaves, plants, trees, vines, branches, sky, encore! I could never make heads or tails of the wild, and, sadly, my compass was having the same struggle. But I had to go, I had to start somewhere. The end of the rainbow wasn't at my feet and the pot of gold wasn't just gonna appear to me.

My feet moved under me but I couldn't help but think that one man's straight is another man's rickety gait and a giant leap for one is a shuffle for another. I assumed that Eddie used a compass and I assumed that he meticulously counted every step he took, but I didn't know for sure. Maybe he just picked a random spot in the woods and dug a hole. Maybe he tried his best to recall the journey that he had made after the fact. Maybe he was never there at all. Hell, for all I knew, the only money scattered about those woods was the loose change dropped by hunters. But I plowed on, because there were no other options left to me. And that's when I knew that The Righted Mind was a total crock of shit. The best thing that I had when I left their care was a promise made to me by one of America's most notorious crooks. Wasn't I supposed to be healed? Wasn't I supposed to be fixed? I sacrificed five years of my life so that I could be *righted,* right?

For over an hour, I followed Eddie's directions precisely. This didn't feel right and it didn't feel wrong, it just felt like I was following a path, but then I came to a creek. He didn't say anything about a creek. He never even mentioned water. I wasn't at a break in my directions, this wasn't a crossroads or a turn. I was supposed to just continue on east, and for a while, too. I decided to put my faith in the shapeless and cold water, which was much easier than putting myself in the shapeless and really cold water.

The creek wasn't all that wide but it was waist-deep. I held my shovel and my pack over my head as I waded across and grew worried that my frozen ass might get washed away with the brisk current. Once I pulled myself out on the other side, I tried my best to squeeze the water from my pants and then ripped into one of my candy bars. I needed to balance out the chill I was feeling with something positive. This worked, for a while anyway. Yes, the chocolate was sweet, the peanuts crunchy, the caramel gooey. My bottled water was crisp and pure and the sun was still overhead, but then it was time to start walking again.

Fuck! What a moron. Alert, alert, retard in the woods. I repeat, retard in the woods. Of all the stupid, boneheaded things I had ever done, this had to take the cake. I had forgotten how many steps I had taken. I could have written it down if I had brought a pen, I could have carved it into my arm with my crappy knife, I could have stayed focused, but no, I'm an idiot. In that moment I was so pissed off that I clutched my shovel with both hands and twirled myself around like a discus thrower at the Olympics. I was gonna launch that heavy lump into the water and watch it wash away. I didn't need that snake Eddie. I didn't need his dirty money. I didn't need this stupid task or those woods. I didn't need to be following someone else's commands anymore, and I didn't need CrimeSpree. It was just a dumb fantasy, anyway. Why the hell should I give what I felt to the American public anyway?

Like an ugly and out-of-shape ballerina who was sloshed on cheap cognac, I fell to the ground in a pile. I cried like a petulant child, kicked my feet at the dirt around me and cradled my head in my hands for an unnecessarily long stretch of time. Once I had calmed myself and decided to stop behaving like a complete pussy, I rose from the ground and noticed my shovel rested just mere inches from where I stood. Well, I'll be goddamned, I wasn't even good at littering. This was actually a relief. As I had said before, I had nothing else to do. I was accustomed to the journey anyway, the in-between time that most people find bothersome. For me, the end result of the journey was often bothersome, or at the very least unfulfilling.

With my head moderately clear, I still couldn't recall the exact number of steps that I had taken, but I knew that I had cleared five thousand steps not too long before I came to the creek. I brushed some of the dirt from my clothes and finished my candy bar. I reached out and grabbed my shovel and begged my compass to point me back in an easterly direction. I checked my watch and saw that I had about four hours of daylight left. I glanced at my paper and the total number of paces that I had left to retrace. It was gonna be a dark night out in the woods.

The rest of my hike was mostly uphill. I couldn't really tell at the time, as nature has her ways of fooling with you. What I mean is that after drying out from my little swim, the remainder of my journey into the undeveloped passed rather quickly, as it was pleasurable, cleansing almost. I could no longer hear the highway, and there was nothing to suggest that man had ever walked the earth. The sun cut through the trees and it cascaded down in ribbons over the flora around me. The forest floor was soft with damp leaves, and it rippled with roots as all the trees apparently were stitched together just below the surface. Up from the land of ferns and mosses rose vines that coiled themselves around the titans of the wild before losing their singularity among the branches in tangled knots. I witnessed as new buds crowned from the ends of nourished stems, and I listened to the speech of the birds as they sang of life's revival. I breathed deeply of the air and held it in my lungs. I closed my eyes and concentrated on the feel of the land and nature's purity as it rested all around me. As I felt the splash of filtered water hit the back of my throat, I regretted greatly not having drunk from that flowing stream. I could only imagine its taste as I absorbed the warmth of the sinking sun against my cheek.

But back to reality. Man, has that phrase ever been followed by anything other than disappointment? I'm guessing not, and my situation in rural New York was certainly no exception. Darkness comes early in the thick of the woods, and I believe I might have mentioned earlier that my trek was of the upward variety. Both of my ankles were beginning to complain loudly, my left especially, as it had never healed properly. Every step was starting to feel like one too many, and as my body became momentarily absorbed into the creeping shadows, I was given a frosty preview into what the night would bring.

With my head down, my ankles swollen, my skin laden with goose bumps, and my breath heavy, I suddenly felt a rush of light as it flooded my new surroundings. I had popped out into a clearing that was a swollen mound of earth, which testified to my climb. It was nearly the size of a ball field and covered with low grass. I walked out to the center and took in the panorama. I felt like I was standing on top of the world, as my vision was filled with nothing but treetops and sky. The sun had dipped behind the trees now, and its exhaustion spread around me in bands of orange as if the whole of the forest had been set ablaze.

I checked my watch. I had arrived within twenty minutes of the time that Eddie suggested it should take me to reach his treasure. I should have left earlier, but sun or no sun, my mood was high because, just as he said, there were fewer trees upon this mound than fingers on my hand. I was close—I could almost feel the money in my fist—and then I saw the tree, the tree like no other. There were a few trees dotting the green. They were maples I think. I couldn't tell for sure. I'm no dendrologist, but they all looked basically the same. They were thick and mighty with massive branches that extended upward and out. It was still early spring, but they were already flush with fresh leaves. The bark of these giants was of a deep brown, and the grain of their hardened skins was true, artistic, almost, in its pattern.

And then there was the black sheep, the misfit, the Buffalo nickel, the square peg, the weirdo. Maybe it was the fleeing sun or the encroaching shadows, maybe it was just the sounds of the forest that tend to unsettle the minds of men, I don't know, but this tree was scary. It grew crooked and without direction. Some branches were thick, others thin, and the leaves they held were sparse. The bark of this monster was dull, a flat black, almost, and it grew gnarled and wildly uneven. A hole had been carved out of the trunk by some manner of beast. It was dank and dark, and, as I stared into that scant abyss, I couldn't help but think about what creature stirred beneath. Perhaps he was the keeper of the gold. But like I had done my whole life, I commenced my search for things that are not mine without a thought for the rightful owner or of the consequences that may follow. I drifted over to the north side of the tree and stabbed my shovel into the ground.

What was I doing? Oh yeah, I was looking for money. I had to remind myself of this because after an hour of digging, it appeared as though I had done nothing more than carve out the world's largest whack-a-mole grid. I was starting to lose hope. As the twinkling of the stars began to share the sky with the last slivers of daylight, I knew I was sleeping in the woods. That was okay, I think I had known that all along, but in every scenario, I had already dug up a fortune. That was a hell of a detail to take for granted, but there was always tomorrow.

Yes, that's right. There was always tomorrow. There's no such thing as there is always tomorrow. What cocky fucker thought that up?

Screw tomorrow, anyway. That was my thinking as the moon wept down onto me from the glimmer of the sky above. I hadn't found anything yet, but I could still see as far as the tip of my shovel. That was good enough for another few, empty holes, and when that failed I flicked on my flashlight and gripped it between my teeth. I was getting pissed off. My teeth were sinking deeper into the dry rubber end of the light and my excess saliva was carrying the stale taste onto my tongue. I was sick of finding absolutely nothing. My legs had hurt before I had ever dirtied the tip of my blade, and now my arms were killing me. I could feel the blisters form on my palms and I felt that telltale sensation of pain as I tore a few open as the ferocity of my shoveling rose with my impatience. It was cold, but I was sweating, and the darkness was so swollen by that point that using my puny flashlight to hold off the black was akin to battling a dragon with a toothpick.

But then I heard it, the telltale sound of metal on metal. My tool made a sound that a shovel should never make when being thrust into virgin earth. I froze, rigid as a stone, in the very pose of my last dig. I felt my heart race and I honestly felt a little nauseous in that moment. Even though I was encased by night and in the middle of nowhere, I took a look around. The noise had sounded so loud to me. Surely someone else had heard it, too. I fully anticipated the emergence of privateers from the seas of black that surrounded me. They would close in and plunder my treasure with their banners high and their swords extended. But wait! I was the priveteer. No, no,no, scratch that, I was the pirate. Sorry, Ed.

I fell to my knees and clawed at the ground. I scooped up the surrounding dirt and flung it behind me. I jammed my fingers under the box and tugged furiously at its coarse and rusty body. It wiggled this way and that but was content in its placement. I then wielded my shovel with new authority and stabbed at the thin roots that stretched themselves over the box. My steel cut through the fibrous veins like a bolt of lightning through the transient clouds until at last there was nothing left to tether the case to the earth.

I pulled the metal tote from its grave and fell back onto my ass. With the box between my knees, my fingers shook as I flipped open the latches on the lid. I tossed it back with such force that the corroded hinges broke apart, causing the lid to sever from the lower half completely. There was a black trash bag beneath and I didn't even bother to pull it out, I just dug in and tore that sucker in half. As the plastic was rent I was given

162

just a peek at the contents inside, which was more than enough to drop my jaw.

My flashlight tumbled out of my mouth and went dark upon the ground. I fumbled around for it and then smacked it off my leg repeatedly until it sparked back to life. As steadily as I could, I guided the beam over the wound in the bag again to study my prize. There was no real sense of order. In fact, this was clearly done in great haste, but it was there. The money was actually there. It had been bound by rubber bands in uneven stacks and crammed into the bag with such disregard that most of the bills were crinkled, some even torn. But it didn't matter. It was a hell of a lot of money. I didn't know for sure how much was there, but a million dollars felt like a conservative estimate.

I laid back onto the ground with the split bag clutched between my hands. I felt the mud under me and I shivered as my sweat conspired with the air to form an icy film over my exposed skin. My lungs exhaled columns of visible breath and my eyes saw absolutely nothing as I allowed my weary lids to close. I took in the sounds of the forest at night as my ears treated my mind to the caroling of the owls and the crickets and the wind as it dances through the trees. Oh, the majestic and enigmatic creations of nature, they have no concerns for things as trivial as gold. They have no idea what they're missing.

Chapter 9

Distractions and an embarrassing lack of maturity

Behind every great man, there is a great woman. Is that how the phrase goes? I know I'm in the ballpark, anyway, so the specifics of the quote don't really matter all that much. Details, mere details. But back to the aforementioned whimsical sentiment: is it actually true? I don't know. I haven't kept company with very many great men. I'm sure that it applies in some cases, though, which leads me to this question, what kind of woman is behind a bad man?

Ah-ha! Trick question, and you guys bought it. Once a con, always a con. But to allay the mounting suspense, I'll put this little riddle together. The answer is women, plural. Lots and lots of bad women. Behind every bad man is a trail of bad women.

All men, all people, have vices. Most of us, however, will never get the chance to indulge these vices, for a multitude of reasons. Too busy, too poor, too shy, whatever, but the vices are there. The rich, married movie star has sex with hordes of women half his age because he can, and the married gas station attendant doesn't because he can't. Are you following along? Give people the means to behave inappropriately, and they will do just that. But this absence of grace doesn't just affect the barbaric and simplistic desires of raging, straight males. No, if it's not sex, then it's drugs or booze or gambling or comic books or cars or adorable little kittens. We like what we like, and, given enough disposable income, we will like the things that we like beyond the limits of what is practical or socially acceptable. We will indulge ours most frivolous wants until they become our needs.

So, what did Mickey Moore do with Eddie Arch's money? More on that in a minute, but for now, note that I just referred to myself in the third person at the exact point in the story when I leapt from hobo to millionaire. See? Expendable money turns everybody into an insufferable, egotistical douche bag. But don't fret, I'm poor now. That won't happen again.

Well for starters, I forgot all about CrimeSpree. Fuck that place. I had just dug up a fortune and I did it with the con-mans' tried and true method of promising to help someone in exchange for cash. This was my greatest con to date. It was my Superbowl, my Nobel Prize in thievery. I was gonna enjoy myself.

I stuck around New York and settled into a cozy apartment located conveniently off of Interstate 390. I bought a Cadillac, not a new one, but I felt the need to roll in a Cadillac all the same. I bought new clothes, comfortable shoes and an assortment of stylish hats. I furnished my apartment modestly but I did splurge on a high-end bed and a TV that was much too large for the space I rented. I even began seeing a chiropractor on a regular basis, as my shoulder and ankle felt it necessary to bark their complaints at my nerves from time to time. I delighted in the things that most people try to avoid. I went to the dentist for the first time in about two decades, and after a trip to the doctor for an exam, it was explained to me that I had high blood pressure. Imagine that.

But it wasn't all fedoras and floss. No, I spent much of the money on women, and I'm not talking about fancy dinners with respectable females. If I could live to be a thousand, I suppose I would carve out some time for that crap, but life is finite and short. I've always had a grasp on that, and as a result, I have always preferred the company of women who drink, smoke, swear, and have sex with people that they barely know. Can you really blame me, though? There's plenty of shit in this tale to sling in my direction, but this, too? No, leave this alone. I was just a tick over forty, I had spent a great deal of my life unemployed and on the move, and the hottest chick that I ever managed to bag was old enough to be my mom. Can't a guy have some fun?

If you travel Interstate 390 north toward Rochester, New York, you'll see signs along the highway that advertise the wares available at an outlet mall located just outside of the city limits. It was in this very location that the Wild-Kat strip club once stood. Great times were had there indeed, but you already knew that. After all, it was cat with a *K*. How very edgy. Or maybe these chicks just couldn't spell. That was very possible as well, but also beside the point. The point being, I frequented this fine establishment, and it was where I procured a variety of lecherous entertainment on Eddie's dime. Come to think of it, I never properly thanked him for that. I genuinely feel bad for it now, but back then, he was the furthest thing from my mind.

It was in the dead of summer and it was a hot one. Rain hadn't fallen in about two months, other than the occasional deluge that lasted all of five minutes and did nothing more than pump excess humidity into the already thick air. During that time, the sun never seemed to tire of searing into everything under it, and the heat was so oppressive that it made the whole of Rochester stink. You know the kind of heat I'm talking about, the heavy kind that makes the air smell of baking asphalt and warm earth. In short, it was a miserable summer. The power grid went down a few times and the price of air conditioners skyrocketed. Which leads me to the reason that I first set foot into the Wild-Kat.

In the apartment building that I lived in, things had gone awry somewhere in the ventilation department. There wasn't so much as a puff of cool air that had flowed through anybody's unit in over a week, and, as you might imagine, I stayed away from home as much as possible. I ate out a lot during that week, and I spent a great deal of time in my car just driving around. I walked around department stores and other places that had air conditioning, and I even went to church one evening. I sat in the very last pew, played with my phone, and nodded off, but I did toss a few bucks onto the collection plate. I'm sure they had a hell of an electric bill to pay, too.

It was day six of my apartment being uninhabitable and the temperature outside was 102 degrees. If you're not sure where it's at, grab a map and look up Rochester, New York. It's practically in Canada and it was 102 degrees. I was starting to think that this was gonna be the test that would break Porrima. Everybody was pissed off and irritable. It was a small miracle that nobody was killed over a cup of ice or an oscillating fan. As for me, I was in the Cadillac on the 390, traveling without any real direction or purpose. I was poking along well below the speed limit, and it was a good thing, too, otherwise I might not have seen the sign for the Wild-Kat. It was about half the size of a proper highway sign and it was made out of particle board. The advertisement was painted on, and it relayed the news to all passersby that happy hour now lasted all day, lap dances were half-off, and the AC was ice cold. Next exit, you say? I was as good as there.

The Wild-Kat was the best kind of strip club. Don't be fooled by the glitzy clubs that feature sparkling clean interiors and valet service. These are show bars, not strip clubs, and let me tell ya, show bars are no fun. The drinks are overpriced, the security is tight, and the girls are way too pretty and they know it. This makes them all snobby and it makes them all business. There's nothing worse than a stripper that's all business. The Wild-Kat, on the other hand, was your typical titty joint. It was placed inconveniently enough outside of town, the parking lot was gravel, and the inside probably hadn't been updated since the Vietnam War. They had three beers on tap, no liquor, a cooler full of canned soda, snack-size bags of chips, and sandwiches! Ah, I love a strip club with sandwiches. But this isn't about corned beef or Mountain Dew, is it? Hell, it's not really even about cold air. No, it's simply about women with daddy issues.

On any given night, even a weekend, there was only a five girl rotation at the Wild-Kat. They were closed on Sundays and Mondays, and might as well have been on Tuesdays too. The Tuesday night girls were a train wreck. There was Darling, who had meth-mouth, Baby, who was just over eighteen and about ninety-two pounds, and Shadow, who had an impressive collection of surgical scars. Candy was older than me at the time and Jinx could have been really cute, but this chick was an epic drunk. She would only dance once or twice a night because she was normally too wasted to stand up straight, and she always reeked of puke.

On all the other nights, the girls were actually pretty good looking, and they were real people, too, flawed people like me. They lived in crappy apartments, drove ordinary cars, and followed corny TV dramas when they got home. What I really liked about these girls was that there was something about each of them that was imperfect, ugly even. Diamond had the body of a goddess and the hair of a hobo. Jasmine was struggling mightily not to be the token fat girl, and Foxxxy had a set of fake boobs that looked great in a bra and a little weird out of one. That's not to say that I didn't approve of her slightly misshapen rack. Let me tell ya a little something about fake tits. They're just like ghosts. How, you ask? If you can touch 'em, they must be real. But the bottom line was that these girls and all the others like them were a blast. I got to know them all on a first-name basis, and at one time or another, I took each one of them into the champagne room for a little extracurricular activity. I also wasn't above a visit to the creepy hot-tub room, perhaps every strip club's dirtiest secret.

I'm not trying to fool anybody. I had money, and I knew full well that much of the affection that I was being shown from those vultures was just an act. I didn't care. The part about having sex with a bunch of different, young women was real and that's why I burned bill after bill at the Wild-Kat. I had something that they wanted and they had something that I needed. Maybe it was the other way around, who knows? But we had an arrangement and we had some laughs. It was a good time, a genuinely good moment in my life, and that's when I met Starletta.

Starletta, what a name. It sounded celestial and mysterious, and, man, was I hooked from the start. The other girls were kinda like my buddies, but not Starletta. No, she wasn't anybody's friend. This chick was an animal, and animals act only on instinct. More specifically, she was a predator. She could smell the blood in the water and I was hemorrhaging the stuff in the form of dollar bills.

It was on a Thursday, the first time that I laid eyes on her. It was just a few clicks past five in the afternoon, and I was in the bar area having an iced tea and sharing a bag of peanuts with Jasmine. There was a baseball game on the TV and it was starting to feel like I was living the charmed life. I had disposable income. I was out in public enjoying sports with a woman in cheap lingerie seated beside me. It couldn't have been better. But then a storm blew in and ripped its way through the Wild-Kat and from the eye of that catastrophe emerged Starletta.

Those of you who have never been seduced by a woman are probably picturing Starletta as the physical embodiment of beauty, with salon-perfect hair and fingernails that could impersonate the twinkling of the stars. She didn't possess any of those things. Starletta, or Andrea, as her parents once called her, had white but crooked teeth and bright red hair that was awkwardly styled with an overabundance of hair spray. She never quite mastered the art of makeup and she had excess fat on her hips. She walked a bit uneasily in her high heels, and she had a crooked nose. She may not have fulfilled the common requirements for physical perfection, but it didn't matter, it never has, because she was the perfect killer. This is what pulls men in and suffocates us. The attitude, the inexhaustible ability to secrete primal sexuality with every word, every movement, and to infuse it in every last goddamn aspect of the human condition.

I never felt Jasmine get up. I didn't even realize that she was gone. I forgot all about the baseball game and I lost my appetite for food, as Starletta was the only thing I wanted in that moment, and it was only her that I wanted to devour. She said all the right things, she pushed herself into me just the right amount, and she stared into my wide eyes long enough to let me know that she could be all mine, provided that I was willing to pay the price.

Without a word, she walked away from me when it was her turn to dance. I had glitter on my lip from where her finger had brushed across it, and my vision was locked upon her ass as the movement of her hips hypnotized me like a fleshy pendulum. From a distance, I watched as she peeled off her clothes and thrust her tits into the faces of the men that seated themselves around the stage. I saw as she squatted down in front of them, and stared in wild wonder when she slowly righted herself. She employed an exaggerated, jerking motion that caused the curve of her ass to gently caress any patron who had been drawn into her web. I was made witness to her profane display of the very essence that forces men from their beds each morning, and as she writhed and wiggled through her set, toxic Starletta never took her eyes off of me.

This glorious torture continued for nearly a month. In between her designated time upon the stage, she was all mine, but this feeling of possession was just a ruse, a part of her game that she allowed me to play. When Starletta was actually dancing, she always kept a safe distance from me, no matter how many fistfuls of dollars I hurled in her direction. If I wanted a private dance, she was too busy or simply nowhere to be found. But then, when I was at my most desperate, she would return, and with this resurrection would come the promise of her absolutely.

She had her meat hooks sunk into me, so deep, in fact, that I still hold affection for her in spite of what happened. I was in love with her, of this I was convinced. I yearned for her, I needed her, I drew breath for her. She was in my every thought and my every action. My independence was robbed from me as I became a slave to her every whim. I was her robot in a skin suit, just waiting for the next button to be pushed.

Click. That was the sound of me pressing the pause button on this lurid tale. But why? Things were just getting interesting. I'll tell ya why, and pay goddamn close attention because this is a revelation. I will expound to you all the very thoughts of the dying man. These aren't the thoughts of the man who has been sentenced to death, and they are not the thoughts of the man who the doctors have stamped an expiration date onto. No, these are the thoughts of the man who finds himself at the witching hour. We think of only two things, and they are both women. We think of the one that we always truly wanted, and then we think of the one that we always truly needed. I'm sorry that it's not about anything more profound, but there it is. And as for me, I am thinking of Andrea and I am thinking of Lucy. You can debate amongst yourselves as to which woman fills which role. That truth is for me alone.

And then it happened, one boiling night when the warmth of my own blood could have rivaled that of the black summer heat. Starletta asked me to take her to my place. No, wait, what the hell was I saying? She didn't ask, she never asked for anything. Starletta begged me to take her home. She hooked one of her perfumed legs around me and panted her commands into my ear. She shook as she spoke and her eyes bulged like she had just thrown back a cocktail of lightning and meth. She practically pushed me out of the club at just after nine in the evening, still dressed in nothing more than her furiously indecent costume.

Out in the parking lot, the gravel growled under the weight of her high heels as Starletta tore her top apart without breaking stride. As the defeated fibers floated down alongside her hips, she thrust her fingers into her hair and allowed the humidity to style it. I watched as the streetlight glow beat down over her, and how it illuminated the new sweat that broke from her breasts. She leaned over the hood of my car like an impatient teenager and tapped her fingernails against the hardened shell of the clear coat. She licked her lips at me and then waved with a giggle in her throat as a few patrons witnessed her erotic display. I clicked my remote and unlocked the door, but Starletta wasn't done showing off just yet. Out from her purse she pulled some lipstick, and sloppily applied much more than was necessary. With her mouth, she smeared that cosmetic paint over my face and then across the passenger side window of the car, leaving juicy red lip prints. It was her way of saying *Starletta was here*. As though I would so easily forget.

When I woke up the next day, things were different, things had changed. For starters, I was given a whole new understanding of what is possible in the sack. The memory from the night before was fantastic and indelible, and it was also the only positive change that Starletta had given to me. She was nowhere to be found, and neither was approximately seventy-five thousand dollars of my, err, Eddie's cash. I was shuffling around my apartment like a zombie looking for her and rubbing the sleep from my eyes when I noticed the ransacked state of my closet. The doors were cracked open and an assortment of shit that I rarely used spilled forth onto the carpet like the closet had vomited. I was stunned still and snapped fully awake at the same time. I felt my heart flutter, and a wave of anxiety washed over me that forced my lungs to strain just to perform their usual duty.

After the disbelief unwound its chains from me, I flung myself onto the floor and tore through the pile. I upturned shoes, some photo albums, an old pair of jeans that I should have tossed a month ago, assorted books and boxes, and a crock pot that I had completely forgotten about. But there was no money. Nope, she found it and she vanished. I bet the evil stripper was wearing a shit-eater from ear to ear when she flipped open that cigar box and found a small fortune. She probably thought she was the smartest slut in the room as she slipped away, but little did she know I had over a half a million dollars in cash spread out over the rest of the place. Sure it was a hit, and a hard one, but my panic was assuaged when I discovered that all of my other hiding spots remained undisturbed.

I was in the bathroom, hovering over the toilet, thinking that I was gonna puke. I had just checked the tank and was relieved to see the waterproof box still sitting on the bottom. It was the last place I needed to check, and everything save for the closet was A-OK, but I still felt sick. Initially my nausea was for the missing money, and then it shifted to the loss of Andrea. My feelings were a mix of heartache, the kind that a scorned teenager feels the first time he gets dumped, and twisted pride. After all, I was had. Score one for Andrea and her alter ego. She had won this round. But as I sat there upon the faded tile with my back up against the peeling wallpaper, I realized that I had purchased something with my seventy-five thousand. Perspective. I was given the perspective that I so desperately needed, and, as a bonus, a helping of focus was thrown into the deal.

I only went to the Wild-Kat once after that night. I went there to ask about Andrea and garner some pity, but nobody seemed all that interested in helping me. For over a month, I hadn't had time for Angel and her bad tattoos, or Cinnamon and her swollen bag of self-consciousness. Come to think of it, I hadn't paid much attention to any of the other girls who were swallowed up in Andrea's shadow, and they were all too happy to throw it in my face. I couldn't blame them. They were right.

It's funny to think of it, but that motley mix of whores with their collection of mental problems and self-image issues taught me a valuable lesson about what it means to befriend someone. Being someone's friend has its perks, but it comes with responsibility, too. I'm not sure I ever really knew that before, but there I stood in the aftermath of Andrea, poorer than the day before and all alone again.

It was time to move on and it was time to get serious. I had spent close to four hundred thousand dollars and wasted about eight months' time whoring around. I decided to rededicate myself to CrimeSpree, and I didn't allow myself to get too close to anybody. I kept to my own company after that, and actually found that going to bed every night at nine-thirty in the evening can be pleasurable. In the mornings, my ears didn't ring with the echoes of bad hip-hop and my cell phone wasn't being blown up by a myriad of people that I barely knew. I already had everything I needed, anyway, the basics for comfortable human survival. My wants were a different story, but I only ever wanted one thing, the one thing that I could never have.

I've brought Lucy up enough by now that I suppose I should concede that I'm not as stable or self-sufficient as I would like to have you all believe. I think now that I needed her to love me, but she was just a box of bones under the soil. No magic, mysticism or truckload of prayers was gonna change that, so I found other ways to cover the wound. I fell in love every day. It was the girl on the morning radio program, and the next day it was the perky chick in the car rental commercials. After her, it was the sweetheart I passed on the street before moving my affection over to the bubbly starlet with the newest pop song. I loved them all from afar and never allowed my fleeting infatuations to drift into the realm of reality. After all, what does reality give you? It makes you realize that your dream girl is flawed and annoying, it makes you pay bills, and it causes you to bleed. Fantasy was better, pantomime never complained, and make-believe kept me warm at night.

Chapter 10

CrimeSpree's first victim...pay up, sucker

Wow, that was uncomfortable. Maybe I had reached that point in my life where I was coming to grips with mortality. Maybe my mid-life crisis came in the form of a pathetic regression into childish behavior. Maybe somewhere in the back of my mind, I was beginning to regret never leading a normal life or conducting myself in a decent manner. I don't know what it was, but as the summer was flickering out, I took a sober look around my apartment. What a loser. I had taped up pictures from magazines and other such publications that featured women I fancied. It was odd, creepy, almost, but mostly it was just sad. After two months of grieving the loss of Andrea and of feeling sorry for myself, I took down the glossy pages and stuffed them into a trash bag. I finally deleted Andrea's number from my phone, and I even emailed Eddie my address. I made the bed and swept the carpet, I got a clean shave, and, with a clear head, I walked down the street to have a quiet breakfast with my laptop computer.

In front of me was two scrambled eggs, a plate of bacon, a side of toast, and two cups. One held coffee, the other, orange juice. My computer sat in the middle of the table, and it segregated the drinks from the things that required chewing. It displayed listings for parcels of acreage that were available for purchase in the area, but the item that was most noticeably placed directly in my face was something that only I could see. It was the unavoidable truth that my old pal Eddie was due to be released in about two months and I wasn't holding up my end of the bargain. I had to get cracking. It was a long time coming.

The land that Eddie planned to use for CrimeSpree had been seized by the state some time ago. I wasn't crazy about this location anyway and so I finally settled on a plot that seemed more appropriate. It was also one of the cheapest listings that I could find, but, hey, it was gonna work all the same.

Once the state of New York thanked me for my interest in future development, I spent close to a week out in the woods with survey markers and an assortment of neon spray paints. I precisely marked off which areas I thought would best serve as the entrance way, the parking lot, the filthy streets that would be, yada yada. I used tape and string to condemn entire sections of the woods to death as I roughly mapped out where the roads should run. I spent a shiny new dime to have aerial photographs taken of the land and had the images blown up large enough to cover the walls of my apartment.

The glossy images became my new wallpaper, and, just like an eight-year-old, I proceeded to draw on the fresh coverings with magic markers. I had four replicas of the same image, and so I played around with some different ideas. I used yellow for the roadways, and orange ink to designate the areas reserved for parking and foot traffic. I used a red marker to sketch the outline of the first three streets, and employed an abundance of abbreviations that I scribbled over areas I thought would be of special importance. Fittingly enough, I used black to mark off the section reserved for the nefarious heart of CrimeSpree and I made a plethora of notations all around the borders. These little blips of thought contained everything from my ideas about what each street should feature to the price of popcorn.

Late one evening, after another day of staring at two-dimensional snapshots of the forest, I was mashing my way through a tepid Hot Pocket when the finer points of what CrimeSpree should be all about finally filtered their way into my brain. Sure, the rough concept had been there for years, and every night I went to bed with the goal of perfecting the idea, but I could never quite pull it together. The land itself was nothing more than a huge square of wilderness with paint on the grass and litter strewn among the trees. The pictures in my apartment weren't any more impressive, either. They were just inflated images of the wild with colorful graffiti smeared over them in a semi-coherent manner. But then I figured it out. I had been trying too hard. I was trying to polish something that was meant to remain ugly and jagged. As I sat there on the couch with some version of a sandwich in my hand and a piss-poor excuse for entertainment on the TV, I saw again the extent of our collective devolution. What I was ingesting wasn't sustenance, what I was watching wasn't entertaining, what I was doing wasn't living. I had become comfortable. I had almost forgotten New Mexico. I flipped open a notebook and started writing.

I'm not sure how long it took me to fill, but I do know this: I did little else besides write during that time. Sure, I got up to use the bathroom here and there, and I paused periodically to hammer down a bag of chips or a bowl of cereal, but I honestly did nothing else besides write. Okay, you caught me in a lie, I did sleep. But this wasn't proper sleep, it wasn't even planned sleep. It was more akin to passing out. Now and again, my mind would have enough of me and it would put me down on the couch or in whatever chair I happened to be folded into at the time. But the pen never left my hand and my notebook always remained splayed out over my lap. I never allowed myself to rest for very long anyway. There were still blank pages and unborn ideas. There was still work to do.

I remember vividly the very second that I came to face the cardboard skin at the end of the notebook. I stared into that flimsy, opaque flap and allowed the exhausted pen to fall onto the floor. I was done. I knew I was done. Yes, I had more ideas, but they were just gonna be useless minutiae if I had kept on going. I had run out of room, and I took this expiration of virgin pages as a sign from the cosmos to stop. After all, nothing in my notebook went unmarked. Everything was stained and altered, for better or for worse. Nothing was pure any longer. Purity is boring and unnatural. My ideas were ready to take form. They were ready for CrimeSpree. I leaned back into the couch and I exhaled the biggest breath of my entire life.

I have a strong feeling that tomorrow's lung function will muscle its way into the top spot, but I'm gonna try not to think about that. Tonight is for setting the record straight, for clearing the air. Tonight is for reminiscing. Tonight is for me.

Where was I? Oh, yeah, heavy breathing. So I shot up off my ass and went on down to the corner to grab a snack. There used to be this deli at the end of my street that served up irresponsibly large sandwiches. They were great, too, but like most of America's food, the source of these yum-yums was a thing better left unseen. The deli was kinda dirty, their equipment was old and outdated, and personal hygiene didn't seem to be tops on the priority list for anybody who worked there. It was eventually shuttered due to health code violations, but I ate there often and without worry. Hell, that's why we're born with immune systems, right? Maybe I just liked to live dangerously. Oh no! How long has that cheese been sitting out? What a rebel I was.

I arrived home at just about the time that the braunschweiger had declared war on my intestines, but it wasn't a bother as I was in for the night. I treated myself to a catnap and some Pepto-Bismol, and then it was back to my notebook. I skimmed my notes, reread the parts I had forgotten about, and scratched out the things that were just plain stupid. I spent the rest of that night and the better part of the weekend tearing out the pages and reassembling them in a more cohesive order. With that bit of spastic editing out of the way, I put my ideas for CrimeSpree on the spinning wheel, as it was high time to see some progress.

During the week that followed I made about a million phone calls, and made countless trips out to CrimeSpree's overgrown location. I met with contractors and state officials. I

179

discussed with them the ins and outs of my project and tried to assemble an attainable goal for completion. I encountered hurdles, but I managed to knock most of them down with the power of persuasion. When that tack failed I simply slicked the necessary wheels with the most effective lubrication known to man: money. What can I say? A little flash of green and things get moving. It's the cost of doing business, I suppose. I hired a band of day laborers to help me with the clearing and most of the grunt work, and by the time that the smell of freshly laid asphalt was in the air, Eddie Arch was on his way to New York.

Eddie picked me up outside my building and it was immediately clear that he was doing alright. He had only been out of prison for a few days, but he looked like he had just strode off the set of a photo shoot for GQ. Don't kid yourselves, he was still ugly, but a suit that commands four figures can put a shine on a lump of coal. It was some sort of silk fusion number in charcoal with black pinstripes. He wore a set of polished black wingtips, silver cufflinks, and a black tie whose sterling stitching shone as brightly as the shoes. He wore a gray fedora and a pair of semi-transparent sunglasses. A pack of cigarettes peeked from a side pocket, but even they appeared elegant. They were housed in a custom chrome box emblazoned with Eddie's initials, and, come to think of it now, I don't think he ever smoked a damn one of them.

Even under his hat, his hair was neat and styled. His formerly gnarled fingernails were clean and even. They even had a certain gleam to them, like he had been using hardener. He had grown a thin beard which was salted by age, while the skin underneath and all across his face was smooth and even. He had made no attempt to acquire a tan. Rather it seemed to me that he had embraced his lunar complexion. His flesh was as pale as bleached bone, and it barely owned a wrinkle. All of that aside, Eddie still didn't look healthy. Yeah, he looked good, but not healthy. He looked aged, old. He looked like a ghost.

We both filed into the back seat of a Cadillac that made mine resemble a cheap knock-off that had been slapped together in a sweatshop of some far-off foreign land. There was alcohol on ice and matching power docks for a myriad of devices. Each side of the car featured touch screens that had software more powerful than that found in many low-level government institutions. There was a smoked-out sheet of glass that segregated us from the driver, and there was an even thicker wall of silence between us.

I still can't understand it, the transformation that Eddie underwent inside The Righted Mind. He was no longer the twitching, sniveling coward who I had met in the chapel. He was calm and composed. His words were carefully measured and weighted. As we drove down the highway, I got to thinking about the failures of that prison again. Sure Eddie had been undeniably changed, but he was no different. That is to say, he wasn't improved. His appearance was elevated, his speech was confident, his clothes were pressed, but underneath all the streamers and bedazzlement, he was still a piece of shit.

As I looked around the car and snuck glances at the opulence that spilled down Eddie's scrawny frame, I also reached the obvious conclusion that devious Mr. Arch had thrown dirt over more than just the modest box that I had dug up. Who knows how many others he had hidden or how much cash he still had at his disposal, but he made sure I got the impression that it was he that was the top dog. He never even asked me about the million that I had unearthed. Not one question, not a peep. He never even asked if I had found it, and, honestly, he couldn't have cared less. I had fired the starting gun of CrimeSpree and that was good enough for him. In fact, he was downright delighted.

I was relieved. After all, I had really only committed about two months' time to our project, but as Eddie poured over my notebook and the pictures I had taken, he assuaged my concerns. I know he tried like hell to mask his pleasure, but that was a task he was ill-equipped to perform. He wore a smile in the corner of his mouth almost the whole way there, and I came within an inch of calling him on it. I didn't have the heart to bust his balls though. I just let the old guy enjoy himself. As he sat there all stoic and reserved, I could tell that he truly thought he was fooling me. He gave it the old college try, but remember, I had been conning Eddie for the better part of a year, and he was rusty. So I just sat there, quietly savoring my victory, and I allowed Eddie to do the same.

Once we arrived over the lumpy expanse of asphalt that would one day hold CrimeSpree, Eddie finally caved and permitted his excitement to take over. He loaded a clip of speech into his mouth and unloaded with enough ferocity to win any war of words. He was simply recycling my ideas, but even I found it hard to keep up. His mind was supercharged as he gestured, and, as he predicted the things to come, I was genuinely impressed. He knew much more about construction and development than I ever could have imagined, and in his mind's eye, he put the pieces in place the way a chess master does when he announces that he's prepared to conquer all comers.

Then Eddie drew quiet again, and suddenly. It was like he was trying to undo his boyish enthusiasm and return to the unemotional man I had greeted outside my apartment. With a fresh rime of snow on the ground, the sun was at our backs and the light touch of the wind was drifting off Eddie's suit as he stepped away from me. He walked a solid fifty feet away and then stopped. He turned around again and craned his neck to face the sky. He looked around, as if to fully absorb and appreciate the abundance of empty space and feral growth around us. That's how it seemed to me anyhow. My mind was feeling a bit overwhelmed then, and as I too looked out into the forest, I felt rather insignificant by comparison. We must have looked tiny, like two specks atop a black postage stamp lost adrift over an ocean of brown and green. But Eddie's perception

182

wasn't mine. He exhaled a breath that could have filled the lungs of a giant and stared me dead in the eyes.

"Mickey," he said. "This is gonna be huge."

Okay. At this point, I still thought Eddie was full of crap. Delusional, really. CrimeSpree was doomed to fail, and I believed this with all my heart and soul. What made me so sure? Because I had experienced the very terror that we were hoping to replicate, package, and sell. I knew the general public wasn't capable of handling such a rush of visceral emotions. Hell, I wasn't getting in line to take part in a reprise of what I had witnessed in New Mexico. It sucked, it was nightmare worthy, and, at best, the memories that I carried convinced me that we would enjoy zero repeat business. I know I intimated before that what CrimeSpree would offer was something that the public needed—I still believe that—but the public at large often rejects the things they need most. For Christ's sake, some people refuse cancer treatments. But who was I to protest? I was due to rake in 30% of whatever we made, and I had nothing to lose. I figured that it would be fun watching CrimeSpree rise like the Frankenstein that it was, and if nothing else, the ride was gonna keep me busy for as long as it lasted.

As you might remember, CrimeSpree opened for business just as a New York winter was unraveling its grip from the land. We had only been operating for a week and already I was having panic attacks. Our streets were deserted, our games went unplayed, and the only soft pretzels and hot dogs that were consumed were those eaten by my very bored employees. With alarming immediacy it became clear to me that we had utterly failed to construct a museum of chaos and violence. Instead, we had built a ghost town. To usually achieve such status, towns must first be raised, occupied, and host some period of prosperity before dying out. CrimeSpree cut all of the fussy business and lively nature right out of the equation. It was a desolate castle that never had a king. It was a graveyard without bones.

After the first month was in the books, the truth grew to unignorable proportions. We were losing our collective asses. During that time, I had four people walk off the job in favor of minimum-wage employment, and it wasn't long before making payroll became a serious problem. I started reaching into my own pocket to pay my crew what was owed to them, while I stopped taking a check altogether. Financially, I was still doing okay, but I could see the end as it loomed on the horizon. Another month or two of commercial disaster and I would have had no choice but to leave CrimeSpree to rot in the woods. I was gonna be flat broke again if something didn't give and soon.

I was seriously pissed off at Eddie too. He wanted to hide in the background, and that was fine by me, but he was also supposed to be the capital behind my creation. I hadn't spoken to him in weeks and he wasn't answering his phone. I couldn't absorb many more hits, and I could no longer tolerate Eddie's absence while our ship continued its steady descent into oblivion. I didn't know what he was up to, but I was determined to find out. Eddie had moved onto CrimeSpree property and settled into an apartment located right at the end of 1st street. His place dominated the entire top floor of our tallest structure, and, by all accounts, I would be his first visitor. He used to collect young women the way children used to collect baseball cards, but that wasn't his style anymore. Eddie had grown truly reclusive.

I parked the car in the empty lot and glanced at the time before I got out. It was 4:30 in the morning and I was betting on that bastard being fast asleep in bed. It was my turn to give him a rude awakening. It was my turn to ask the questions. I walked briskly through the lot with only the sounds of shifting leaves at my back and the jingle of my keys at my side. I unlocked the front gate and hopped one of the seldom-used turnstiles. I started down 1st Street and very quickly found that the silence that it hosted was just as unsettling as anything we had purposefully created. In the dead quiet of the early morning, it was eerie to view. The shuttered vendor stands, the dilapidated facades of buildings that stored nothing, the cold light bulbs, the bent signs, the graffiti and the cracked asphalt.

I quickened my pace, and, for the first time, I found a little faith in CrimeSpree. The place was deserted, I knew this for a literal fact, and yet I was still uneasy. The burnt-out ghetto that surrounded me was just a fake. I had built the goddamn thing, but still I quivered. As I felt my nerves twitch, I became excited anew about seeing my park reach its potential. I wasn't being a pussy, I was honestly scared and I knew others would be as well. This street wasn't even designed to be frightening and yet it was. I had to find a way to get people in the door. They had to feel this, they had to hear the same haunting song that I did.

I entered into Utility Building #1—not a very original name, I know—and flicked the lights on as the door eased shut at my back. The bulbs above me sparked to life and illuminated the vast space of the ground floor. There were utility hookups and other such things that are necessary to power any large establishment. There were cans of paint in the corner, props we hadn't found any use for, and leftover bits of lumber and shingles. The concrete floor was heavy with dust, and the walls were made of dingy cinder-block. Plastic pipes, electrical lines, and junction boxes traced their way over the stone like elaborate industrial tattooing. I walked over toward a freight elevator through that vast area that knew no organization.

The elevator didn't need to be as shitty as it was, but we were all about pinching coin, remember? As that clunky sucker woke up, I heard the groan of its cables and I watched the rough insides of the building go by as I passed through its innards. Up at the top, I slid the heavy door aside and stepped into another world.

What a self-indulgent prick. Eddie really must have thought he was something special. I mean, come on, a marble fucking floor? Yep, the floor of the hallway that led to Eddie's

185

apartment was marble. The walls were painted green, and inlays of real silver had been pressed into them in intricate designs. No fewer than four chandeliers hung from the arched ceiling, and each held enough crystal to power any mystic device from a fantasy novel. They bled light down onto the rows of statues that lined each side of the hall, and gave a soft ambiance to the delicate features of the porcelain figures. A set of double doors was placed at the end of the hall and they were as red as the aftermath of any sacrifice ritual. The handle and lock set were custom made and coated in pure gold, of all gaudy things, and, get this, you needed a skeleton key to activate the tumblers.

I beat my fists onto the wood as violently as the Porrima in my blood would allow and then waited for a reaction. Nothing. I banged at the door again and again and again, and not a damn thing changed. Like a complete idiot, I kicked the barrier as hard as I could. This also did nothing, or so I thought. Years later, I would learn that my action had earned my foot a hairline fracture. At least I used the leg with the good ankle. I took a descent back into the warehouse, poked around a bit, found a sledgehammer, and returned back upstairs.

It was a plan easier conceived than executed, but I persuaded the lock to open eventually. I stuck my hand through the wound I had carved and flipped open the latch. The doors glided out toward me, and a soft amber glow revealed a state of urbanity that was downright nauseating. I had taken only two steps into Eddie's massive, one-room apartment and already I had seen opulence that would have shamed the whole of Rome at any time in its history. The floor was, predictably, marble and I could only guess as to what comprised the walls, as fine art and silk tapestries covered every available inch. The ceiling had to be twenty-feet in height. It undulated softly in an even pattern and was fully decorated with a mosaic made of tile. Each piece measured only one square inch, and their collective body depicted a colorful array of gods from religions ancient, extinct, and those still fervently followed. Across from where I stood in absolute disbelief was a row of windows that stretched the entire length of Eddie's palace. They ran straight to the floor, they arched where they touched the roll of the ceiling, and all but the center were built of thick stained glass. The only clear window in the place, it stared out into the untouched state of the forest. It was poignantly clear to me that Eddie didn't want to look at CrimeSpree.

As I walked through this testament to human indulgence and excess, there was plenty of stimuli to overwhelm the mind. The television was two hundred inches wide, the grate of the fireplace was made of ancient iron salvaged from a famous shipwreck, and the silverware was gold. Eddie had more statues than most people have friends, and a half a dozen display cases were packed with priceless items. Some were small, some were large, some were beautiful, others ugly, but all of them were expensive. The china was Royal Copenhagen Flora Danica—I found this out later, too, I'm not that savvy—and the kitchen cabinets were crafted from hammered copper. A fish tank the size of a Jacuzzi posed as the coffee table, and busts of exotic animals stared in at a visitor from each corner of the room. Eddie didn't even hunt. Even the damn toilet bowl was encrusted with jewels. I guess there is nothing quite like the sensation of taking a shit on a fortune. But that was the point for Eddie. He had won, he had beaten the system.

I can't remember it all now, that would be impossible. In my mind, it has all just become one obnoxious blur of gems, precious metals and ego. I truthfully can't even recall wandering around the place, and I don't even remember the exact moment I saw Eddie. I don't recall it with any notable clarity, anyway. But I do remember one thing. I remember the smell. That was unforgettable. People are afraid of death. Don't be, but be very fucking afraid of its smell. Now that is something truly unholy. If a god of love and light actually exists, the stench of a rotting corpse is his absolute antithesis.

Forgive me for telling a little white lie earlier. One person did, in fact, die inside the gates of CrimeSpree. Eddie was splayed out on the couch with his bony legs agape, his arms flat at his sides, and his head cocked to one side. He was wearing only a bathrobe, which was clearly old, but yet it still had its tag. It was from a thrift store and it had cost him eleven dollars. I bet he never got tired of wrapping himself in that rag and then stretching out upon a piece of furniture that cost more than most people would spend on a new car. Eddie was funnier than I ever gave him credit for being. I suppose it's because it was near impossible to catch Eddie enjoying himself. He liked jokes and he liked to be clever, but he only behaved in such a manner when he was sure no one was looking. I always found that strange. But fuck it, right? He could have been the funniest man to ever walk the earth or he could have been the most socially awkward malcontent to ever crawl out of a womb, it didn't matter. Both guys were telling the same joke now anyway.

You people are sick. You want the gory details, don't you? Alright, here goes. Poor Edward had been on the couch for quite some time, as evidenced by the corpse rot that tethered him to the cushions. The flesh that had been stretched over the backs of his hands had now collapsed and it fell into the gaps between his bones. His feet and the lower portions of his calves were swollen and purple. For all I knew, they might have been like this before his heart had exploded inside his chest, but I was fairly confident that the splits around his ankles were new. All of his nails were mildly yellow, as were his gums as they began an arid recession from the surface of his loosening teeth. His mouth was open, and the telltale signs of dried slobber were caked along his lips. His thin nose had been whittled down even further by the knives of decomposition, and his eyes were on their way to falling deep inside his skull. The flesh of his face shrink-wrapped his cheek bones and the passage of every minute vein that swam just below the surface was outlined in congealed blood and decay.

I threw up in the corner and staggered my way out of the pharaoh's tomb. On the way down to the street, the elevator tussled my guts and I spit up again. Once I had reached the open air, I dropped to my knees and felt as beads of cold sweat tumbled down from my brow. I shook the way we mammals tend to shake while in the grip of influenza, and I tried desperately to draw calm and even breath. I exited 1st Street without any of the fears that had followed me in, as my mind was frozen onto the still image of the rotting earthly remains of Edgar Archibald Stapleton.

As I waited for the cops, I wondered if they were even gonna bother to send an ambulance. Hell, they could have sent a station wagon. But that was just a passing wonderment, a comical valve put into use to relieve some of the pressure that the sight of death instills. What I really thought about, what really wound its laces into me, was the aftermath. I couldn't stop thinking about the series of differing moments that will inevitably follow each of our lives. How would Eddie's obituary read? Who would come to mourn? Would the public lash out against an incompetent system once it was revealed just how much money Eddie had managed to hide? How long would it take for life to return to normal for all those who were affected by Eddie's death? Ah, now, that's the question, that's the yardstick. Your value will be accessed by the impact that your absence creates. It's not fair or right or even wrong. It's not really all that accurate in some cases, either, but it is what we do as an organized society that likes to write things down.

So with the history books that chronicle the misdeeds of the now nonexistent hungry for fresh ink, let me tell you what happened next. The scent of Eddie's death was as common as any other, and its odor called the vultures. Old whores greedy for one last score bobbed over the surface of the muck marsh dug from the lawyers that came before them. Forgotten relatives tossed their names into the inheritance hat, and the state could barely keep the drool wiped from its mouth once pictures of Eddie's apartment hit the news. The Righted Mind claimed a right to some manner of compensation, and even a couple of my employees demanded raises. Of all the damn nerve. The cash-cow was dead, you dumb asses.

At the present moment in time, we are still not through the shit-storm kicked up from the passing of Eddie. The saddest part about it all is that almost no measurable time has been spent on the memory of Eddie the man. It has all been about money, bad behavior, and who deserves what. But don't let yourself get misty eyed, not even a little. Eddie brought all of what followed his expiration on himself. He wrote his epitaph long before his heart underwent a complete meltdown. Which is why I didn't shed a tear for the guy, either. Truth be told, I didn't even like him. He was a business partner, nothing more, and I preferred it when he stayed out of the way. Any day that I avoided talking to Eddie was a good day. He was a bucketful of the dried fecal matter that collects inside the underwear of dirty adolescent boys. He was scum. The sadness that I spoke of was only for the hard lesson taught by Eddie's death. The lesson being that a full human life can amount to nothing more than a trail of receipts and disparaging remarks. It's not sad, it's tragic.

Eddie left everything to me, everything that he could, anyway. Most of what he had in possessions was seized and auctioned away, and my cut was greatly diminished by the lawyers that had been hired just to ensure that I got something. But at the end of the day, Eddie willed every available dime to me, a man he barely knew. Alright, put the hammer down on the horn of the sadness train, because here it comes again. I was the closest thing to family that Eddie had left, and I think we shared a total of three meals together, including our time spent in prison. I was the closest friend that he had, and I don't think either of us ever referred to the other as such. I know I sure didn't, but I was all he had. Or maybe Eddie really believed in CrimeSpree. Maybe he wanted it to continue. I find that way of thinking highly improbable. The only thing that Eddie believed in was money, and he liked to acquire it in dubious fashion. I think he saw CrimeSpree as a rip off, and I think that's why he wanted it funded. He liked to cheat people.

I'm no saint, I like to rip people off too, or at least I used to. But unlike the dead and buried Mr. Stapleton, I believed in CrimeSpree, and with him gone and his money in my pocket, I found a new focus. I provided slightly better wages for my employees, improved sections of the park that should have been done before it opened, and I advertised. All throughout the spring, I bombarded an area of one hundred square miles with billboards and annoying radio spots. I bought air time on the local TV stations, and I took out full-page ads in the few newspapers that still survived. It was sink or swim time, now or never. The public would share in a little of what I had experienced so long ago in New Mexico, or I alone would die with the fading memory of that sensation of abject fear. And it was all made possible by Eddie. Thanks, pal, that's the last goddamn time I'm gonna mention your name.

Chapter 11

A lifetime of violence

Poetry is a mirror which makes beautiful that which is distorted.

The poet Percy Bysshe Shelley said this, and it is this observation that could be applied to CrimeSpree. Yes, there were blueprints, checklists, and other such things that are required to erect any business, but it wasn't so neatly put together. My desk overflowed with stacks of papers and invoices, but they all came after the fact, after the poetry. The poetry being the murder that I had witnessed. It was the inspiration, the muse that directed me to do things that were beyond my conscious control. No preplanned outline could have raised CrimeSpree. It was its own animal, and it grew and evolved according to its instincts.

Once our first summer of operation was underway, business was booming and I no longer harbored any fear of watching the whole thing turn belly-up. We were making money hand over fist with a product that didn't even come close to giving anyone equal value for their money. Okay, maybe the food, the drinks, and the games were reasonably priced, but you didn't need to travel all the way to CrimeSpree to grab a snack or win a prize. What I'm talking about were the *rides*, as we called them. The fourteen replicas of urban horror.

I said it before and I'll say it again, we put on a poor representation of the past. But the past always comes back around, doesn't it? It sharpens it teeth and hones its ferocity, and it lays in wait like a savage quietly stalking the night's conquest.

It started sometime in July, if my aging memory serves me correctly. I was in my office, just zoning in and out and killing time. I had my feet up on my desk and I was taking shots at the garbage can with wadded-up pieces of paper. The MLB All-Star Game was playing low on my computer, and I was contemplating going home early. It was a Wednesday, the park was kinda slow that night, and there was no real reason for me to hang around. But then there came a knocking at the door like the barbarian on the other side was trying to beat it down.

Good old Clint Ruin was on the other side and he was positively freaked. He was wearing a plaid suit with high-top tennis shoes, and he was without his bulbous hat. I had never seen the top of Clint's head before and now I knew why. His hair was thin and wiry, and it spread out like a crop left to die upon an abandoned farm. There was a weird lump on one side and a large birthmark on the other. It looked more like a rash or a blood spatter, as if he had been shot up through his mouth, but with the offending bullet never finding its way out. With the absence of his hat, it was clear that Clint had been in a big hurry to find me. His face was slicked over by sweat and his eyes were rattling around in their sockets like one of his boyhood seizures was coming back for a rematch.

"It's real, boss, it's all real. It's all come real."

He must have spouted that vague affirmation twenty some odd times before I finally told him to shut up. I physically plunked him into a chair and hurriedly grabbed a bottle of water from the fridge. He sucked it back like it was an elixir designed to rewind the hands of time, and then motioned for another before even taking the first bottle from his lips. With a half a gallon of water wetting his insides and with two crinkled containers languishing at his feet, Clint finally decided that it might be a good idea to take a breath.

"It's gone too far, boss," he said, slowly, while wiping new sweat from his face.

"It's finally gone too far."

Clint was right about a lot of things, but who can say for sure what is too far and what is not far enough? Is the porridge ever *just right*? At this point, I still didn't have the faintest idea

193

as to what had spooked Clint, but as I look back on it now, that was the beginning of the end for Porrima. The spiral had begun, and, like a great whirlpool above the drain to oblivion, we were all gonna get sucked down.

Apparently a rather rough brand of shenanigans had taken place somewhere along a dirtied and darkened stretch of 4th Street. As you may recall, 4th Street was the avenue that featured simple assault, and it was one that permitted our guests to travel in a group. This made it an unlikely stage for things to get out of hand, but that's where it happened. It was the good dog that finally bit, it was the tidal wave from a serene lake, it was the cancer in an otherwise healthy twenty-five-year-old body. It was flat-out fucking unexpected and it was shocking.

A group of five friends who all hovered around legal drinking age set off down 4th Street looking for a little adventure. Predictably enough, one of my employees emerged from the shadows to torment the uneasy band of sheltered suburban youths. This kid was no older than those he stalked, and assuredly he was just as nervous. Like a proper ghoul, he slunk behind the pack scuffling about and making just enough noise to make his unwelcome presence felt. In keeping with his training, this kid rushed the crowd just as they could see the end of the road and the safety it offered.

Sorry, Dean. I'm sorry about what happened to you. Dean, of course, is not his real name. After the incident, he quit CrimeSpree, and I took it upon myself to never use his name in connection with the park. But it wasn't as pretty and simple as all that. I found him in the parking lot. Well, I had found a brutalized approximation of what Dean used to be anyway. He was walking as fast as he could down through a row of cars, and under the glow of the moon, he glistened with a pink lacquer of warm blood and sweat. As I ran behind him, I called his name but this only served to hurry his pace. He wanted nothing to do with me. He didn't want to explain what had happened, he just wanted to get the hell out of there. I can't blame him. I still remember what it was like that day in New Mexico. I remember running through the desert and feeling as though every other human soul was my enemy. No amount of words or reassurances could have soothed me back then. I didn't want to be caught either. Like I said, Dean, I'm sorry. I should have just let you get away.

By the time that he had reached his car, Dean was spent, he was done. He dropped his keys to the asphalt, and, rather than pluck them from the ground, he just followed them down. Down to the baking black surface he fell, like a bag of trash flung into the back of a garbage truck. He laid there silently in a heap, just waiting for the compactor to come upon him and finish the job.

His mouth was open wide and his chest heaved as though all the oxygen in all the sky couldn't sate the needs of his lungs. Through the quivering hole in his face, I saw the reddened spaces where five or six of his teeth had been just fifteen minutes before. The lower cup of his jaw overflowed with blood, and this pool bubbled and popped like the surface of a witch's brew. His right eye was swollen shut already, while the left side of his head housed a crinkled and crude representation of a face. His forehead was lined with scrapes, as though he had been dragged behind a speeding truck, and entire tufts of his springy brown mop were missing. Three of Dean's fingers were clearly broken, and one of his shoulders appeared to be slightly out of joint. I glanced down at his pants and saw that one of the legs was red and sodden with a menagerie of bodily fluids. As he twisted in agony over the pavement, the movement of that leg made a sloshing sound with every swing.

After the initial shock of what lay at my feet subsided in negligible fractions, I flipped open my phone and called 911. Before I could even stammer out exactly what had happened to the agitated operator on the other end, Dean used the last of his strength to rise and slap the phone from my hand. He used his dry leg to kick the device under a line of sleeping autos and stared me dead in the face with his one, blood-shot eye. His pupil was enormous and all the veins that normally hide themselves in the background of the sclera became visible and enraged.

"Leave me alone."

His tone was menacing, short and authoritarian, and I knew he was as serious as a heart attack, but I still tried to make peace. I searched around for his keys, unlocked his car and helped him get inside. He slumped back into the seat and closed his one good eye. I thought to wait around, you know? I wanted to make sure that he was gonna be alright, or as alright as he could be. But he wanted me to leave, he had made that clear, and I didn't listen. With one very concise request, Dean had warned me that he was now a monster worthy of fear, but Porrima wouldn't let me listen. It didn't allow me to understand him. So, like an idiot, I stood there after someone had threatened me. I guess I just thought that he didn't have it in him. Who did back then, anyway?

Dean reached out the window and grabbed me by the front of my shirt, and in one brisk motion, he yanked my face down to his level. My bottom lip smacked off the top of the door and I immediately felt a rush of blood on my tongue as my teeth carved a crude design into my mouth. After the haze and the water fled from my vision I looked at Dean, and the new condition of his appearance reflexively caused me to jerk away. With his angered grip, Dean made sure that wasn't an option for me. He wanted me close, he wanted to give me a good look at the tenderized meat that hung over his skull and he wanted me to listen.

"Leave me alone," he stammered, through bloody gums and a grate of stained teeth.

"Leave me alone, or I will fucking kill you. I will fucking kill you!"

I left Dean alone after that. He never showed up again and he never called. I never received a medical bill or a call from a lawyer. The police never showed up and asked nosey questions, and I did as I was told. Besides, Dean was just one element of this shit-storm.

So, the scene of the crime, as it were. 4th Street in all its grimy glory, with the shuttered storefronts, the busted streetlights, the slight odor of something moldy, and the abandoned cars. Clint Ruin was there, spazzing out of his mind over a puddle of blood and Dean's teeth, as was that pack of five twenty-somethings. Each one of them wore varying degrees of disbelief, but they all shared one thing in common. Not a damn one of them could figure out what they did wrong.

In the instant that poor Dean decided to perform his job to the fullest, one of the males in the pack thought it was time to finally act like a cornered animal. As he felt Dean's arms wrap around his waist in an attempt to tackle him to the ground, the young man instinctively brought the battle to his attacker. He spun around and raised a knee to the bottom of Dean's chin with a force strong enough to dislodge the attacker. Dean fell to the surface of the street, disoriented and with a sore mouth. That's where it should have ended. That's where it usually ended. One fright, one reaction, and then a lot of running, but that was just the beginning.

By all accounts, the scared boy with the powerful knee stood over Dean for a moment with his eyes wide and electric. He tried to speak, but adrenaline had robbed him of language. He looked to his friends as though searching for an answer to this riddle, but they were just as shaken as he. What could they have known that he didn't? They were just as sheltered and as clueless. The situation that had swallowed them was bigger and far more fearsome than their lily-white collective. Their surroundings were a bleak beast with long teeth that promised only the arrival of continued horror and an ever-escalating vulnerability.

I think this is when the boy's brain flushed the Porrima right out of him. He glanced at his companions and saw the abject weakness in their individuality. The two other young men were naive products of the 8th Day Era like he, with no scars or lines of experience on their faces. They weren't men of action. They were barely men at all. The girls were even worse. The two females were rather skinny, and they clutched each other tight, not knowing what else to do. They couldn't run to one of the boys, as that had grown all too confusing long ago. Like many other groups of friends edging their way into adulthood together, these anonymous people shuffled relationships between one another like playing cards through a deck. They were frail, useless almost, but united, they were five against one. The math was easy and it came in the form of a tennis shoe to the side of Dean's face.

They broke upon Dean like a wave over a beach, and then over the town beyond. All five of them were called to action by the first kick, and they unloaded on him with the ruthlessness of a Howitzer. After the first minute, Dean coiled himself into a ball, but this didn't stop the bombardment. In a circle of violence, they kicked and punched the limp piece of meat below them, not knowing how much was enough to secure their safety. One of the girls even grabbed a large bottle that had been discarded in a gutter and beat Dean with it until the paltry strength within her spindly arms caused it to break over his back. They walked down 4th Street as children and they walked out as adults, seasoned and seared by the fires of violence and fear.

So I suppose now I will be called a monster again for stealing away the innocence of children. The problem with that is that these people were not children, they were grown adults who didn't possess the faculties necessary to deal with fear. That part of them had never grown up. The world for them remained rose-colored until that night on 4th Street when it became blood stained. They were taught a valuable lesson, they

198

learned something about themselves that only a despicable act can teach, and they discovered that Porrima had failed. It was a great iron wall that kept the violence out and allowed the conscience to snooze in the corner. But there were cracks in that wall and when the violence came rushing in, there was nothing on the other side to say enough is enough. And Dean almost died because of it.

Having people beaten into a pulp was never my intention, that much should be clear by now. Believe it or not, CrimeSpree was supposed to be fun, but in order for it to be fun, it also had to be dangerous. Chlamydia is no fun. Banging slutty girls is a blast, if you follow. Sometimes good-times and inconvenience go hand in hand.

Dean floated off into obscurity, and the five friends who put him there were all relatively pleased with their experience. Sure, they were a little upset, but they all had a good time and expressed something very familiar to me. Each one of them said that they felt alive, more alive than at any other moment before. Four of them even vowed to return to CrimeSpree. So that left only one more mess for me to clean up, and, admittedly, I had done little scrubbing to this point, but Clint Ruin was gonna be different.

Before I could even put it all properly together, he had fled out of 4th Street like a madman with his limbs flailing and an odd howl trickling out of his throat. Clint didn't show up for work for a week and nobody seemed to know anything about where he went. I would like to say that I tried everything in my power to contact him during that time, but it was a truly impossible task. That looney bastard didn't have a phone, he refused to use a computer even though that must have made his life horribly inconvenient, and no one even knew his home address. He preferred to pick up his checks at my office, and in the rare event that I did need to mail something to him, it always just went to a post office box. I can only recall maybe three times that I saw Clint ride in a car that had a GPS system.

He didn't trust the stuff, and when Clint didn't want to be found, he did a damn good job of hiding himself away.

But Clint Ruin always showed up for work and he was always on time. Something wasn't right and I was getting concerned, but, much the same as he did months before when CrimeSpree first opened, Clint simply appeared to me. Like a ghost from the fog, Clint walked up from behind me and introduced himself as though we were complete strangers.

I was sitting in the diner at the end of 3rd Street getting ready to start my day with a modest breakfast and a hulking cup of worry for my strange friend. I had my back to the entrance, and as I sipped at my coffee I stared into the far side of the restaurant. There, beyond the tables, the booths, the waitresses, and the gray, checkered linoleum floor were the doors to the abyss. A set of industrial barriers the color of faded slate stood silent and motionless in the corner of the room right of my vision. On the other side were the turnstiles and the choices. On the other side were the fourteen paths of CrimeSpree. As I thought of Dean and the absence of Clint Ruin, I came to realize that my simple calculations had been wrong. There weren't just fourteen paths of CrimeSpree, the paths were limitless. They were as diverse and as enigmatic as all the dark expanses of outer space. The journey taken was going to be different for everyone. It was going to be special.

It felt appropriate to me that this aspect of CrimeSpree was barricaded off and segregated. It wasn't meant to be seen by those too cowardly to experience it. After all, death is frightening. The way into CrimeSpree was like a death, but a welcome one. Entering into CrimeSpree proper was akin to killing off all that made you hesitant and fragile. The adventure would strip you down to raw nerves and leave you to twist in the wind like a bloodied bed sheet on a line, helpless against greater forces. But after death comes rebirth, and as this sentiment knocked around inside of my noggin, I turned my eyes to the door that slept at the other end of the wall.

There it was, the exit from all the horrors of CrimeSpree and the avenue to new life. It was a plain door like any found in a nondescript office building. To look at it, you would never know its purpose. But when it opened and when you saw the faces of those that emerged from its womb, you knew immediately of its power. It spilled forth a parade of survivors, the very people who had sought out fear and spit back into its face. The very people who were fighting Porrima. Of all the protests against Porrima that were staged during the 8th Day Era, this little door was their champion. It was the only one that ever changed anything, because it changed the mind. This door and its mate created the perfect metaphor for the relationship between the mind and the person that contained it. Something was going in and something different was coming out.

I grabbed myself a refill of coffee and sat back down for another think. And what did I think about then? Dean, and if I had done the right thing by erecting CrimeSpree. I would revisit this inner conflict later with Alice Spenski and Adam Markson, and again with a few others who don't merit inclusion into my story. In time, after Clint Ruin walked off the face of the earth, I would again question myself and my choices. I still contend that my intentions were good. With CrimeSpree, all I ever wanted to do was to make us whole again. Not better, not worse, just real. But what do they say, the road to hell is paved with good intentions? That makes me wonder what the road to heaven is paved with. Maybe it's not paved at all. Maybe it's just gravel and dirt.

I'm fading, aren't I? I'm wandering a bit and, admittedly, I'm getting tired. I haven't stayed up for this long in decades, but it's okay. I have better things to do at the moment than sleep. I don't think I would sleep very well anyway. There's plenty of time for that later.

Clint spun the tires over the gravel and snapped me out of my introspection with a rough tap on the shoulder. I paid him enough. He really should have bought a nail clipper. He slid himself into the opposite side of the booth and helped himself to my cup. Before he even said a word, Clint drained it down, fixed another coffee and brought back a clean mug. He placed the fresh brew back in front of me and held the empty mug out in front of him, patiently awaiting a fill. In his mind, this made sense.

I looked across the table at him like he was the product of a shared nightmare by Walt Disney and M. C. Escher. His appearance was a jumbled collection of cartoonish aspects, all tossed together and mashed into a universe that knew no order. He wore a Vietnam War Era flak jacket overlaid with a Frankenstein tie. It was silk and comprised of about three others that had been chopped apart and stitched back together again. A chunky necklace made of beads and other cheap craftwork materials was wrapped around his left wrist, and a fresh tattoo of something illegible was scrawled over the back of his hand. He was topped with a new bowler hat, and by new, I of course mean to say that it was a threadbare treasure found at a thrift store. He had pierced the orange brim with assorted rings, and Clint wore a set of contacts that had formed his irises into star-shaped designs.

"I'm Clint," he said.

"Yeah, I know. So where ya been?"

"Oh, yeah. Sorry, boss."

"I'm not mad. I'm glad to see ya back. I was just wondering where you went."

"I went out."

"Out? For a week?"

"Yeah, I just went out."

"Fine, fair enough. Hey, I'll buy you breakfast."

"It's after noon," Clint corrected me in a voice that made it seem as though the procurement of pancakes was a thing of impossibility beyond a certain hour.

"Okay, how about we call it lunch and I'll buy you a burger?"

"I usually have ham for lunch."

"If I buy you something edible will you put it in your mouth?" I said, content to play Clint's silly game.

"I like you, boss."

"We've been over the boss thing. Mickey will do just fine."

"Sorry...boss," said Clint with a serpentine smile.

We sat across from each other for over an hour and we didn't speak nearly as much as you might imagine. Our conversation came in sputtered chunks that contained things of value and things of no earthly consequence. We talked about our food, the weather, and Clint's fancy new hat. He really wanted to discuss physics, for reasons that I and the whole of science are ill-equipped to explain, and we shared our thoughts on diet soda. Having a conversation with Clint was like traveling from point A to point B while taking every detour that the rest of the alphabet allows. It was a meandering road, it was weird and it was often frustrating, but eventually, it led somewhere.

We didn't get around to the Dean incident and the ramifications that would follow until Clint had finished gnawing through his ham and cheddar. And that's when Clint and all of his esoteric wisdom caught me like a surprise left-hook to the blind side. He said something that spun me around and sent me to the mat of moral debate. I was down among the murky unforseen and unintended results of my way of thinking, and the ref was counting fast. I was gonna lose this debate, this battle of minds, and by all that is proven fact, I knew it.

I'll be honest. I was overmatched. After all, Clint'd had a week to prepare and train, and I had done nothing except logically sort out the issues that 4th Street had dealt me a handful of days back. Shame on me for thinking in measured steps. I sympathetically thought of Dean, and tried to estimate the amount of compensation that he should receive. I thought about the kids who had put the hurt on him, and I tried to understand their differing reactions to that night. I took some delight in the fact that I knew I would have repeat business, and I felt a connection to all involved. Even Clint, as we all now shared an intimate knowledge of fear. I shuffled these emotions and the facts of the case in some form of order, and then went about my work. I was moving on from it, it was over, the book had ended. Or so I thought.

Clint was a fan of Chaos theory, and in defiance of this field of study, he set about making predictions. He put forth the idea that everyone involved in what had happened that night on 4th Street was irreparably changed, and so far, I was in agreement with him. He suggested that the minds of Dean and his five attackers were now strengthened against Porrima and that this made it possible for them to supersede its will. He went on to say that these six people were now unfettered and free to do as they wished. As a result, they could potentially expose others to a variety of unsavory behavior. Given time, those six would become legion, until the walls of Porrima fell like dominos, until, boom, you guessed it, chaos.

The possibility had never crossed my mind. To me, CrimeSpree was just a night out, an open-and-shut experience of the dark, nothing more. What the hell did I know? I was just a con-man, a cheat. I wasn't the type that could be bothered with consequence. God damn it, Clint, you were right. That bloody dustup on 4th was a shot from a popgun that turned into machine gun fire that grew into air strikes that devolved into nuclear war upon the streets of America. But we'll save the unraveling for later. First, let's delve into my utter dismissal of Clint's assertion.

No way was I buying that garbage. To me, CrimeSpree was still just a patchwork imposter of the real thing. The only aspect of life that it was poised to change was my tax return. I took Clint's words to heart, but all the while that he was preaching the end of the world, I was fashioning my counter argument. In my estimation, all that we had learned, the only thing that Dean and his friends had taught us, was that CrimeSpree worked. It was running the way I had envisioned, and it was giving people that elusive feeling of shadowy dread that they had come to find. It was a success. We were just doing our jobs well and earning our pay.

That was about the point in our exchange when I pulled myself from the mat and finished off Clint in the late goings of our match. He didn't want to be a part of something detrimental, and CrimeSpree wasn't; I had convinced him of this. Why, it was nothing more nefarious than a successful business that gave its customers value for their dollar. As Clint exhaled a hammy fog in my direction, I could tell that he was relieved. I had eased his worried mind, and he agreed to stay on and play his part. He agreed to continue to participate in our little charade.

When the end came, this is why Clint disappeared, of this I'm convinced. He thought I had lied to him. He felt like I had led him astray. He believed that I turned him into the freak that nature had costumed him as since birth. But I never lied to Clint. I was wrong, but I never lied. I thought I was telling him the truth. It's just a shame that I couldn't see the truth back then. To this day, I think about him, I wonder about him. What happened to you, Clint Ruin? I'll never know, that's for certain, and the world will probably never know either. We may be better for it, though, because when I think of all the many ways that Clint could have chosen to bid adieu to existence, none of them seem very pleasant.

A month had passed since Dean took his leave of CrimeSpree, and life returned to normal. Clint was back to filling his role as the zany MC of 17th Street and business at the park plodded along predictably and without incident. Violent crime remained locked in its cage, and the avenues of middle America certainly didn't run red with the blood of innocents. Everyone still took Porrima and it continued to work. The bone of contention that had momentarily wedged itself between me and Clint revealed itself to be nothing more than a tiny blip on an otherwise vast radar screen. The summer died away quietly and profitably, and as the winter closed in around us, the savagery that had befallen Dean began to fade into memory.

A mild winter settled over New York and most of the Northeast as year one was coming to a close for CrimeSpree. It wasn't in the plan, but we found it necessary to shorten our hours of operation during the winter, and we were only open to the public four days a week during the first two months of the year. This came as a blessing, though. It gave me and my employees the time we needed to seriously evaluate the park and improve on the things that had gone overlooked. We upped our security, and we practically doubled the amount of medical personnel on staff. Clint filmed a brief instructional video that laid out the pros and cons of a visit to CrimeSpree. It could be viewed at the park and online, and we encouraged our patrons to educate themselves on what lay in store for them.

In Clint's haphazard and rather hilarious presentation, he even went as far as to strongly dissuade people from visiting certain areas of the park. As you may suspect, I wasn't too thrilled about this tack at first, but there was an underlying genius in Clint's warnings that he had not foreseen. His video of caveats and advisements only made our most barbaric streets more popular. Hey, every fourteen-year-old wants to watch porno, right? Money by the pound, money by every pound of flesh.

I saw what Clint was trying to do, and I also saw what he was actually doing, and so I decided to take advantage of it. I suggested a policy that would bar entry into streets like 12th and

15th until any given patron had first visited at least five of the other, less vicious avenues. Clint thought this was a great idea and he thought I had the safety of the public in mind with my policy of preparedness. It might have worked that way in some cases, but what I saw was a way to generate more revenue. Sorry, Clint.

Things worked themselves out anyway. The fresh spring that arrived brought with it a new start and a second chance for my progressive vision. Business was better than the year before, and incidents like the one that involved the rearrangement of Dean's face were nonexistent. Among all of the changes that we had made, maybe Clint's wacky video and my disingenuous policy were actually working. Hell, maybe they were even positive for all involved.

In our second year of operation, nothing all that remarkable or spectacular took place. It started to feel like I had finally made something out of myself. I was running an honest, albeit unorthodox, business and the morale at CrimeSpree was high. My employees were happy and the misfit child that Clint Ruin had always been finally seemed to find his niche. The money was steady, the protests against my enterprise were low. It was the perfect year. I even snagged me a live-in girlfriend for the better part of that year, and life seemed like it was at last smoothing itself out into a path that led to somewhere that made sense.

Everyone gets one for free, isn't that what they say? I suppose that the second year of CrimeSpree was my free one, so to speak. It was my moment of calm and relaxation. But it was just a dull moment with the power to bore you all to death. So let me say this, if you're lucky, your life is as boring as mine was during that time. A mundane existence can be underrated, if you're catching my logic. Everybody wants peaks in their lives, but we all forget that the valleys are soon to follow. But what's even worse, we never appreciate the things that we get for free.

I know I didn't, at the time. I never allowed myself to fully taste that slice of time that disappeared all too quickly.

As it turned out, Clint was on to a little something when he was musing about Chaos theory. Some things just take time to materialize. It occurred to me some time back that Dean and those who injured him had absorbed a lifetime of violence on that fateful night when their worlds and fists collided. Given the era that these people knew, that incident was too much to take in, far too much for one night. As I said, it was a lifetime of violence that was poured onto them all. They were wet dogs and when it came time for them to shake off the filth, the drippings would one day come to cover us all in its stain.

Chapter 12

The unraveling (yours and mine, respectively)

So, if you're still all with me, then I feel that it's relatively safe to assume that everyone has at least a shaky grasp upon what things were like for my daring enterprise. The first year was a bit bumpy with obstacles met and then overcome. The twelve months that followed fit snugly into the category of smooth sailing, as all systems checked out A-OK. Which brings us to the third year of CrimeSpree's existence upon the face of our strange little planet. How did that go again? Oh, that's right. Not well, not well at all. In fact, the third year was cut short by a government raid, a swath of arrests, and the permanent shuttering of my masterpiece. Why the hell did that happen? I mean, was it really necessary? We'll delve into those questions and a few others in due time, but first, let us gather around the table again, because old Uncle Mickey wants to tell more murder stories.

A while back, when I found myself among the presence of Tweedle-glee and his corpulent sack of perspiration and foul odor for a companion, I encountered a revelation. I had deduced, quite correctly, that murder and other violent crimes still took place right under Porrima's nose. Yes these events were rare, so rare, it seemed, that the enigmatic and transitory powers that be decided to brush them into a corner lest Porrima be exposed for her failure to bat a thousand.

Did you know that just three years into the 8th Day Era, there was a serial killer roaming about? I thought not. This fucker was pumped full of Porrima just like the rest of us, but on the weekends there was no calm, no racquetball, no jogging around the park for this individual. Nope, the off time for this phantom assassin was spent a-hacking, a-stabbing, and a-killing. Her name was...wait, what? Yes, her. I said her. Her name was

Leslie Cannon, and the world knew very little about her until nearly fifty years had gone by since she first discovered a flare for butchering the long pig.

It has been estimated that Leslie, with her small frame, brunette ringlets, and square reading glasses, dismembered somewhere close to eleven people. Eleven people went missing from the same area of the same state around the same time, and in an era where the fear of violence was beginning to recede. This caused quite a stir, and it begat candlelight vigils, prayer circles, and a few concerts that purported to be fund-raisers. In other words, these disappearances spawned a bunch of crap that has never aided in the recovery of anyone. Sorry, but hopeful thoughts don't exactly comb forests or drag lake bottoms.

The bodies were found, all of them, if the reports are to be believed. But the public at large wasn't privy to this information until the 8th Day Era earned the more fitting title of Generation Lost. You see, as each severed hand, head, and foot was found, they were systematically bagged, burned, and disposed of. Eleven people, that's a lot of pieces, and each one was incinerated like a scrap of common garbage. I can't fathom just how much man-power and how many different agencies the government dedicated to the recovery of Leslie's playthings. Remember, if just one body, if just one head had been found by a regular citizen, Porrima would have become Leslie's next victim.

This blood carnival took place in Montana, and the lazy excuse of multiple bear attacks was chosen to explain away all of the missing townsfolk. And as for Leslie? Well she was found dead out in the wilderness, half decomposed and wet under the rain of a budding spring. The disappearances stopped at that time, as well. What a coincidence, huh? It was said that the pretty receptionist who was nearing her thirty-ninth birthday had perished due to a rock climbing mishap. Her family found this odd. After all, Leslie didn't even like camping and she held a certain disdain for many outdoor activities. But that's what they said. You know, *They,* those bastards.

Leslie Cannon, with a name like that, she was built for violence. Okay, it's pronounced Ca-non, but let's get this straight, Leslie was a weapon all the same. She was the 8th Day Era's monster. It may be even more monstrous yet that her victims were never given the burials that they deserved. Their families were never told the truth, and Leslie got the funeral that any likeable young woman who died a tragic death would get. And this was all done in an effort to protect Porrima. Eleven innocent people were scrubbed from the material plane, and one serial killer was denied a trial. I don't mean to suggest that Leslie deserved one. It just makes me wonder who was actually tasked with the duty of killing the disturbed Ms. Cannon. And yet I'm despised for the things I've done. At least I was always honest about CrimeSpree.

Alright, I'll put the brakes on the pity train before it really gets rolling, and I'll move on from Leslie. There's not a whole lot more to discuss when it comes to her, anyway. But there were other unsavory deeds which unfolded during the 8th Day Era. Oh, how terribly scandalous.

Utah was the state that received the Porrima head start, and as of this present moment in time, not a single scrap of murderous evidence has been unearthed from the soil of that state. This still doesn't mean that Porrima worked, it merely suggests that the drug was successful in curbing violence, but as Leslie had showed us, a downturn and a complete annihilation are two separate things. Which again leads me to the point that Porrima was a failure. Man, how long do I have to roar about this subject?

So, one state and one perfect record. Do any of you wish to venture a guess at how the other pieces of our fine union fared? Anyone? Not as well as Utah, that's for sure. I'm certain that other nasty spates of savagery could be found in Montana during the 8th Day Era if anybody cares to do a little digging, but hey, Leslie was enough. And yes, she was the worst, nationwide. She was the most violent American over the course of three decades. I bet some other shit went down during the 8th Day Era, though. What do you guys think? Let's have a peek.

There was that little incident in New Mexico, which, oddly enough, remains unconfirmed to this day. A man was beaten to death outside a bar in Kentucky. Pennsylvania was the stage for five murders, all of which took place in the same county, and Georgia was the scene of a hazing death. So far, ten Virginian women have come forward to say that they were raped during the interminably long 8th day, and Alaska can claim one admitted cannibal. His ravings have never been substantiated, but could you really blame the guy if he is telling the truth? It gets cold up there.

Over our collective skin the bruises formed, the hymens were rent, and the bodies piled up around our feet, but nobody seemed to notice. The crimes listed above and the many others not mentioned all had one thing in common: they were shielded from view. The public was never told of such things, we were never warned of the danger that still hid under our beds. Instead, the messes were cleaned up by the now exposed and defunct PPA. That's Porrima Perfection Alliance, just in the event that you haven't picked up a newspaper in the last decade or so.

These guys were the worst. Just the very concept of their work was immeasurably more deplorable than my goals for CrimeSpree. Although to be fair, the guys at the top of the PPA and the politicians who secretly supported them haven't fared much better than I, but that's neither here nor there. It was one thing to simply clean and cover up murders, rapes and other assorted monstrous activities, but it was the lengths that the PPA employed to ensure the integrity of the ruse that were truly unbelievable. Witnesses to such undesirable events were paid to keep quiet, they were threatened, more than one was admitted to a mental hospital, and a few simply vanished.

Perhaps they went rock climbing with Leslie. An elderly couple unexpectedly moved abroad, exiled is more like it, and the outrageous claims of violence made by most others were ignored altogether. I fit into that category. The words of a penniless drifter with a criminal record didn't carry much weight back then.

The remains of the dead that inconveniently cropped up were dealt with fairly easily. After all, it's not that troublesome to list someone as a missing person when you know full well that they're never gonna claw their way into the *found* box. But what of the damaged living? The raped and the beaten, the people who still had tongues and memories? Well, they received much the same treatment as those unfortunate enough to witness the yeti of barbaric behavior. When the persuasive inclinations of money and threatening speech failed to quiet the victims, they became victims all over again. Most just disappeared like specks of matter into the vast stretch of space.

You have to understand just how much was at stake when it came to the new and improved America. I don't mean to suggest that you should agree with the PPA or the agencies that aided them, but you at least need to understand the role of each piece on the board. Since the thirty-odd years of the 8th Day Era, there have been one hundred and thirty-six reports of murder that have come to light during that time. There were roughly sixty rapes and another four hundred or so beatings that Porrima was designed to weed out. That's somewhere in the neighborhood of six hundred victims of violent crime over a thirty-year stretch. That's nothing, even if that number is doubled, even if you count the witnesses who needed quelled, that's nothing. In fact, it's not even worth mentioning. Ah-ha! Enter the PPA.

They took a very scientific and measured approach to their duty. If just one brick is crumbling, you don't tear down the whole house. That could get pricy. Money, it all came down to money. Admitting the failure of Porrima, dumping the drug, restructuring law enforcement, absorbing the lawsuits and the panic, it was all too much of a risk to take. We're talking trillions of dollars, maybe more, maybe even too much to properly calculate. America took on Porrima, and then we were stuck. I suppose Porrima was a god after all, and gods, real or imagined, like to be in charge.

This wasn't enough to unravel America from Porrima, was it? Nope, the PPA kept everything in check, the injections kept us complacent and a hard truth kept curious minds at bay. Think about it, if an infinitesimal number of mostly faceless people had to be sacrificed to ensure that the whole of the nation could live in perpetual safety, which line would you file into? Don't be a hero. As I said, think about it. Picture yourself with duct tape around your mouth and a broken nose. Taste it, taste the blood as it slides down the back of your throat. You can almost feel the sweat as it courses through your knotted hair, can't you? It's no fun being restrained, free to experience nothing but helplessness. Now feel the cold steel of the business end of a gun as it is pressed into the side of your throbbing temple. Just a little squeeze, one click, and in an instant your brain no longer resides inside your skull. It is a chilling scenario. Now picture all of that happening to someone you've never met, and then feel free to answer my question honestly.

So, that leads us to another, inevitable question. What was it that was the catalyst for Porrima's undoing? The answer, very simply put, was CrimeSpree. Finally, I can take credit for something.

Oh, where did it all begin? Now that's a real riddle wrapped inside of a mystery that's been forcibly stuffed into an enigma. Nobody really knows, not even me. The beginnings of the end were too small to notice at first, even for the PPA. I can guarantee you this, though. It all started to come apart a lot sooner than anyone could have predicted. Yeah, I'm pretty confident that a good spell before Adam Markson blew his brains out and a few clicks in time before Alice Spenski's vagina was invaded by strangers, it was already too late. CrimeSpree wasn't open for three full years, and it was already too late.

So what vague shit am I hemming and hawing about now? Crime, that's what. Real crime, too. The kind that scares people, the kind that hurts. White-collar crime doesn't frighten anybody. Sure it's inconvenient, it can fuck your life up something proper, but it doesn't give you nightmares. White-collar misbehavior doesn't make scary faces in the dark, and it doesn't carry knives, but something wicked came crawling out of the shadows after an extended catnap.

So here's how it all went down, how all the dominos knocked into one another. As it happened, a visit to CrimeSpree stuck with people a hell of a lot longer than you might imagine. I'm talking everybody, too, even those that were too chicken to venture past the controlled atmospheres of the first three streets. I always thought that it was gonna be one specific event at CrimeSpree that would impact a patron. I thought that's what people needed and I made that the goal of the park, but it wasn't that at all. It was the entirety of the experience that actually changed the mind. It was much the same as when your mind tricks your eyes into seeing things that are not there, or when you believe the visions of an impossible dream. Being at CrimeSpree was one big trick, and it fooled the mind into thinking that it was in legitimate danger. This sensation then convinced the brain that the Porrima soup sloshing around it was no longer working. This, of course, is when that old bitch instinct showed up, and then it was all over for the medicine.

Most people didn't act out. No, no the change was more subtle. You see, after a few hours had been spent inside the park, the mind started to wash itself of Porrima. It was a defense mechanism, a way of prepping the body for the potential danger that the future promised. In short, my customers developed a natural resistance to the drug, and, as a

215

result, they became reawakened to violence. More visits, more resistance. The more intense the experience, the more resistance. It was two-plus-two-equals-four until somebody got punched in the face. The answer to the problem was an old one. It was violence. It was an option open to them again, maybe for the first time in their lives, and it was an option that many exercised at one time or another.

It took a while for the authorities to put it all together, because the primal nature of violent crime began to act like itself again. It was random. There was a gang initiation here, a spousal abuse case over there. All of a sudden, reports of rough muggings and sporadic episodes of violence were making the news reports again. These events, when plotted on a map, concentrated themselves closer to the eastern side of the United States, but as time went on, the stain crept out. It all started slow, too, but like a boulder down the side of a greasy slope, things sped up rather quickly. The reports of violent crime really began to raise attention right around the start of CrimeSpree's third year, and by the time we were shut down, the reports of such behavior had multiplied every month.

Let's be clear about one thing, though. We didn't just go back to sixty without first starting at zero and then hitting up all of their numerical buddies along the way. In the beginning, the crimes were pretty benign. Well as benign as true violence can be, anyway. But we kept plugging along through beatings of ever escalating intensity, until, at last, we danced hand in hand with murder once again.

I know I already revealed to you all that some people had always been immune to Porrima's influence, but that was the PPA's department. Those incidents were few and far between. In other words, they were easy to deal with. This was different, the CrimeSpree effect. Too many moles were popping up at the same time, and the PPA was ill-equipped to whack each and every one of them. And then it happened, just like cosmic justice. Some poor sucker got himself killed, and the cleanup crew was nowhere in sight. There was no denying this one. Murder was back from vacation. Porrima had failed for all the world to see.

It's a little redundant to spell out the end. Some people committed violence, others saw it, their brains responded, and then they in turn could comport themselves in a violent manner as well. This was just survival, it was nature being herself. Like a wildfire out of control, our brains were turning out the lights of Porrima one by one until the house was dark, and this was taking place all across the country. Think of it like an outbreak of disease. If some illness spread rapidly through touch and simply through sight, with no management solution set in place, in a nation of over three hundred million people spread over thousands of miles, how could it be stopped? That's what they never counted on. Our brains finally throwing up a wall to Porrima. And to think, we just needed the slightest nudge.

An entire nation tap-danced over a sheet of thin ice for thirty years. We grew soft and lazy, we became sensitive and naive, and, man, when we all fell through, shit went crazy. Like an atomic bomb set off in our collective sleep, everything changed in an instant. One day all was shaky but relatively quiet, and the next, well, it was different. In under twenty-four hours, less than one full day, whole cities burned, riots claimed lives by the dozens all over America, and no one was safe.

I'll be honest, this scared the shit out of me. The first aspect of my fear was a reasonable one. It was the realization that I could be harmed. And I'm not talking about the Beelzebub in a trucker cap that I found in New Mexico, no, now brutality could potentially come from anyone. The second portion of my fear was strictly a fiscal one. I was going to go out of business! That's right, I didn't have the market cornered on violence anymore, it was everywhere and it was free again. Why travel to CrimeSpree when you could just find a random dark alley in your own neighborhood?

So, the end, the unraveling, as I have so eloquently titled it. It arrived sometime in May, and it was the alarm clock that stirred all of America from our lethargy. The night before was fairly close to any other. Sure, it was a bit violent for the 8th Day Era, but all was still relatively calm. The reports of crime that were filtering in seemed distant to most people anyway, unreal, even. Many of us simply assumed that Porrima had encountered something of a speed bump. Nothing's perfect, right? Even the news outlets with their insatiable bloodlust for anything sensational and scandalous downplayed the curious incidents that had popped up as of late. This new violence wasn't gonna last, and it certainly wasn't here to stay. That made it unworthy of attention—after all, some celebrity just landed himself in rehab. Now that, people, is news. But the new morning that arrived was a strange one. The sun came up and the rooster crowed and the monsters tore away our sheets as they all cried in unison. *Wake up, time to die!*

God, that was an awful day, it was truly awful. I'm not going to pepper this information with wry wit or humor. I don't think I'll be a smart-ass either because not a shred of it was amusing in the least. The sickest of shit had been flung, and once it struck the blades of the societal fan, that filth was cast onto each and every one of us.

At just after six in the morning, a gunman walked into a daycare center in Maryland and killed one child for every bullet in his tool. Before most people had left their houses for work, three major banks were robbed using the old-fashioned techniques of muscle and vulgarity. One such incident even ended with an explosion that produced four fresh corpses for those in the funerary business. A man was stabbed to death by his wife as he slept, and a high-school nerd was lynched by a pack of meat-headed thugs. A group of teens took it upon themselves to cull the homeless population in Morgantown. And five suicides were streamed live on the internet.

218

By noon that day, a murder had taken place for every state in the union and fistfights sprang up like dandelions over a new spring's lawn. Word was spreading fast through all channels of the media, and the realization that something chaotic had descended upon us was unavoidable. I was at home, frozen in front of my TV as I watched the serene nation that I used to know come apart in blazing color and smooth pixels. It was hard to breathe. I felt as though I couldn't even blink, because every time I did, a fresh hell was seemingly reported. It happened that quick, and the logical thinking that this spiral would eventually reach its end began to feel wholly illogical.

As I sat there with my muscles tense and the heartbeat strident from adrenaline, I knew that this event was my generation's tragedy. Growing up, we had all read about the attacks on Pearl Harbor and the Kennedy assassination. We were told of September 11th, 2001, and how that day forever changed the nation and those who had lived through it, but we never truly understood what it all meant. I suppose no generation can really understand the impact of a nationwide tragedy until they come to face their own, and on that day in May, the reckoning showed up for those of the 8th day. It was the jagged birth of our defining moment, because all of our lives would now be measured by what we did *after this.* It was our great marking stone along the infinite road of history.

This catastrophe was unlike any that had preceded it, and it proved a fitting end for Porrima. She was a beast the likes of which the world had never seen, and her death was just as unique. Make no mistake, what happened that day was an attack, but we did it to ourselves, and I'm not just talking about one single day near the start of spring. No, we had sealed our own fate long ago when we fancied ourselves wise enough to leash the mind. Porrima has no side effects, that's what they always said. Well fuck you. Some things just take a while to surface, and when Porrima's failures rose up in us, we freaked.

An inexplicable reaction took place as our brains rejected the drugs, and, quite specifically, we lost our minds.

By evening, my television screen was filled with the colors of red and black as fires blazed before the backdrop of nightfall. Entire cities were ripped to shreds by riots, whole malls were looted of goods, and thousands of American citizens had been killed before the military launched a campaign against its own people. And that's when I stopped watching. I clicked the remote and tossed it across the room. It landed into the garbage can and that seemed like an appropriate resting place for it. I remember slumping back into the embrace of my couch and actually crying. I wept out loud like an orphaned child, and to this day I cannot point to any one reason as to why.

Back then, two things were going on at the same time. I was curled into a ball, overcome by the gravity of the day while thousands of people all across the country were being subdued with teargas and tasers. The Army flooded the streets and they very concisely revealed to us the full potential of a human being unfettered of Porrima. Sure, some people died, and in much the same manner as those that needed quelled after the Solution #499 disaster, but I gotta hand it to the military, they did a fine job of mopping up the mess. It was almost as though they knew the day would eventually arrive.

I don't think I slept that night. The sounds of sirens and of things being destroyed were foreign noises to many ears back then. Like everyone else, I was unsettled and sick, to some degree. I must have nodded off or passed out somewhere during the night, though, because I don't have a memory of the sun peeking up over the curve of the world. When daybreak came, it swept over the country like a celestial flashlight washed over a shipwreck at the bottom of the sea. The images that were put under the bright lights of day were stark and frightening to adsorb. They were impossible to believe. Our perfect nation was now stained with blood and ash. Whole towns lay crippled, and buildings of all descriptions still emanated warmth from the fires that had eaten them.

In a twisted reprise from the night before, I found myself in front of the TV again. But this was gonna be different. It was day one after the disaster. It was the start of the tears and the denial and it was time to pick up the pieces. The dead needed to be counted and named, and the arrested needed to be processed and questioned. Ah, the questions. They formed conversations that begat answers, because that's what questions do, and all of the broken fingers pointed right at me. Once all of the messes had been swept up it was pretty clear that a common denominator was involved: my lovely park. Yep, it was six degrees of CrimeSpree as the government traced the evil right back to its root. Every perpetrator, every aggressor, they all had either visited CrimeSpree at one time or another or had been violated themselves by someone who had. And that was enough for the democratically elected kings of our country to order CrimeSpree to the grave. The minions came and they smashed in my doors, turned over my operation, arrested my people, until at last all that was left was to deal with was me.

I'm gonna put that off for now. Reliving this all in memories that I've tried mightily to forget has been no fun, so you'll have to forgive me as I put off my own end for as long as possible. Which brings me to the totality of Black May. That's what it was called, or, rather, that is how it is remembered. Black May, yeah, it never made sense to me either, after all, the blood and the spike in violence really only lasted for one day, but I suppose that month just stands to symbolize the end of thirty years of medicated peace. Not that it matters, but I'm pretty sure that Black May is also the name of a heavy metal band. Oh how quickly we forget the true meanings of historical events.

Black May fell in line nicely with all of America's other disasters in the sense that it immediately effected very few of us. Sure, a few thousand people died and a couple billion dollars in damage had been done, but that's still a relatively small amount for both categories in a nation as big as ours. The fact of the matter was that most of us did like I did. We just watched the chaos from our climate-controlled homes. Some of us probably even went to the fridge for snacks. But disasters never abate quickly. Okay, so they show up with a loud bang and an attitude that screams, *look at me!* But they endure far beyond the initial banging and clanging. People tend to assume that hurricanes only affect the cities that they soak, but this is inaccurate. Hurricanes displace people. They drain populations from one area and cause them to swell in another. As their implications move these people from place to place, they also inject these new environs with fresh attitudes and culture. In time, towns and even entire cities can be permanently changed from an event that unfolded many states away and years before. You see, it's not the impact, necessarily, it's the reverberations. They're what get all of us in the end, the consequences.

Porrima was the first victim of the reverberations. At the dawn of that new morning, she died quietly and without fanfare. It had taken a while, and for that maybe all of the doctors and scientists that created Porrima need to be extended some credit, but their experiment ultimately failed. After that, things moved about in a predicable manner. Some people lost their jobs, while new areas of employment opened up for others. Class-action lawsuits were filed and many politicians were run out of office. The rest of the world just laughed at us, and more than a few nations intimated that the arrogant Americans finally got what they deserved. In time, true crime returned as some of us rediscovered the satisfaction that only physically harming another can bring.

The rates of violent activity spiked a bit after Porrima's funeral, but soon enough, they leveled off. Our appetite for barbarism eerily returned to almost exactly where we had left it at the start of the 8th Day Era, thirty years before. Eventually it began to feel as though that whole stretch of time was just a fanciful dream. We collectively washed Porrima from our systems much quicker than anyone dared to predict, and it seemed like the whole era was in danger of one day being forgotten. Oh, but you're forgetting the revelations aren't you? Yes, they came trickling out one by one. The lab experiments and the underhanded deals that pushed Porrima into our veins. We watched the reports and read the blogs that spoke of the hidden murders, the PPA, and we as a nation sat down for a speed-date with Leslie Cannon and her hobbies. I'm telling you, it's the reverberations, they get everybody.

But this knotted yarn has never been about everybody, has it? It hasn't been about you, either. Nope, all along it has been about me and the things that I've done. And just like a shockwave over still water, the tremors found their way to my front door.

By the end of Black May, I knew that CrimeSpree's run was just about up. The weather was nice, our reputation had never been more alluring, and the number of people through the turnstiles suddenly dropped like an anchor through ocean waves. We weren't the real deal anymore. We had become the cheap imposter that I always knew CrimeSpree to be. That was a real kick in the pee-wee's too. Business was going great, Alice had just taken her walk and Adam Markson was still alive.

There are nights in your life that you'll never forget. Everybody gets a few, a handful, maybe, for better or worse. These memories are so strong, so impactful that they will even ignore the ravenous appetites of Alzheimer's disease and other such varieties of dementia. I've had a few nights like that, and one of them involves Alice Spenski.

Man, did this girl get fucked up at CrimeSpree, but Alice never looked at it in that light. She didn't see damage on her skin. I'm not even sure that she felt pain, because after the procurement of an ice-pack and a few aspirin, Alice was ready for a snack.

I was in the diner hanging out in the back with the cooks, sipping on coffee and swiping fries from random plates when Alice walked in. In an instant, everything went quiet. None of us knew what had just happened out front, but it was an ominous silence that fell over the diner. To this day, I swear I even heard the compressor on the freezer as it switched off. This little girl staggered in with her clothes shuffled and torn and her hair decorated with dried blood like the tinsel that Satan might use on his Christmas tree. Her face was swollen, a few bruises rose to the surface of her fair skin and three of her fingers were splinted and wrapped in stained gauze. She limped her way through an audience of frozen faces until she reached the counter. With a groan of authentic pain, Alice pulled her voodoo-doll body onto a stool and rested her pounding head in her hands.

"Can I have some soda, please?" asked Alice to no one in particular.

Her words murdered the quiet like the roar of a thunderstorm bottled into the empty confines of an old steel drum, but still, nobody said shit. Alice was served her twenty ounces of syrup and flavoring by a rigid waitress who assumed the role of deaf-mute. The Midwestern blonde used the straw like a vacuum, and, as she motioned for a refill, the painted fingers of her other hand ripped through the tangles in her hair.

What the hell happened to you. That's not a question, it is just six words that some dum-dum strung together and spat in the direction of Alice. It was also the start of her proper life. If you can remember back to the beginning of this nonsense, then you will recall something similar that once happened to me. Oddly enough, I was also in a diner when some dope asked me a question that would change my life, or, rather, begin it. If I had never heard that absurd query, *what year is it?* none of this may have ever happened. But I heard what I heard, and it was a gunshot that signaled the start of this crazy race. Without that strange encounter, I can't say for certain if I would have gotten into that diesel murder machine. And if I would have said no to that ride, well then, everything else just disappears. Clint Ruin and his Chaos theory strike again.

My meaningful life began that day so long ago, and when Alice heard her six special words, her life was permitted to commence as well. What had she done up until that point? Nothing, not a damn thing of note, Alice will tell you that herself. So, back to the epiphany, yes? The black powder and the spark.

"What the hell happened to you?" asked a faceless voice with a percolated cadence.

Alice heard what we all heard, but for her, it was different. The words had meaning, real meaning, and they resonated with the most abstract dimensions in her mind. As the words floated into her ears and then faded off, she lowered her head and sucked back another gulp of her beverage. Alice then swiveled her seat around and faced the captivated gallery. She stared into them with knowledge in her gaze and they all looked upon her with anticipation.

By some measure, I suppose that Alice did describe what had happened to her, but she never truly answered the question that spun her around in the first place. That was unimportant, the scars to come, the physical remains of something much more profound. But Alice spoke, and she spoke in detail of her time spent among the grimy embrace of 15th Street. She barely covered the actual assault. It was simply the means to a greater end. What Alice discussed was the profanity of the incident and the poetry that entwines itself with every experience worth experiencing.

From the back of the house, I could hear Alice's words as they rang clear as bells. It was so silent, the cooks even turned off the fryers and the ovens, as we all just wanted to listen. I remember as my employees and I were pulled out of the kitchen and toward Alice like a pack of zombies straggling their way to a brain buffet. Her speech was consuming, her oration so powerful that it commanded the attention of every ear that it reached.

I stayed mostly out of sight and leaned my lanky frame up against a wall. I shifted my eyes from Alice and then to the sea of faces that surrounded her. She had slid herself onto the edge of her stool, while those around her were frozen and fixed in place. It was surreal to see as those who came in simply to mash through a cheeseburger were now seated on the floor with my cooks. With all the chairs full of asses, the onlookers formed a half-circle around Alice and they gazed upon her like she was a prophet. It was the busiest my diner had ever been and I didn't make a dime, but that was okay with me. It was a truly profound moment for me, and it was when I knew, unequivocally, that I had done the right thing in erecting CrimeSpree. As I watched Alice gesture, as I watched her eyes swell and her lips recede as she became a puppet to her tale, I knew I had been made a witness to history.

I can't recall exactly what she had said that night. I was more or less absorbing the moment and not necessarily the details. That night has become the righteous angel sent to expunge from my mind the devil memory of New Mexico and Interstate 40. It was the antitheses of that horrible day, and it finally made sense of all that was once scattered and lost. When I watched that man being beaten to death, I knew something was wrong, and it wasn't just the obvious. I knew something was wrong with us. But then, years later, as I allowed myself to melt into Alice's speech, I felt like every American was on their way to being put back together. It was emotion that had been missing all along, it was feeling and the authenticity of human experience. Alice had suffered and bathed in these sensations, and she was spilling her wisdom onto all present.

A crooked smile crept into the corner of my mouth, but it wasn't the kind that usually surfaced once I had made a con or banged a drunk chick. This smile was real and it was educated, because I had the knowledge that Alice had. And, for the first time in my life, I watched as my efforts set about bettering the world.

So giggly grins and hugs all around, right? After all, this was history, a defining moment for mankind that would reverberate out into every corner of the nation. And we were there to experience it in the flesh, there in rural New York, we all were a part of something important. It was a celebration of the mind, and we all damn knew it, as a handful of Americans had just seen the light that Porrima had always shielded from their eyes. Alice Spenski, with the jerky articulations of her arms and the dry-throat croak of her words, had just taken the first steps into a lifetime of accolades and literary awards. For crying out loud, her works are already studied in schools. And me, the unwitting architect of this honest madness, I was shown that what I had done was the right thing to do. I was shown that my life was, in fact, worthwhile. But being right is never easy, it's never simple or plainly spelled out. It can be confusing, and it often calls for tough decisions to be made. *Right* saw fit to have a girl raped and *right* put a gun down Adam Markson's throat. *Right* sparked riots and it's the reason why Clint Ruin simply vanished. It sort of makes me wonder if *right* is actually *wrong* in disguise. Either way, whatever it has been; right, wrong, up, down, black, white, thick, thin, bloody, beautiful, it has all led to this.

Chapter 13

You can't kill murder

They're gonna hang me in the morning. Read it again, understand it, because these are *your* words, the ones that will change all of your lives. This whole tale has been nothing more than a big fucking circle and I was the unlucky rat that was chosen to run around it. There's a fundamental problem with circles, though, for no matter how hard you try and no matter what approach you employ, you always find yourself back at the beginning. Nothing's changed. Sure, maybe you've gotten older, a snazzier cell phone might have been introduced, but the circle never budges. It stays the course and just waits for everyone caught in its ring to see things its way. The circle always wins.

Twenty years ago, I was sentenced to death by a judge whose face I can barely recall, but I do clearly remember the sound of his voice as I heard the word, DEATH. How fitting, capital punishment was reinstated in honor of the man who was blamed for the resurrection of murder. I must say, I feel like a fairytale princess on the eve of her super-sweet sixteen.

Oh, my! You did all this for me? You built those shiny new gallows for me, and that rope is all mine? Oh, you really shouldn't have.

Seems barbaric, doesn't it? Hanging, I mean. But it's quick and cost effective. Bullets run about a buck or two, electricity is pricy, and certain gases can be volatile to store. I suppose that I could have conned my way into lethal injection, but I'm somewhat uncomfortable with needles. So it's the dangling for me.

It's almost over, though, and I'm relieved. I'm tired. Twenty years is a long time to spend anywhere. I'm willing to bet that even resort spots get pretty goddamn boring after twenty years. Two decades in prison, and I'm ready for it all to be over. This has been real prison, too, hard time, as they say. The snugly ideas of The Righted Mind are long gone, and as I sit here in my chilly 6' x 8', I almost pine for Texas. I'm so tired of bland meals and stainless steel toilets. I'm tired of buzzers and metal, and my patience for violence ebbed away far back into the past. I'm tired of teardrop tattoos and shakedowns. I'm tired of my cinderblock, and the grain patterns that I've memorized, and I can't spend another day peering out of my state-issued rectangle of sky. But most of all, more than anything else, I'm tired of losing Lucy.

It's been a long night, and, oddly enough, it's been much the same as the seven-thousand or so that have preceded it. You would think that it would be different, more profound, it's not. It's just the last one in a long line of a pattern with no variance. It's been a dark night just like all the others. Fatigue is everywhere and the nuttiness that isolation offers is just as tempting as it's always been. As I've sat here hunched over this notebook and blabbering into an aging audio recorder, I've thought about pretty much the same things that usually churn themselves around inside my brain. I've dedicated time to my formative years and I've contemplated all the many ways in which things might have turned out different. I've thought about my travels, my restlessness. I've looked back fondly on the few friendships that I managed to make and I've slowly retraced the indelible memories of women like Andrea. Everything that went into the formation of CrimeSpree seems impossible to me now, almost like it must have happened to someone else. If I concentrate hard enough, I can still feel the heat of the desert and the humidity that hangs in the air during a Southern evening. I can still recall the faces on the bus that liberated me from Texas, and I can still smell the greasy funk that clung to the inside of Darlene's diner.

Memories have a way of getting cloudy, though, and by the time you find yourself in advanced years, you'll understand.

It's just simple math. You can only lob so much shit into the mental closet of storage before some things topple over and others tumble out completely. You begin to question the reliability of your own mind, and you doubt the authenticity of events that supposedly involved you directly. Hell, I've been found guilty of things that I don't even remember doing, and I cherish certain memories that could never be proven to have ever actually taken place. That's a real heartbreaker, and Lucy has wiggled herself into that category.

She just feels like a memory from a dream to me now, and I hate that. I'll never know the degree of her happiness with me, and I'll never know if it could have actually worked out between us. I can't say for sure if the memories I have of her and the experiences we shared are photocopied images to be believed, or if they are just fanciful renders constructed by my mind in a fashion that pleases my subconscious. I'm tired of thinking.

How surreal it is, to write the end as it happens. I suppose I'm lucky in some twisted, demon-deal sort of way. After all, it is me who gets to play the lead role in yet another circumstance that few people will ever know. And so I guess that brings us to the topic of regret, and whether or not I possess such a sensation. The simple answer is no. My life hasn't been good, bad, or indifferent, it has just been life. My personal journey through the riddle that nobody has yet been able to unravel. It began, things happened, and now it will finish. Underneath it all, much the same assessment could be applied to anyone who has ever lived. Julius Caesar, Marky Mark, Abe Lincoln, Jesus Christ, Jackie Chan, all the same. Okay so the plot points might vary from case to case, but guess what? It's all still birth, stuff, death. Thanks for playing.

It's winter in New York and it's cold. I can feel the chill as it bleeds into my cell, and I am starkly aware of the ebbing black outside my window. My cell floor is littered with empty cans of soda and a discarded E-cigarette, as the battery gave up a while back. Those things are usually not permitted in prison, but I managed to whine my way into a few luxuries for the last hurrah. I suppose I could kill myself. The cans could be ripped into makeshift blades and I've heard stories about guys that can fashion explosives from certain batteries, but why bother? When your remaining time can be measured in minutes, you might as well lie back and let someone else do the work. That's always been my style, anyway. Besides, a witty zinger might come to mind as I'm being personally escorted to the big shebang. Now who would wanna miss that?

Remember back to when you were a kid and how every storybook was constructed to teach the reader a lesson. Now listen up, because that's all kiddie-land bullshit. Not every tale is designed with a lesson in mind, not all of them are built to instruct. Not every story has a moral. Don't disparage Porrima, don't slander those that framed the 8th Day Era and don't feel bad for me, just accept my story for what it is: a rhyme with no reasons.

I don't like to repeat myself, but maybe you can understand me better by lending a second look to something fatalistic that I jabbered on about a while back when things seemed sunnier. Forever is a word that we toss around way too much. If you ever really stop and think about it, forever doesn't actually exist, it's just a made-up concept. Did you know that in about a trillion years or so, every single galaxy will be as far away from each other as the universe is presently wide? In simpler terms, everything will one day be so far apart that not one little star will twinkle in the skies above. Not even light is forever. So, now that the science lesson is over, let me say again that time will eventually forget about me. It will forget about you, too, and everyone you have ever known. A time will come when everything that has ever been done by everyone who has ever lived will no longer matter. When you think about it in those terms, this whole charade feels a bit empty, doesn't it?

Yes, it does, the answer is yes. I know this fact won't delay the inevitable, but it at least gives me a small measure of solace.

I can see as the world outside is turning from solid black to luminous gray. The morning has arrived and the end is nigh. Don't panic. It's not *the* end, it's just mine. In the distance, I can hear the heavy doors of my wing as they are being forced open one by one. I can hear the boots of the guards, my uniformed beefcake valet, and, if I stay real quiet, I'm pretty sure that I can hear the anticipation of the crowd. The execution may not be televised, but it is open to the public.

I'm happy about that. Let them watch, let them observe what I've given back to them. Let them indulge again of the flavors that I saved from the clutches of modern medicine. Let them witness the closing of the circle and let them see with naked eyes the fruits of my labor. And just like any properly seeded yum-yum, I've got some swinging to do. It's time to put down the pen, to string the rope, and to drop the bottom out from under the last vestiges of the 8th Day Era. Just don't be afraid to wave hello to the bestial and natural face of mankind. It may be a bit startling.

- END -

Acknowledgements

Thanks to Meghan Miller for her incredible editing work on CrimeSpree.

Thanks go out to my friends and family, for their support and understanding of my work. To my Mom, Dad, and my sister for their incredible support and for always being cool with my weirdness. To Rachel, for so many things, but especially for allowing me the time to disappear into the computer for hours at a time and to drop all kinds of cash into my many passions and hobbies when there are bills to pay. And a thanks goes out to my cats for being goofy and amusing at the times when I'm anything but.

About the author

Rich Hayden was born and raised in Pittsburgh, PA, and still resides in the area with his girlfriend, Rachel, and cats. CrimeSpree is his debut novel, and, unless outsourced, will never appear in audiobook format. The yinzer accent is much too thick.

www.ingramcontent.com/pod-product-compliance
Lightning Source LLC
Chambersburg PA
CBHW070616130626

46556CB00001B/383